THE TORCH

'Prime Minister. My name is Jonathan Fraser, Colonel, now retired, late of the Twenty-second Regiment, Special Air Service and formerly Fourth Hussars. You can establish my identity from the army list.'

'Just one moment. I was told that this call was from the Soviet Embassy.'

'You have not been misled; this call is indeed from the Soviet Embassy. This building is now under the control of myself and my men.'

'They did it!' Hammond said as though to himself. 'They went and bloody did it.'

THE TORCH

Glover Wright

ARROW BOOKS

Arrow Books Limited
17–21 Conway Street, London W1P 6JD

An imprint of the Hutchinson Publishing Group

London Melbourne Sydney Auckland
Johannesburg and agencies
throughout the world

First published by Hutchinson 1981
Arrow edition 1982

© Geoffrey Glover-Wright 1980

Made and printed in Great Britain
by The Anchor Press Ltd
Tiptree, Essex

ISBN 0 09 929090 1

To Harry

Contents

PART ONE
Decision

I

The gates, at each end of the private road, were of wrought iron fixed into solid arches of stone. They were lit by four old-fashioned electric lamps. A few feet inside the gates, a green painted guard-house sat between two drop barriers to stop unauthorized vehicles entering this sensitive area, which houses many of London's foreign embassies.

It was after midnight when the two black youths saw the tall, upright figure of their victim quite clearly, as he passed under the four lamps. They leant against the railings on the Park side of the Bayswater Road, their eyes bright in their faces from the effects of hash. The joint was dropped through the railings and they began to follow their mark. As they passed the gates, the two constables on duty gave dead-eyed looks as the youths laughed provocatively.

The man they were following turned left and made his way towards one of the smaller side turnings. He turned left again, stopped for a moment before an entrance to a mews, and drew cigarettes and matches from the pocket of his camel overcoat. Straight-backed and brisk in his movements, he struck a match and lit a cigarette. The sudden flare of the flame haloed his face, and cast dark shadows above his lips and eyes, where the iron grey of his moustache and thick eyebrows stood out in relief from the contours of skin drawn starkly across bone. He removed the rolled newspaper from under his arm and strolled into the darkness of the mews.

The two youths broke into a silent run, their feet cushioned in tennis shoes. The mews ended dead. There was no exit. Black garage doors glistened in their gloss paint, blind witnesses of violence. The muggers passed their mark and turned lithely like dancers, one holding out his palm, pink and wet like a dog's tongue. The other struck it with his own and smiled widely.

'Bread,' he said, 'or you're fuckin' dead!'

The man raised his eyebrows in an expression of surprise, which could have been at the slang, the obscenity, or the sud-denness of the encounter. The grey eyebrows dropped as he thrust the newspaper, folded end first, into the inverted U of the stomach under the rib cage of the speaker. The mugger folded over, his lungs ejecting air, and his stomach its contents.

Even before the black face hit the paving, the man turned and, with a sharp grunt, as though from some hidden pain, kicked sideways at the kneecap of the other, crushing the cartilage with the thick leather sole of his brogues. Deliberately shaping his right fist, he chopped both the fallen figures behind the ear.

The encounter had lasted no more than a few seconds and barely a sound had given away the violence of it. With quick movements, the man positioned the first youth so that he would not choke on his own vomit, and retrieved his cigarette from where it was slowly burning a hole in the trousers of the other. Satisfied that neither of the muggers was more than severely hurt, he walked quickly to one of the lock-up garages, opened the doors with a key already in his hand and started up the dark green Jaguar XJ6 inside. He drove out of the garage and secured the doors again, before driving from the dark into the brighter street lights.

As consciousness returned to the two muggers, the residents of the mews were awakened by a high scream of intense pain. A scream peculiar to the recipient of a knee-cap wound and uncannily female in register.

Some way past Enfield, on the main London to Cambridge road, there is a small village, which most drivers pass through without noticing. The narrow left-hand turn-off at the mouth of the village crosses a stream, via an unexpectedly severe hump-backed bridge, before heading off into tall trees and green meadows. Further on, between tall pillars, is a gravel driveway leading up to a large Georgian manor house.

For many years the building with its extensive grounds had lain unused and empty, and it was only within the last three that a company, registered in Jersey, and known as Spartan Leisure Limited, had secured a lease. The property was part of a trust fund and the ownership uncertain, but the trustees and the estate agent were satisfied with the substantial rent the Jersey company had agreed to pay.

According to the estate agent, their operation, an 'away from it all rest and recuperation centre' as their expensively produced brochure described it, was run in a highly efficient manner. He noted also that Spartan's clients were always male, with the exception of occasional weekends, when the manor reverberated with the sounds of far from Spartan living. He had tried, on some pretext, to approach the house but had been deterred quite firmly by the hard-looking groundstaff who kept the place well patrolled. Naturally he'd protested, but the men had very clearly stated that Spartan's clients paid a great deal of money for the course, and that included absolute privacy.

Spartan Leisure was in fact owned by a retired colonel, formerly of the Fourth Hussars and the Special Air Service, although that ownership would have been extremely difficult to prove in a court of law. It was just one link in a chain of holding companies, which fronted for some very lucrative businesses indeed. In the City, that mecca of high finance, Colonel Jonathan Fraser's profile was so low as to be non-existent, and his presence on the boards of certain companies so lightweight that he was considered ineffectual. Fraser was a shadow in the corridors of moneyed power, regarded merely as a fighting man who'd caught a bullet in some Middle East rebel war and been invalided out with sufficient private money to live his rather introverted life without having to rely on his army pension. In fact, the small City bank who regularly cashed his pension cheque was of the opinion that there was not much in the way of private income, as he drew regularly from these monthly credits.

The truth was somewhat different. Colonel Fraser was, in terms of hard cash and easily convertible assets, a sterling millionaire. He was also a fanatic. A man who commanded the absolute loyalty and blind devotion, to the point of worship, of the men who had served under him. The British government, shrewd and calculating, tapped this power source whenever the need arose, and used Fraser to form military units that could never, in any circumstances, be attributed to the official Establishment.

However, as in business, Fraser was never seen to be at the front of any operation. His role, once again, was shadowy. He was in a deadly position, between the Establishment and the highly profitable business of private warfare. Fraser negotiated with the paymasters, and recruited the recruiters.

The position carried with it the necessity of total trust in the motives and aims of the government, and the knowledge that, in some cases, men were being sent to their deaths as part of a considered plan.

If the government had understood the kind of man they were using as their go-between – if, for instance, a psychological profile had been asked for – they would have realized that they were running a considerable risk. In late 1975, when secret arrangements were made for a military involvement in Africa, that risk had become critical.

The débâcle which followed turned Jonathan Fraser against all that he had formerly stood for. The deep-set values of his own generation and class were swept away as though they had never been. He knew that, deep in the core of the Establishment which he supported and of which he was a part, a cancer was eating steadily towards the surface. He was betrayed. Shamed before those who respected him. They were *his* men, who rotted in stifling squalor in these concrete block-houses. Men for whom, ultimately, he was responsible.

Fraser had contemplated the measure of this – and calculated the cost.

Eventually, Colonel Fraser had pleaded ill-health, in the form of severe injuries suffered from an exploding mine in the Omani rebel war years before, and phased down his activities on behalf of the British government. Much of his newly found spare time was spent relaxing amid the amenities of Spartan Leisure and one autumn morning he sat in the empty breakfast room of the manor reading the front page of the *Daily Telegraph*. The leading story was a breakdown of the previous day's events outside the Embassy of the USSR, where certain political groups were demonstrating against further expansion of the already considerable Soviet diplomatic presence in the United Kingdom. As a secondary item the *Telegraph* reported an attack on two West Indian youths in the same neighbourhood. The report inferred no connection between the Anti-Embassy-Extension demonstration and the brutal assault. The police were continuing with their enquiries, and were interviewing the youths in hospital.

Fraser folded the paper over, rose, and walked through the

main entrance hall of the manor on to the sweeping gravel forecourt where the Jaguar stood.

He drove the car to London with authority and economy of movement, using bursts of speed when necessary but content to wait in line whenever there was no alternative.

In the City of London, Fraser entered a small private bank where he withdrew a substantial sum in cash. This he carefully secured in his briefcase before walking some distance to the premises of a firm of solicitors.

There he was greeted as a valued client by a senior partner and they settled down to business. He passed over various deeds to properties, owned by himself directly, or through holding companies, then appointed the firm as trustees of his estate in the event of his death. He handed over a sealed envelope containing his will. Whilst the partner made notes he dictated certain arrangements and conditions regarding the eventual distribution of his wealth.

The solicitor deduced that his client was clearing his affairs in a way that could only indicate recent bad news regarding health, but Fraser assured him all was well and that he was simply taking precautions. They shook hands and Fraser left.

The weather in London the next morning was considerably colder and chilling rain warned of a premature winter.

Paul Stratton hated it.

Turning up the collar of his raincoat, he angrily pulled a thirties-style peaked cap over his thick, black hair, and walked the streets of the capital. His miserable progress entailed stops at certain small hotels in the Victoria and Earls Court districts of the city.

When changing districts, he travelled by taxi, for he was not a man given to using such utilitarian forms of transport as buses or the Underground. He lived in hotels, travelled by taxi, and owned nothing, save the clothes and basic necessities taken, as needed, from his large leather suitcase.

Paul Stratton was a soldier between wars. A combat veteran, in a nuclear world, where foot-soldiers should have been obsolete, but were not. Instead they had become specialists, highly trained experts, indispensible in the small but vicious wars around the globe. And, because there is no place for the ultimate weapon in such conflicts, the best men were worth their weight in gold.

Stratton, in mercenary jargon, was a 'twenty-four-carat bastard'. His parents, tea-planters in British India, had enjoyed the very best the Raj could offer, but when the rocky marriage of Empire and Mother Country finally succumbed they found themselves back in England. The difficult adjustment was made and the large Stratton family settled down to a new life.

Almost at the very moment of receiving the results of his final examinations, Paul had applied successfully for a commission in the army, but soon discovered that he had left one smothering family for another.

Not wanting to give up the possibility of action or the discipline the army offered, Stratton cast around within the structure of the military establishment and found an élite cadre of individuals who comprised a very different family indeed. He became one of the very few accepted by the SAS. He was home.

While serving in the Oman, he had received a cable which informed him that a charter airliner travelling to Spain had vanished without trace. It had been only two weeks earlier that his mother had sent him a letter, proclaiming with great joy that the entire family, including various wives and children, were pooling their resources and flying to the sun together.

'And that!' he thought, in the stark moment of shock, 'is that!'

He applied for compassionate leave and returned to England. The missing aircraft was never found and, finally giving up hope, he left the empty shell of his parents' home in the London suburbs and made his way to headquarters of the Twenty-second Regiment, SAS, in Hereford.

During his period in the Oman, the regiment had lost its commanding officer, and the moment he stepped through the check-point, he sensed a strong almost fanatical force driving the hardened troopers. Later, in the presence of a tall, sandy-haired colonel with amber eyes and a fanged moustache, he understood. The new commander was that force.

The men had already christened him 'The Wolf', but his real name was Jonathan Fraser. Stratton continued his journey through the rain, armed with a list of names, having one thing in common. They had all served under and felt the power of that man.

He bore a message for each of them : The Wolf needs you.

And the pack was gathering.

That evening, Colonel Fraser, at the wheel of the Jaguar, skirted the walls of Buckingham Palace and headed towards Victoria. The meeting before him he anticipated impatiently. It was one step further forward in an otherwise grim day.

His regular visit to the Harley Street specialist had changed nothing except for the replenishment of painkillers, which he took cautiously, like a smoker trying to cut down.

The specialist had murmured quietly to himself as he studied the small dark shape, almost perfectly triangular, on the X-ray plate. And Fraser, as he sat staring at the inside of his skull, felt, in one agonizing memory of terror, the jeep lifting towards the sun, hopelessly losing the race against the white-hot fragments of metal which followed.

He had lived the pain again. The cushioned seat under his buttocks being pierced, driving his torn body backwards, so that one final sharp fragment entered neatly into the base of his skull as cleanly as a surgeon's scalpel.

At Victoria, Fraser bypassed the main-line station, turned the nose of the Jaguar towards the river and pulled into a street lined with small hotels. He parked the car and entered one of them.

Inside, tucked behind the webbing of a notice-board, he extracted two envelopes addressed to Paul Stratton. He pocketed them and palmed the bell on the small counter. A short, portly figure appeared, his front covered by a striped blue apron.

'Stratton?' Fraser enquired.

The man jerked his head upward. 'Thirteen,' he said, then touched Fraser's arm with plump fingers, gently restraining him. 'There's a woman !'

'That's all right,' Fraser assured him, pulling away.

He took the short flight of stairs to the upper storey. Thirteen was at the end of the corridor.

'Paul?' he called, knocking, and heard movement as sheets were tossed off and feet hit the floor.

The door opened a few inches, and the odour of strong

tobacco and women escaped through the gap. Part of a pale face appeared, one eye, the pupil almost perfectly black.

'Can you get rid of the girl without too much fuss?' Fraser asked, his voice low, not wishing to offend her. The face inclined in agreement.

He moved away and leant against the papered wall, arms folded.

The door was still ajar, and in the circular mirror of the dressing table, he could see the naked body of the girl as she dressed, her full breasts swaying as she moved, her dark pubic hair like deep shadow. The sight did not stir him. He felt detached, like an old man watching children at play, aware that a part of his life had passed and would never return.

It was a moment of loneliness; even desolation.

The girl pulled tight denims over her white thighs, and struggled with the heavy zip. Moving faster, as if being urged on silently, she pulled a sweater over her head then tossed her hair to free the trapped ends. He turned his face aside as she left hurriedly, then stepped into the room.

Stratton had opened the window, and the curtains billowed inwards. Almost immediately the air cleared, and the smell of the city replaced the musky atmosphere. Stratton sat on the hastily made bed, legs outstretched, pulling deeply on a thin, evil-smelling black cigar.

'Pretty girl!' Fraser said, closing the window.

'I should have got rid of her sooner. Sorry!'

Fraser dismissed the apology, then dipped into his breast pocket and tossed the two envelopes on to the bed.

Stratton's dark eyebrows lifted. 'Two more! That certainly gives us plenty to choose from.'

'I've a place in Putney,' Fraser began. 'It's empty just at the moment. Arrange a party. Plenty of girls – some men too. A few women over the top if you can. And no drug-users, drinkers only. We can't afford that sort of trouble at this time! Have our own men arrive so that they're part of the crowd. It's probably an unnecessary precaution, but worth taking. The house stands with a row of others, but it's detached and there's good parking. It's divided into a duplex apartment on the first and second floors, while the ground floor is taken up by the caretaker and his wife. Make the party on the first floor and we'll have the use of the second.'

'The second has its own locking door?' Stratton asked.

Fraser nodded and took a card from his overcoat. 'Yes, but not its own entrance. Everyone goes in at the front door. Here's the address.'

Stratton swung his legs from the bed. He was tall, with the hips of a bullfighter.

'When?' he asked.

'This weekend. Saturday. That leaves two more days. We should have some more affirmatives by then.'

'We don't need them!' the mercenary protested.

'We will,' Fraser said firmly. 'The men who are settled we don't want. We only need the ones who don't really give a damn.'

A tight smile creased Stratton's handsome face. 'Like Paul Stratton!'

'Like Paul Stratton, like Jonathan Fraser, like anyone fed up with this tired, uniform, predictable, utterly boring world!'

'*Are* you?' Stratton asked, the question stronger in his eyes than on his lips.

Fraser's smile broke under the moustache.

'I? I want to sleep for ever.'

'You're quite sure about this? No doubts? Regrets?'

'Doubts? Of course I have doubts! But only of the final outcome. Regrets are something I have never suffered from. It does no good to look over your shoulder at a road you've already walked along. Anyway, it never looks quite the same if you walk along it a second time.'

'Saturday then,' Stratton said as Fraser turned to leave. 'Time?'

'Nine should be adequate.' He opened the door and left.

2

The disturbances outside the Soviet Embassy were, by Thursday morning, causing some concern. Commander James Vere, of the Special Branch, received a telephone call from the

Permanent Under-Secretary at the Home Office, a feared and hated man who concealed his motives like a stiletto blade.

'Commander,' the pompous voice brayed, 'the Minister wants more than just the routine reports from the Uniform Branch. What he *really* wants is something in depth!' The tone implied that the Minister did not know his own mind. 'You do understand what I mean, Commander?'

Vere's florid complexion darkened. He tapped his pipe sharply on the edge of a crystal ash-tray, spilling glowing embers on to the blotter.

'Perhaps the Minister would care to detail his requirements to me personally. In writing!' he said heavily. 'That way there will be no problem with crossed wires. I wouldn't want to be treading on any sensitive toes, or duplicating reports!'

'There is absolutely no question of duplication, Commander,' the Under-Secretary interrupted, furious at the implied challenge. 'It appears to me to be very clear what the Minister had in mind.'

'Under-Secretary, I still feel that this is a purely local incident that should be handled by the Uniform Branch.'

'This "local incident", as you choose to put it, is touching a very sensitive area. A *very* sensitive area! We are in the process, ah, that is to say . . . the Foreign Office is in the process of establishing sound relations with the Soviet government. Or haven't you heard of the word *détente*, Commander?'

'I am completely familiar with the word. Indeed it is that very policy which gives me the most trouble with dissident groups!' A silence fell on the line. 'Under-Secretary?' he enquired.

'Commander Vere,' the voice returned portentously. 'I realize you have many problems to deal with. But I must emphasize that the Minister requires those reports at the earliest possible moment. I hope we understand each other fully?'

Vere sighed and began to button up the front of his waistcoat.

'He'll have them!' he replied curtly.

'Excellent! *Everything* to *me*, personally. Oh! While you're at it, copy the Foreign Office Adviser. Doesn't hurt to show them that we too are aware of the bigger picture!'

Vere waited for the cut-off and slammed the phone down hard.

'Swine!'

He stabbed at his intercom. 'Get me Hammond!' he said, his anger evident.

Chief Superintendent Colin Hammond was at his desk, two offices down the corridor, when he was buzzed by the Commander's secretary.

'Go straight through,' she said tartly as he entered.

The girl had joined them after being with SIS and she still felt it was a step down the ladder. Hammond had once made the grave error of referring to SIS as 'the spooks' and she had never forgiven him.

'*Come!*' a voice blared.

The chief superintendent entered the inner office and stood before the walnut desk.

Vere's head was lowered over a report and Hammond noticed, as always, the strong growth of white hair on his superior's head. Unconsciously his hand moved upwards and touched his own thinning dark strands.

'Here you are, Hammond,' Vere said, holding out a handwritten list of instructions. 'Read, inwardly digest, bloody well implement and get back to me as soon as humanly possible.' He looked up, his eyes fire-hot. 'Sooner!'

Hammond raised an eyebrow as he glanced at the paper.

'All we need to do on this, sir, is use the basic technique for observation and identification at demonstrations. The only difference is that this is happening daily, not just a one off.'

'Just give me a daily report until the thing blows over,' Vere sighed. 'I am aware of the procedures!'

The chief superintendent opened his mouth to speak but Vere forstalled him with a raised hand.

'Don't tell me, I know already. You haven't the manpower. Well, you'll have to make do, just like the rest of us. Get out there yourself for a change, instead of sitting in that monastic cell you call an office, dreaming up improbable solutions to impossible problems. We are all aware of the capacity of your cranium. Let's see what you can do with your feet!'

Colin Hammond's problem was that he was one of the new

breed of policeman who had come into the force with a university degree, and had spent only a minimum period in the lower ranks. To make matters worse, he came from a working-class background which he had never fitted into but which, perversely, would not let him go. He was in that no-man's-land reserved for those whose abilities lift them out of their social position but do not ensure entry to a higher social plane.

'You're not one of us!' his father would say, whenever the opportunity arose. 'You're a brain! You'll end up one of the bosses, blast you!'

The old man was dead now. The heat from the furnaces finally sapped his strength and dried him up. On the day he died, he was shrivelled and small. Hammond was glad his father had not lived to see him enter the Special Branch. That would have been the final blow! The Branch were always the ones who kept close tabs on the militant left-wingers in the unions, and his father had been among the most militant on any list of subversives.

Hammond had a large domed forehead, almost bereft of hair, except for the very top and sides of his head; large brown eyes that, in the open air, peered liquidly at the world as though protesting the assault by the weather; sallow skin and a strong mouth and chin, which, even at the age of thirty-nine, rarely looked as though it needed shaving.

At school, the one thing that had saved him from many severe thrashings from those envious of his mental prowess and the obvious favouritism of the teachers was the simple fact he was strong, although not physically big. He had to thank his father for that, as never a day passed without the importance of physical strength being impressed upon him. The old man had known, with shrewd wisdom, that the boy would need more than his apparently prodigious brain to survive the reality of life in industrial England.

'Brains is all well and good,' he would say, 'but what happens if you get them bleedin' knocked out then? Eh?'

Hammond learned his lesson fast. After a school fracas in which he came off worst, he joined the local amateur boxing club and in a matter of weeks there was not one bully who had not a sound and painful reason to keep well out of his way. He kept his kit at the gym and his parents never found out. Hammond did not believe in flaunting strength. He believed that, like the brain, it should be evident only when used.

He returned to his office and sat behind the metal desk. The room was without any personal touch and could accurately be described as austere. Two grey metal filing cabinets and a couple of hard straight-backed chairs made up the rest of the furniture. One hook, behind the door, took his coat on a wire hanger.

Checking the duty-roster, he shook his head ruefully, proceeding to juggle names and times, jotting details on a scratch pad, until he felt satisfied enough to move on to other operational problems.

Two hours later he made phone calls and arranged a meeting in his office with the men whose names he had pencilled on to his pad. His briefing was clear and precise.

'Check faces for known anti-Soviet agitators – Zionists, right-wing groups, both the sensible ones and the lunatic fringe. Also the residents' protest group. And don't forget the left wing! Just because this is an anti-Soviet demonstration it does not necessarily follow that the left are at home with their feet up. The left are almost *never* at home with their feet up. Theirs is a very heavy commitment. They live their beliefs. They'll be out there sizing up the opposition and also doing what we'll be doing – that is getting names and faces for little black – or red – books. Watch, too, for new faces who look as though they are more than just sensation seekers, or want to have their granny see them on *News at Ten*. You never know what you might turn up! We always need new faces for the files. If we *have* to mount this operation let's have a good trawl and see what we can pull into the net.'

With that, he'd sent his team out to the area, with the firm promise that he'd be making trips to the trouble spot himself at regular intervals. He could not know that he had been placed at the centre of a fanatic's vision of a personal *Götterdämmerung*.

Paul Stratton stepped from a taxi on the Friday evening and threaded his way through hopeful young men, as they posed against railings watching for stray girls. The entrance to the discothèque was subterranean, a door below street level, down dangerous steps. He was a member and the doorman tilted his head towards the bar without greeting.

The music was like the sea, full of raging curls and flat calms, and the voices of the crowd like gulls, muted one moment, then shrieking. Stratton cut among them, forcefully but without touching.

The bar was small and set off to the side; he ordered a brandy and sank it, his hand still around the glass for another. Behind him loud Arab princes splashed Dom Perignon in silver buckets and drunkenly toasted pale blondes, their wrists captured by Cartier bracelets in dull gold, the designs identical, as though bought by the gross. One of the Arabs looked at him, fearing a male loose and dangerous, and gathered in his flock, cosseting them with more wine.

Stratton looked up, and past them, into the flashing room where the music was loudest and where bodies jerked as if raked by machine guns. Taking his brandy, he stepped into the discordant firefight, the eyes of the girls following him. He had to force his way through the volume of the music like a surfer through breakers. The brandy heated his blood and his dark eyes, now accustomed to the flashing lights, found others that were on him. He began pulling in the camouflage for Fraser's private party.

Jonathan Fraser had stayed at his club for the nights of Thursday and Friday as, on Saturday, he had a full day ahead of him. At eight o'clock the porter's desk woke him by telephone and coffee and toast came up to his room ten minutes later. He ate as he dressed.

The evening before Paul Stratton had telephoned to confirm that arrangements for the party were going well, but Fraser could tell by his voice that he was tense, and from experience knew that the moment the phone came down on the receiver, Stratton would be out looking for a woman.

Fraser drained the last of his coffee in one gulp and left. His Jaguar was in the club's small car park, and he drove to Shepherd's Bush, stopping to purchase more cigarettes, then checking the road carefully in his rear-view mirror before moving off. He approached the premises of the arms company only after passing the building and circling through side streets until he was satisfied there was no surveillance. Stopping a quarter of a mile away, he walked the difference and at his destination his business was conducted swiftly, all arrangements having been made in advance. Final signatures were made and a pick-up date and time settled.

Paul Stratton, in the meantime, was spending his Saturday morning at the house in Putney. The caretakers, husband and wife, were set to work removing dust sheets and covers off the furniture, polishing and cleaning. It was well into the morning when the van arrived with its cartons of liquor. The caretaker and the van-driver hefted these up the stairs and Stratton paid the driver from a flat wad of notes clamped in a gold money-clip.

As he settled with the man, a well-preserved 1960s Ford Zodiac with wide chromed wheels and aubergine paintwork grumbled to a halt, settling heavily on its fat tyres. Stratton jerked a thumb towards the upper windows of the house and the pretty youth inside grinned before unloading his bulky disco equipment with unexpected strength. He was still testing his equipment through headphones as Stratton completed his own arrangements in the upper half of the duplex apartment. Satisfied, he locked the connecting door to the upper floor and pocketed the key, then tapped the disc-jockey on the shoulder, indicating that it was time to leave and assuring him that his equipment was absolutely safe. He also assured him that, if he brought either drugs or gate-crashers with him that evening, he, his drugs, his equipment and his friends would all go the same way – out of the window from the first floor.

Stratton, who had recruited the caretakers as barman and general help for the evening, told them to be ready at eight o'clock. Finally he made the disc-jockey drive him to the nearest taxi-rank.

Fraser, meanwhile, put the remainder of Saturday afternoon to good use. At a specialist car-mart in south London he selected a green Range Rover with only 8000 miles on the clock. He paid for the vehicle in cash, registering it under the name of Spartan Leisure and including it under that company's insurance cover. He then acquired an Austin van and arranged for it to be painted to match the Range Rover. Collection of the vehicles was arranged for the following week.

The afternoon traffic was heavy as Fraser drove to a large sporting and outdoor equipment store where he made one purchase only. This was an oil-fired lamp, more like a ground flare, of the type which gives an open flame, effective in all weathers.

He took the package containing his purchase and walked into the street, his mind burning strong and free and the cold numbness of his internal wounds suddenly glowing with warmth and bright pain.

Evening crept over Putney like a rolling mist, damp, and laced with the pungent smells of oil and factory residue. Along the Thames, houses crept close to the river, the green tongues of their lawns lapping with blackened edges at the spoilt waters. Sound pounded through the brightly lit windows of one of them.

Paul Stratton stood inside, against a small bar in the large lounge, and watched dancers in the centre of the room as they began the first exploratory sexual assault on each other. Everything at this early stage was done with the eyes and with carefully chosen words, delivered with practised innuendo. Here and there the bolder ones touched bodies in the attempt to gain quick submission before moving on to another soft battleground.

There were more girls than men and, as it always was with Stratton, he could not resist the temptation to fill every area of his vision with female flesh. At no time in his thirty-five years had he failed to demolish, in one overpowering onslaught, all the barriers women put up against his blatant sensuality. He had two basic needs. Violence and sex. Without the regular fulfilment of both, he knew he might just as well be dead.

Fraser entered the room, and Stratton pulled his dark eyes from the bodies of the girls. He eased himself away from the bar.

'They're arriving,' Fraser said.

A tall girl made her way through the dancers and placed her body against Stratton.

'Ann,' he said, as though it didn't matter. The girl moved herself against Fraser and the drawn face stiffened.

'Go away,' he said.

The girl shot him a glance, then drew herself away.

'Later?' she asked with eyes already floundering in alcohol. 'Go away!'

The girl stumbled, falling into the dancers, who swept her up.

'Sorry,' Stratton murmured, cradling a brandy glass. 'Drink?'

'One of those if you would.'

Stratton poured.

'I'd better see the men,' he said, and stepped into the pressing bodies, moving through them with unaccountable ease. Fraser watched him, for a moment unaware of the crowd or the music. Then he picked up the glass.

The door to the upstairs flat was opened for Fraser by a man whose face he knew well.

'It's been some time, Cornwell. How are you?'

'The better for seeing you, sir.'

'You're abroad aren't you – just now?'

'Abu Dhabi, sir. The Gulf. Weapons instructor. Good money but a waste of life, sir.'

'Rank?'

'Adviser, sir.' A grin etched more lines in an already wrinkled nut-brown face.

'Then the Arabs don't know what a bloody good RSM they're wasting.'

Fraser climbed, gripping the polished hand-rail. His heart pounded and his nostrils flared as he heard the voices of a large group of men waiting upstairs. The music below was muffled, like a distant barrage. He opened a door and entered to the flat staccato of trained soldiers' feet coming together but blunted by soft civilian shoes. He estimated forty.

Slowly and deliberately he walked through the tight ranks standing before the rows of chairs. Each face he recognized unfailingly and put a name to. Now and then he stopped and spoke to a man, questioning him on personal matters as though no time at all had passed since they had last spoken. Finally he stood facing them at the head of the long room.

'Gentlemen,' he said. 'Almost all of you have travelled a long way to be here. I thank you all for coming. Please sit.' He moved towards a blackboard and easel set in front of the curtained windows. 'By now you will all have realized that every one of us in this room has, at some time or another, been a member of the Special Air Service and, at some stage, you have all been under my command. You may have been thinking that this is some sort of reunion. Well, in a way it is! How many have we, Sarn'-Major?'

'Thirty-eight, sir. Five former NCOs. Thirty-three troopers no longer serving. Includes myself, sir.'

Stratton passed a list into Fraser's hand and the colonel continued.

'I see from this that apart from six of you, the rest are still engaged in soldiering in one form or another. What are those six doing?'

'Security guard. Sir!'

'Salesman, sir.'

'Driver, sir. Artics.'

'Sir!' came the threatening tone of the former RSM.

'Sir.'

'Paramedic. Oil rigs. North Sea oil.' The voice was upper class, Eton and Oxford with a patronizing hint of London as if seeking acceptance from the other ranks. 'Bloody cold, sir!'

Stifled laughter zigzagged through the rows, causing the RSM's fingers to curl and uncurl themselves behind his back.

Fraser glanced in the direction of the voice.

'Ah. James Dewey. North Sea oil? Seems you've realized your dream of joining the Establishment at last.'

'Next,' the RSM barked.

'Bouncer, sir. The Lyceum. Sir!'

'Unemployed, sir.'

Again Fraser turned his head towards the voice.

'Any particular reason?'

'Can't stay in a job, sir.' The man shrugged his enormous shoulders as if the weight of the ceiling pressed down on them. Gently he folded his six-foot-four-inch frame back on to the chair, the weight causing it to groan.

'A common problem among men like us, Murray. I shouldn't let it worry you.'

'That's all,' Stratton interjected. 'We have details of the others already.'

'Fine. Then we'll begin.' Fraser began sketching with chalk on the blackboard. 'Over the past few weeks I, with the aid of

Major Stratton, have been contacting former members of the regiment – certain former members, that is – who might be interested in this . . . shall we say . . . *family* reunion!' He completed the drawing on the board. 'You are unaware that I am a wealthy man. A *very* wealthy man.' He added a small triangle to the chalked drawing of the skull. 'I am also a walking, talking, dead man.' He did not wait for a reaction. 'That gentlemen is shrapnel,' he tapped the board with a fingernail, 'and this is my head. If that steel splinter moves further I shall be dead. Before I die I wish to make one final gesture that will make this bored, pampered world sit up and take notice. I want also to experience action once more. I do not, in any circumstances, wish to die on some street in London whilst frantic shoppers step over me in their eagerness to buy before the Christmas rush.' He smiled briefly. 'I have no dependents. You are my family. My beneficiaries.'

A rumble began in the room, cut short by the ominous voice of the RSM.

'Hold yourselves. Colonel speaking.'

'All of you here tonight will receive a cheque for £1000.'

'Quiet!'

'Some of you will, in time, receive more. Others, perhaps only one, will survive to have it all.'

The word 'survive' hung in the air like a headsman's axe.

'Correct,' Fraser said. 'I used the word survive deliberately. We shall be carrying out a final action.'

'To begin with,' Stratton said, taking over, 'there will be a period of training to acclimatize you for the operation. You will find that some of the techniques used may surprise you. At the end of this period, a certain number of you will be accepted as suitable for the operation itself and the remainder will be paid off. The special training period should take no more than ten days and for this you will receive a further £1000 each.' Stratton stopped. 'Before I continue I am going to read a small part of Colonel Fraser's assessment of the operation:

Because of certain aspects peculiar to this operation, which, according to the turn of events may become a holding action, it is estimated that casualties may be extremely high. It is probable that there will be no survivors.

Stratton let the words settle over the seated men before continuing.

'If any of you wish to take the £1000 already promised to you by Colonel Fraser and leave, now is the moment to do it. The envelopes laid out in the table outside the door bear your names in alphabetical order; a cheque is in each one. There will be a short break during which time you may go out of the room to collect your envelopes, smoke or use the bathroom. At the end of the break we shall assume that those back in the room have accepted the odds against survival and wish to carry on. Those who do not return go with our good wishes. Two further points should be made before we take the break. Both are of the utmost importance.

'One. Those who elect to stay will, from tonight, be under our rules of war. Desertion, cowardice, contact with the authorities or the media resulting in the exposure of secrets, or damage to the mission, will all be dealt with in the same way. A hearing before the colonel, myself and the senior NCO. If a verdict of guilty is arrived at, the offender will be executed immediately by a bullet in the back of the neck. We accept the word of those who choose not to stay that this meeting will remain secret. If it is evident that this mission is blown by any non-combatant, our rules of war will be applied. Finally, if . . .,' Stratton emphasized the word heavily, '. . . if there is a survivor, or survivors, of the mission, the amount Colonel Fraser referred to when he said the survivors could have it all, is around £1,000,000 sterling. But the odds against anyone living to see it are one hundred to one. You have twenty minutes to make up your mind.'

Stratton counted the envelopes at the end of the break.

Eleven cheques were gone. Most had torn open the envelopes and removed the cheque, leaving a scribbled note on a scrap of the paper. Different words, which in the end said the same thing. 'I've got a reason to live.'

The RSM reported to Stratton.

'Twenty-seven volunteers, sir.'

'I take it you're volunteering, Sarn'-Major, and not just administrating?'

'That figure includes myself, sir.'

'Good. Still a bachelor?'

'What woman in her right mind would stand my sort of life, sir?'

Stratton smiled bleakly.

'Better form up the men. Colonel wants to address them.'

'Sir.' Stratton nodded to Fraser and handed him a large envelope. The volunteers filled the seats in the front rows, leaving the empty spaces behind them. Fraser stood before them, legs braced apart.

'Some time ago,' he began quietly, 'people I believed to be agents of the British government approached me with a proposition. They wanted to help, militarily, a certain government in Africa, to prevent that country falling into the hands of Marxist-backed forces. I now know that their real intention was, by discrediting British mercenaries and making them appear inept, barbarous killers, to stop once and for all any Western mercenary involvement in the African continent, thereby giving a clear field to Soviet-aided Cuban units and Marxist guerrillas. We all know that they succeeded in that intention.'

He paused, opening the flap of the envelope and extracting twelve ten-by-eight inch grainy photographs, each bearing a different face and obviously blown up from passport shots. 'You probably do not recognize these faces. Nor do I. I did not recruit the men – that was left to others. But I was the prime mover in that disastrous enterprise. *I* set the ball moving. *I* delivered and sanctioned the use of funds passed to me. *I* fell into the trap and delivered the bodies for slaughter and the pathetic remnants for trial and execution or a lifetime's incarceration in appalling conditions. The twelve men still held in Africa are imprisoned in a group of blockhouses. The temperature inside each cell is 130 degrees. The size of each cell is eight feet by five feet. Most of this space is taken up by two rough-cast concrete platforms which serve as beds for the two occupants. No mattresses are provided. Their daily diet is one glass of water, a bowl of rice and one salted fish. The fish is served uncooked with head, tail and entrails intact. The only light and ventilation is from a small unglazed window in the shape of a Maltese cross. The average sentence of the twelve prisoners is twenty years apiece. There is little likelihood that conditions will improve during these years.'

With his face ravaged by anger, he held the photographs over his head. 'Gentlemen, we are going to bring them back!'

At approximately ten minutes before midnight, as Saturday passed into Sunday, a motor coach crossed Putney Bridge. Set in the front window was a card bearing the legend 'Spartan Leisure. Strength of Body and Mind'. The occupants, sitting in the unlit interior, detached and coiled tight inside like parachutists waiting for the green light, watched London drift by.

The never-sleeping city breathed contentedly, unaware.

Jonathan Fraser sat alone watching the dawn break over the Hertfordshire countryside. The manor was silent and the light breakfast that he ate he prepared himself. Spartan Leisure bookings had been phased down a month earlier, the few outstanding reservations being cancelled owing to the need for 'urgent renovations' and the domestic and ground staff were happy to take an unexpected paid holiday during the period of work. Within the following two weeks, although they did not know it, they would all receive redundancy settlements equivalent to three months' wages, plus bonus, and a note that Spartan Leisure Limited was being wound up.

The kitchens and store-rooms were well stocked and there was now no reason for contact with the outside world except in special circumstances.

Fraser studied the growing light and listened to the first small treble sounds of birds. In a detached and unemotional way he wondered how many more mornings he would live to see.

3

Hammond arrived at the Special Branch Headquarters early on Monday morning, his mind ready for whatever the day would bring.

In his office he cleared his desk of routine matters, then studied for the fourth time the terse minute from Commander Vere instructing him to continue 'with greater endeavour' to supply up-to-the-minute reports on the Embassy demonstrations.

Included in the papers on his desk was a copy of the report made on the attack on the two black youths in the Notting Hill Gate area. Although having originally pushed it aside as being unrelated to the task in hand, he found himself studying the details of the wounds inflicted on the victims with growing interest. He hesitated for a time before lifting his telephone, and calling the inspector in charge of the case.

'Inspector Graham,' he said. 'My name's Hammond, Chief Superintendent, Special Branch. I may be wasting your time and mine, but this report on the beating up of those two black kids – I've been copied on this, and having read it, there's something odd – about the injuries I mean.'

'I thought you people might find it interesting, Chief Superintendent. Bit of a hard case who did that one.'

'You think it was one man then?'

'Don't take a blind bit of notice of what those yobs told the papers. They may not have any form – yet – but those two are muggers, sure as I've got a wife, kids and mortgage. They just tangled with someone who hit back – and how! No bloody "gang of whites". More like a trained pro! Para, or someone with that sort of background.'

'Russian security guard – something like that?'

'If they give 'em that sort of training, yes.'

'The blow they each received behind the ear? That sounds exactly like a classic karate dokko strike. If it was, they're lucky to be alive! That's a killing blow – only an expert could dish that out without having a couple of bodies on his hands.'

'Well, I'm not up on that stuff. All I know is that those two buggers probably got what they deserved.'

Hammond mused for a moment.

'What's the chance of getting the truth out of them?'

'None I should think. They'd never admit to taking a beating by one bloke! Don't forget they're bloody heroes now – victims of dormant racialism and white-oriented society. Bloody muggers, that's all they are.'

'How important would they feel if the Branch took an interest in their case?'

'Important? They'd be preening themselves ready for their next TV spot.'

'Couldn't have that. It would have to be kept quiet. We like to know when the Russians have got killers on the streets, but we don't have to let *them* know that we know.'

The inspector laughed.

'Your day must be like one long Chinese puzzle, Chief Superintendent.' He paused. 'Mind you – you could read them the Official Secrets Act . . . scare the pants off 'em that will. Hint that they were almost topped by an Ivan with karate belts by the dozen.'

'Are they fit to move?'

'Not a chance. They've got 'em up at Northwick Park – you know, the biggest most modern hospital in Europe or wherever. Typical that they'd put 'em about as far away as possible!'

'OK. Can you get down yourself – say this afternoon?'

'Any time after two.'

'Make it two-thirty then, Inspector. Northwick Park Hospital. Better arrange for a room where we can talk to them.'

'Huh! Don't worry about that – they're both secure and comfortable in a private room.'

'Equal rights?'

'Yeah! Wish I had 'em.'

'Two-thirty, Inspector. I'll meet you in their room.'

Hammond replaced the receiver. Probably a wild-goose chase, he thought; but then the Special Branch did like to know of any stray professional killers who were at large in England.

The Edgware Road took Hammond to the Kingsbury turn-off and he cut through the rows of suburban semis to the hospital complex. Graham was waiting, almost pawing at the floor, as Hammond entered the private room. The two youths lay propped up against pillows in beds parallel to each other.

'Try to make it as brief as possible, please,' the Ward Sister cautioned as she left them.

'Now this is Chief Superintendent Hammond of the Special Branch,' Graham warned. 'And like the name implies, he's special – very special! So let's see how your story sounds to him, shall we?'

Hammond sat down on a chair facing the two beds.

'First of all,' he started, 'I have to tell you that none of this conversation can be repeated to the press or the tel . . .'

'Who says!' one of the youths yelled, cutting right across him.

34

Graham moved forward but Hammond waved him back.

'This says so. Read it both of you. That's called the Official Secrets Act, and it gives me more power over you than you could ever begin to realize!'

The youths barely got through the first paragraph of the Act. 'We don't know fuck-all about secrets. We was attacked – that's all.'

'You certainly were attacked! The man who gave you those injuries was more than just a man in the street. That man could have killed either of you at any time.'

'There was no one fella. It was a bunch of 'em. Honkies. Jumped us they did.'

'In a cul-de-sac – a dead end – why? Jumped you why?'

'For our bread a' course.'

'They hadn't fifty pence between 'em when they were brought in,' Graham muttered.

'We was mugged!'

'Gawd love us,' the inspector breathed, raising his eyes to the ceiling.

Hammond lowered his voice theatrically.

'The man who attacked you may well be one of the deadliest professional killers in the world! He may even have been Carlos – the Jackal.'

'Nar! I seen the photos of that Carlos, this geezer was thin – had a 'tash. . . .'

'You stupid fucker!' the other black shouted.

'Let's start with the moustache,' Hammond began, rising from his chair.

Graham walked with him towards the car park.

'That didn't take long,' he said as the Special Branch man got into the car.

'They're only kids,' Hammond replied.

'Not on a dark night up a dead end they're not.'

'Sounds like an army man. Officer, by the estimated age and description.'

'Where does that lead you, sir?'

'Lead me? It leads me absolutely bloody nowhere – except up that dead end. They were just unlucky those kids – picking on a man who knew how to handle himself.'

'Sounds to me as if they were *lucky*! They could be on the slab now instead of lording it in a private ward.'

Hammond shook his head.

'No. The man was no killer. He simply protected himself to his best ability. Unfortunately for the muggers, that ability was very high. I don't think, Inspector, that you or I are likely to hear of him again. Goodbye.'

Paul Stratton, like Colin Hammond, had begun his day early. In Enfield he hired a heavy-duty Mercedes van and drove it to where Fraser was waiting in the Jaguar. The six-foot-four-inch Murray was crammed in the back of the car.

'Here are the documents,' Fraser said. 'Nothing will go wrong.' Stratton nodded, and crooked a finger at Murray, who crawled out of the Jaguar and sighed with relief as he slid behind the wheel of the van.

'You have the directions,' Stratton said, pulling his cap over his eyes. 'Just get us there and back in one piece!'

They arrived at the warehouse of the arms company at ten-forty. The collection note was duly handed over and three wooden crates were loaded into the cavernous rear of the Mercedes. The note stated that they were for delivery to SultArm Ltd (Oman), via the British representative, ArabGulf Clearing and Forwarding Agency, an organization which had a relatively uncomplicated working procedure. In all instances goods needing clearance and shipment were air-freighted via private jet-liners belonging to the rulers of the oil-rich Gulf States. This, along with the British stance on the realities of the tremendous potential of the Arab market, made life very simple for the company. Fraser, behind a perfectly legal screen, owned ArabGulf.

Within the cases were samples of a new model automatic assault rifle, plus a liberal supply of ammunition. Also included in the batch were a number of NVDs (night vision devices), flash suppressors and Mecar grenades. The end-user-certificate was signed by a bona-fide representative of the Omani government and listed the weapons as samples for testing with the view to replacing the Fabrique Nationale 7.62 SLR currently used by the Royal Omani Forces in their fight against the rebels.

Fraser had obtained that signature and the order, but the

rifles and hardware would never arrive; they would be held up through some bureaucratic delay and by the time alarm bells started to ring it would be too late. The rifles would already be in use, and the ArabGulf Clearing and Forwarding Agency would have been liquidated.

Paul Stratton smiled under the peak of his lowered cap as Murrary bowled the big Mercedes up the A10.

Stratton and Murray arrived back to find the men stripped to blue Spartan Leisure tracksuits and canvas shoes. They were in great spirits and, in the security of the cellars, eagerly prised open the boxes before stripping the assault rifles of their protective oiled-paper envelopes and grease.

As the RSM formed the men up, Stratton picked up one of the weapons and hefted the weight in both hands. It was an unusual-looking gun, with a pistol grip halfway along the slab-sided body which housed the breech and moving parts. The wide magazine was set behind the trigger unit, and the butt consisted only of a plate at the rear of the metal body.

'Your attention, please,' he shouted, his voice hollow in the deep chamber. 'This is the gun we'll be using. It's a new and highly rated weapon. The arm is manufactured by Sterling, and is calibrated at 4.85 millimetres. The weight is 4.12 kilograms, fully loaded. Operation is by gas, with forward-locking rotary bolt. The rate of fire is 700 to 850 rounds per minute. It also has the capability of firing Mecar grenades directly from the muzzle. All the weapons are fitted with a times four magnification optical sight, and we shall also be using night-sights.' He passed the gun to the RSM. 'One room has already been sandbagged for familiarization and testing of the guns. The RSM will be in charge.' Stratton smiled briefly at the men and left.

Johnson Cornwell, the diminutive RSM, known familiarly in mercenary circles as 'Jack' after the famous prizefighter, kept an iron grip on safety procedures in the confined space. All the men were warned that any weapon, loaded or unloaded, if turned away from the firing line still in the horizontal position, would be treated as being, in his words, 'readied for deadly intent'.

Cornwell paced the line of men, checking every detail mercilessly; shouting instructions when a weapon jammed, or a magazine was fumbled when smacked in fast during a rapid-fire sequence.

The men, although ex-SAS troopers, were ragged – which did not surprise Cornwell at all. He knew the kind of rag-bag armies some of them had been serving with as mercenaries since their discharge. Getting them to think as a unit would be tough, he thought; there's not one below thirty – and that's a difficult age to start taking strict discipline again.

Everything went well for two hours, with only two of the weapons declared useless for combat owing to repeated jamming.

Finally, Cornwell joined the line and completed the test on the last weapon himself, before calling a halt to the firing trials. With a new Sterling still cradled in his arm, pointing directly down the firing area, he removed his ear plugs and ordered the men to detach magazines and check the breeches, before stripping the weapons for cleaning. Raising his own weapon so that the barrel was aimed deliberately high, he assigned a man to retrieve, and set aside for spare parts, the two jammed guns. Turning, he ejected his empty magazine, and was tugging his last full one from his pocket to replace in the ammunition box when his unprotected eardrums were blasted by a sound so loud that he thought that the foundations of the house had given way.

With the Sterling cradled to his chest he crashed to the cold gritty stone. Shaking his head violently, he tried in vain to reduce the high-pitched whistle that filled his ears. With dread in his eyes, he looked towards where the group of volunteers had been standing.

They crouched, frozen in mid-movement, their hair and blue tracksuits covered in white dust shaken from the walls. Two bloodied bodies lay blasted against the brick in deformed shapes, as if dropped through the ceiling from some great height.

Cornwell swivelled his eyes across the width of the cellar, and found the paralysed figure of a man with a raised, smoking weapon, his finger still on the trigger. As if mesmerized, the man turned his shocked white face towards the hard grey eyes, the gun tracing an arc in the same direction.

'Put it down, Pete!' a shaken voice spoke from among the group of men, but the gun kept turning. With death staring at him across the cellar the man tightened his finger on the trigger.

The clunk of the mechanism as it jammed was obliterated by the ripping thunder of the RSM's gun. One arm severed at the shoulder, the jerking body climbed up the wall, held there a foot off the ground by the force of the bullets.

Cornwell's gun clicked on the empty magazine and he turned to face the men.

'Who spoke?' he asked almost wearily.

A man stepped forward through the bunched troopers.

'Me, Sarn'-Major. I told him to drop it.'

'I know what you said. Do you know what you did?'

'I ...'

'You gave him time to fucking think! That's what you did! Count how many men are behind you.'

The man swivelled his head, his eyes flicking fast.

'Seven.'

'That's right. Seven. And two dead.' The RSM pointed a finger at the body of the man he had shot. 'That stupid bastard pulls the trigger on a loaded weapon he assumed would be jammed until the sun fell out of the sky, and you tell him to put it down!' The spittle flew from his lips as he roared. 'He'd have cut the lot of you in half when he realized what he'd done – just to get out of here alive – and you tell him to put it down! You brought him out of shock, you stupid fucker! You're a liability!' He turned away from the man, then swung round and shot him twice through the forehead with a small .22 automatic.

As the body jumped, in spasms, on the stone, he pushed it over with his canvas shoe, and placed a foot between the shoulder blades. From two inches away he severed the spinal column at the neck with one bullet. The body sighed, and shuddered once, like a jelly, before flattening to the cellar floor.

'And the rest of you bastards! You stood there waiting to die! Put your hands above your heads!' Cornwell stood, looking up at them from his five feet six inches of height. Fourteen hands were raised, some of them reaching the ceiling.

'I can't see one weapon in any of those hands. There's forty fucking guns littered around you!' he screamed. 'Not one of you went for them! You're a bunch of cunts! Next time I'll let you all die. Clear this filth up.' His thick ginger eyebrows, which, until that moment, had never stopped jumping on his face, stilled. He looked them over once more with cold murder in his eyes, then with disdain turned his back to them and walked with short steps out of the cellars.

That evening the entire group, now reduced to twenty-five, sat at the long table in the dining room with Fraser at its head. Stratton to his right and Cornwell to his left. The evening meal was eaten in silence. Paul Stratton watched the glum faces with foreboding, knowing the disastrous effect that unexpected and needless death can have on the morale of soldiers keyed up for an operation.

With the meal completed, Fraser stood up and addressed the men.

'Today's unhappy events,' he began in quiet tones, 'prove that the unit is without cohesion. This can of course be rectified. But the hard lesson that was learned today in the cellars of this building is that you are not yet prepared to react immediately and without question for the protection of the unit. The group can only carry out the strike and hold the objective if the safety of the greater number is assured. There may be turncoats and there may well be those who will break under the strain. I assure you these are not idle words! The full nature of this operation is unknown to you. The safety of the greater number must be the highest priority at all times.' He placed both hands on the table and leaned forward. 'Tomorrow, gentlemen, you will all be subjected to certain stress tests unlike anything you have previously encountered. I urge you now to put today's incident behind you and prepare yourselves with a good night's sleep.'

With a curt nod to the group he left the room.

The men began their Tuesday at seven. After they had break-fasted well, Stratton informed them that they had an hour to take fresh air and exercise and warned them that they would not see daylight again until the next morning. At nine o'clock all twenty-three men, including Cornwell, were led by Fraser and Stratton to the prepared stress cells deep in the bowels of the manor where they were to face the twenty-four hours of extreme disorientation techniques that Fraser considered would be sufficient.

The two cellar rooms were empty except for old sacking thrown in a heap in the corner of each. There were no toilet facilities, no food or drink and no daylight penetrated the white-washed brick walls. The men were told to strip naked, before being divided into two groups of twelve and eleven. As the tracksuits, shoes, socks and underwear were tossed aside the volunteers joked and laughed, like a rugby team on its way to the tub. Stratton wondered grimly if they'd still be laughing in a few hours' time. He doubted it. He'd set up the equipment.

Each of the cells was equipped for sound reproduction with powerful speakers bolted into the stone and caged in mesh. Other electrical devices were surprisingly similar to those used in fashionable discothèques. Strobe lamps with a pulsating flash ranged in speeds from a split second of pure white light between moments of darkness to the rushing flicker of an early silent film. Liquid wheel projectors cast indescribable images on to all the walls so that the reality of distance and dimension were lost. Ultra-violet beams darkened everything that wasn't white, and lifted that non-colour to a bluish glare, causing the unpleasant effect of an imaginary membrane over the eye. Laser-light projection traced endless lined patterns through the air with such three-dimensional impact that only touch removed the certainty of their genuine existence and finally, a bank of high-wattage spotlights were powerful enough to make men cower under their blasting beams. Every device was there to induce varying degrees of disorientation.

Eight small closed-circuit TV cameras covered the two stress cells. The pictures from these were fed to an adjacent room where a monitor was linked to each camera.

The volunteers entered the two cells and Stratton secured each heavy door with padlocks. Satisfied, he joined Colonel Fraser in the control room. The TV monitors, power amplifiers, tape decks and mixing controls for sound and light were set, bizarrely, in empty wine-racks, for the room was one of the manor's small wine cellars. The two men sat facing the array of wires and electrical hardware, surrounded by rows of fine vintage wine in dusty bottles.

In the light of one cobwebbed hanging bulb and a red low-wattage desk lamp, they set to work; one greying and wolfish with the fanged moustache, the other, dark and saturnine with black hair falling over his eyes. Monotonously they began the litany of calculated terror.

To control a man you must first control his mind; to control his mind you must first control his senses; to control his senses you must have absolute control of his environment. This is the dictum of brain-washing. Fraser began the long journey from the last to the first. Somewhere along that road he would become omnipotent; the nearest thing to God that the twenty-three incarcerated men would ever know.

The process would follow certain definite paths, along which the men would be taken in controlled conditions. Fraser meant to test them and bend them to his will – not to destroy them. The first path was isolation. In the darkness each man would begin after a time to develop intense concern with himself. The breathing or movements of the others around him would slowly cease to exist. He would effectively be completely alone. The control of his perceptions would follow. Darkness and bright light alternating between other more weird effects would fix his attention totally on his predicament, for he would always be returned to the blackness and his own inner being. Later would come degradation, as he was forced to fulfil the normal functions of the body in the same environment in which he existed. He would find this difficult and demeaning, but nature would take its course. Debilitation and exhaustion would overtake him as his body was denied the nourishment it was used to, and the sleep it relied upon. These sustained tensions would eventually weaken his physical and mental ability to resist. Some, however, would find the hidden reserves of strength that smoulder in all men. Fraser waited patiently for that fire to rise and feed his torch.

In the cells, the men lived death as they sat lined against the cold brick walls in darkness. For hours they sang and told jokes until their repertoire and enthusiasm was exhausted. Then perceptibly their spirits began to slump.

The two crouched figures in the control room watched them on monitors tinged pink by the infra-red filters on the cameras. Muscles slackened and mouths started to gape open, as the onset of sleep soothed their nervous systems.

The sudden white pulse of a strobe, an infinitesimal moment of time and light, snatched them back to reality and scrambled their nerve endings. The sequence was repeated. Momentary sleep. Sharp light; almost imagined. Anger crept into the grumbling of some. Sleep. Light. Sleep light. Sleep. Light.

'Fuck this!' a voice said.

The monitor in the wine-cellar showed a figure in the first cell crawling across the stone floor towards the bundle of sacking.

'Cover my bloody head!' he said aloud.

Cold lips kissed his hands as he pulled the sacking away and the bundle fell heavily on him. He shrieked, pushing madly at the dead thing that lay on him. Bedlam! They crawled through the dark like animals to the terror-stricken man, their hands, with the soft jerky movements of the newly blind, touching and shying away from the bodies of the men killed in the cellars the day before. The group in the second cell would not discover their gruesome companions till much later, when they were all half-demented. Their experience would be much worse.

Fraser's voice filled the first cell, gentle and soft like a concerned father.

'They died for no reason. No cause. They failed to protect us. Leave them. They are nothing now.'

Filtered light filled the cell, a warm glow that sent terror scuttling away like rats into the dark. Singing began again.

The light faded slowly and they were unaware of the creeping darkness until it engulfed them. Stratton, working from a check list and a digital clock, flipped two switches which activated the four liquid wheel projectors in both cells. Inside the cells, the hard stone of the walls seemed to dissolve, and all around them the undulating patterns pitched their minds headlong into the nucleus of the universe.

Unconsciously they edged their bodies away from the wall and into the centre of the cells. It was as though they were atop a stone monolith soaring high into the stratosphere and beyond. At first, the awesome spectacle brought a feeling of wonderment, but this was not to last, for an aching loneliness fell over them; separating them, and leaving each man solitary and bewildered. Sounds began, so distant, that they were like a sea lapping at the base of the monolith, far below in the black depths which were, surely, beyond its hard stone edges. The men backed further away from the walls so that they sat eventually in a tight group. Together, yet utterly alone.

The voice, for that was the origin of the sound, was on a tape played back so slowly that all the human characteristics disappeared, yet its message infiltrated their minds on a subliminal level, so deep, that they could not know it. The phrase of four words took a full minute before it began again. 'The Torch must burn.'

Gradually the bright blues, yellows and scarlets of the undulating patterns, dulled to the deep crimson of blood, the patterns pulsing like human tissue under a microscope.

Every man began to adopt the foetal position as though triggered by some soundless command. Their loneliness ebbed as they sat or lay, knees raised and hands clutched to their chests, in the warm encircling womb of pulsing red.

Fraser's voice sunk in echo filtered through the red walls.

'We are one family. We share the danger. We share the reward. Each is as the other. The Torch must burn. We are one family. We share the danger. We share the reward. Each is as the other. The Torch must burn. We . . .'

'We are . . .'

And on. And on.

Sleep.

Light.

Blinding white light that penetrated the thin membrane of the eyelid and scorched the iris.

Darkness.

Silence.

Sound.

Voices pleading. Voices cursing and hurling abuse. Soft female voices offering themselves and then swearing foul obscenities.

Darkness.

Silence.

Radio static.

Voices amplified by loud hailers.

'Surrender. You have no hope. Give it up. Surrender. You have no hope. . . .'

Soft red light. Fraser's voice. 'We are one family. . . .'

Machine-gun fire.

African bush sounds.

A firing squad under command.

The crash of the rifle volley.

'*Bastards!*' a man screams and a scuffle as he is held down in the darkness.

Fraser and Stratton watched the screens grimly. The strobes were set in action, varied speed settings making every movement an animated cartoon of life.

Men vomit.

A body rises to defecate in a corner, the air turning putrid immediately.

Thirst.

Hunger.

The creak of a pump being pulled. The velvet rush of liquid into a glass.

Eggs frying, bacon crackling in the hot fat.

No ventilation. Dark mucky air like thick swamp water; so thick you could almost touch it.

'The Torch. Keep the Torch alight. Fight. Fight with your mind. The Torch . . .' and on and on.

Stratton and Fraser took turns to sleep, and ate pre-prepared snacks and black coffee, the monitoring of the equipment becoming almost as great a torture as the technique itself.

Until, finally, it was over. At nine o'clock the next morning, Paul Stratton opened the locked doors of the first cell and the smell hit him.

The waste of the human body mixed with sweat and vomit had made a wall of rotten air that collapsed as the door was opened, like a dam bursting. He gagged and made sure he held a handkerchief over his mouth and nose at the second door. Out of the cells stepped men who looked totally broken in mind and spirit but their eyes lit up with a fire that Stratton had never witnessed before as they saw Jonathan Fraser and heard his voice. He had bound the men to himself so closely that there was no limit to the lengths they would go for him.

But for Stratton the manor became cold, and for the briefest moment he felt, for the first time, like an outsider.

4

After the ordeal of the stress cells, the men were provided with a meal and ordered to sleep through the remainder of the Wednesday. Fraser, who rarely seemed to need more than two or three hours' sleep at a time, told Stratton to put his head down until two o'clock that afternoon.

Alone once more in the great house, he sifted meticulously through the analyses he had made and, by the time an hour had passed, the polished walnut of the large oval table at which he sat was covered with twenty-three neat white piles, each a detailed account of one man's reaction to the controlled tests. Some were set to his right and others to his left – a division of supreme importance, for it divided those who would certainly live from those who were likely to die. A tiny curl caught at the corner of his dry lips, as he thought that the division was also significant, in that some would leave the manor that evening with an extra £1000 to their name, while those who remained might, if their own personal gods smiled on them, be more wealthy than they could ever have dreamed.

Carefully, without missing the importance of the smallest detail, however irrelevant it appeared, he studied the details that each of the men had given to Stratton at the house in Putney. What emerged, in his final analysis, was a clear picture of the life of each volunteer since he had left the rather special confines of the SAS.

Fraser knew exactly what he wanted. Men to match his own instincts. A pack of wolves.

A discreet rap at the panelled door stopped him at his task. He frowned as he checked his watch.

'Paul?'

The door opened and Cornwell stepped inside. In his hands he bore a laden tray.

'Sorry to disturb you, sir, couldn't sleep, what with my head flying around in those crazy clouds you showed downstairs. Thought you might need some lunch.'

Fraser leaned back on the chair, his crooked grin breaking his lined face.

'Crazy clouds!' he laughed incredulously. 'Cornwell – does nothing affect you?'

'I slept most of the time, sir. Switched off, if you get my meaning.'

'I noticed.'

The RSM's face was set, without a hint of humour in it.

'I went through the baby brother of that treatment, Colonel. Korea. I saw a lot go under with it. Released me in '54 they did. Shipped me to Hong Kong first. Some Yank doctors were running these tests there . . . to see if POWs were affected by the so-called brainwashing the Chinese and the North Koreans had given us.'

Fraser frowned, this time more deeply.

'There's nothing on your record to show that you'd under-gone brainwashing techniques.'

'I lied, sir. Told 'em I'd not been used. I could see straight away that anyone who admitted they'd been got at was looked at a bit sideways! Didn't affect me anyway. When the Reds got tough I found I could turn off by causing cramp in my legs. Curling your toes up and setting the calf muscles off – that sort of thing. The pain shut out the lights and the sound.'

'Didn't anyone discover you were using this method?'

Cornwell shook his head very slowly from side to side.

'In that place, Colonel, you told no one anything. If you did the Chinks had it next day. In the end they gave up – put me in with the Turks. After that it was OK. Nothing touched *those* buggers!'

Fraser tugged at his drooping moustache, then, with a grimace, reached for one of the small piles of white paper.

'I wasn't going to take you, Cornwell,' he said quietly.

The former RSM stood quite still. Fraser held a palm up to forestall the torrent he knew was coming.

'It was basically a question of taking men along who had not much else going for them. Men like Murray or . . .' he reached for another pile of paper '. . . or James Dewey. The losers, Cornwell. The ones who'd stick it out to the bitter bloody end because I'd shown them the rainbow – there to be grasped and pulled down out of the sky. The misfits, the dreamers and the losers – that's what our tiny army is going to be made of, Cornwell. You've got something working for you out there in the Gulf. You'll end up with no money worries, and be able to enjoy life – comfortably !'

Johnson Cornwell leant forward, planting clenched knuckles on the table so firmly, that the blood was forced away, leaving white circles on the flesh. Colour rose up his throat and filled his face with a deep flush of anger.

'Colonel. I'm going with you if I have to kill all those bastards in their beds so there's only you and me left. You say I've got something working for me out there with the Arabs ! Well, let me tell you, *sir*. Let me tell you what I've got. I've got six days a week of screaming my head off in a language that most of those rag-heads don't understand ! I've got one day a week which I spend getting blind paralytic drunk, trying to forget the six evenings I sit on a bloody iron cot, staring at bloody concrete walls and listening to the scream of a bloody air-conditioner and my empty bloody life ! That Colonel Fraser, *sir*, is what I've got !'

Stratton stood in the doorway, one black eyebrow raised.

'Come in, Paul,' Fraser said. 'We've just got the first member of the strike-force.'

Stratton moved forward and pulled out a chair, sitting with his long legs stretched before him.

'Welcome,' he said with grim humour. 'So who else is on the list ?'

'The two former officers. Stewart-Smith and James Dewey.' Fraser replied, jaw set, ready for the protests and ready to defend his decision.

'A suspected traitor and a failed medico,' Stratton said, crossing his legs.

'A simplistic judgement, Paul. Stewart-Smith was just about the worst possible choice the army could have made as an undercover intelligence officer in Ulster. God knows, he didn't lack courage nor was he a bleeding-heart liberal; he was an intelligent and sensitive man who happened to see both points of view. In Northern Ireland such self-indulgence is madness.

'It's suicide.'

Fraser nodded.

'So he lost sight of reality. The army slung him out and the Provisionals shot him. Where did you find him ?'

'In the bar of the White Bear, a scotch in one hand and a

Walther PPK in his pocket – one round in the magazine. I checked it. It seems he was in the last of a long series of bars.'

For a moment there was silence. Fraser broke it.

'So he's fireproof! He's dead already – suits us ideally.'

'He's unstable.'

'The conditioning will rectify that,' Fraser replied.

'Mr Dewey's a good man, sir,' Cornwell put in. 'He might have been busted and there's not much he takes seriously but he knows his stuff. We'll need someone to do the patching up.'

Fraser stared forward.

'Dewey was court-martialled for desertion in the field – Oman to be precise. He left wounded and dying men to return to the nearest well-equipped hospital literally holding the pieces of his commanding officer's body together with his hands. Inexcusable conduct? Yes. But I'm alive today and that is exactly the sort of loyalty we need. There'll be no place for tradition or honourable conduct in what we are about to do. We'll be outside the law and its restraints – but that cuts both ways.'

'The rest?' Stratton asked.

Fraser shuffled his papers.

'Fowler, Andy. Irish wife, raped and killed in London while he was on his third tour in Belfast – thought she'd be safer over here I suppose. Burned across both breasts with the words SAS WHORE. Cigarette ends. Fowler got the news and sandbagged a couple of known Provos – doused them in petrol, then phoned HQ. When the patrol arrived he flicked the cigarette he was smoking at them. Right now he's ready to kill anyone who gets in his way. That is exactly what we need.

'Mclennan we all know. Black Watch, SAS, mercenary. Toughest man in the regiment. On the scrap heap. Too old. Very, very, bitter. Major Stratton found him with £2.50 in his pocket trying to hustle a contract overseas. Same answer – age. He's young enough for me.'

Fraser lit a cigarette and sifted through the rest of the paper.

'Murray. Similar situation. Not the brightest intellect – but a good loyal fighting man. On the streets now – not much of a place for men like Jimbo in civilian life. He'll stick it through! Lippmann, Friedrich. English mother. National service here – made the regiment – good trooper. Later joined the Legion.'

'Deserted and on the run,' Stratton added.

Fraser shrugged.

'Everyone deserts the Legion, it's almost compulsory these days. Needs the money – desperately.'

Stratton reached forward for the lists.

'Johnny Hubbard. Explosives. None better, but a lunatic of the first degree. Cracking safes nowadays – keeps his hand in – he says. Sammy Cohen. Communications. Can't fault that, couldn't get a better man.' He took up the next sheet and grunted. 'Walters, Carter and Peterson – there's a legend!'

'Crazy bastards,' Cornwell murmured.

'The best close-quarters men in the business,' said Fraser. 'I've used them on the toughest contracts. They're worth a couple of platoons with light automatic weapons – what's that ridiculous name they use?'

Stratton smiled, 'The Guns of August. All born in August '39 – lifted it from the book. They'll go just for the chance to raise hell. Money's a secondary consideration.'

'Which leaves only one man,' said Fraser. 'A special man for a very special job. The only one of the strike-force who will have to work entirely alone – no support – no back-up. Completely detached from the main group, but vital to our existence.'

'Roberts,' Stratton said immediately. Cornwell nodded in agreement.

'He'll do a job for you, Colonel. Works best alone. Nobody really knows him and not many try. He can kill you so quietly you wouldn't know you were dead – then he'd step over you as if nothing had happened.'

'He'll come,' Stratton said firmly. 'Roberts needs the money more than any of the men. His mother's dying of cancer here in London but he wants to get her over to some genius in Switzerland. That might sound like hearts and flowers but I'd never risk taking it as anything less than a very serious reason.'

'He wouldn't see the joke,' Cornwell stated. 'Roberts was born without a sense of humour. To him everything is deadly serious.'

Fraser gathered in the papers. 'Where we're going, gentlemen, everything *will* be deadly serious.'

When the men surfaced in the early evening, the spacious dining area had been set up as a briefing room. Standing on a table was a model of a compound of block-houses in white painted wood.

All the men were led into the room by Cornwell after they had eaten, many of them still bearing on their faces the ravages of their ordeal. They sat waiting for the appearance of the colonel, but Stratton entered alone and stood behind the model. He handed a slip of paper to Cornwell, then addressed the assembled men.

'We have now reached the stage where the final choice has been made for those comprising the strike-force. As you already know those who have not been chosen will receive payment of a further £1000. I should make it clear that Colonel Fraser has picked the team to make the strike with certain factors in mind. These are unknown to you, and have nothing to do with your undoubted abilities as fighting men. There are other considerations which had to be taken into account and go far deeper than you realize. The RSM will read out the names of eleven men. These will please leave the room and wait in the main entrance hall of the building. They will comprise the strike-force. The rest will please stay seated. Sarn'-Major?'

'Sir! These men to wait in the main hall. Roberts. Fowler. Dewey. Mclennan. Lippmann. Hubbard. Murray. Stewart-Smith. Carter. Walters. Peterson. The rest stay where you are.'

The eleven left the room quietly; not one looked back. Stratton passed over a bundle of envelopes to the RSM to be distributed around the remaining men.

'These contain three items. One, your second cheque for £1000. Two, cash to the value of £300. Three, an airline ticket to a holiday resort in Europe. In the interests of security you will find that your destinations are varied; you will not all be going to the same place or travelling together. The RSM will return the passports we collected from you in London.' Stratton paused, and searched the faces of the seated men with his dark eyes. 'One final thing. As an insurance that your loyalty to Colonel Fraser remains unchanged and that none of you decide to make some extra money by going to the press or to the representatives of any government, I contacted, after the strike force had been finalized, two men you all know well.' He named two ex-mercenaries who now made their living as contract-killers and who were infamous for their efficiency.

'They have all your names, and will receive, tomorrow, photographs and details of your whereabouts. They will be held in readiness until our strike time, which is known only to Colonel Fraser. If by then nothing has been leaked, they will be called off. If, on the other hand, the operation is blown, I shall personally confirm the contract – on all of you. Is that quite clearly understood?'

The names of the two ex-mercenaries were enough to make Stratton's threat perfectly clear.

'Sarn'-Major,' he said, handing over.

'Sir. Now some of you have got night-flights and others first thing tomorrow but transport is ready and waiting now, so get yourselves together quickly. The driver's been told he's not to stop for anything or anyone until he reaches Gatwick Airport. So do what you have to do now – and, friends, just remember what Major Stratton told you.'

The men filed out of the house, through the side door, where the same coach that had delivered them waited to take them away. Jonathan Fraser stood behind a darkened upper window and watched them go.

It was strange, he thought, the ones who are to live, leave with the faces of those about to die. He turned away, ready now to meet those he'd chosen to die with him.

The eleven men lounged in the spacious hallway of the mansion. Some leant against the walls, arms folded and heads lowered in thought; others sat on the ornate gilt chairs, like reluctant princes. Not one of them could be described as young and most had lost any illusion of youth long before they were out of their 'teens. They were exactly what the fanatical colonel was looking for. Men out of place and out of time. Professional soldiers who'd served their time and paid their dues. Products of a society that created them, ejected them, and finally outlawed them. Lauded heroes in war and a sacrifice to conscience in peace. A pack of wolves, led by a mesmeric man, part-crazed by pain and betrayal.

Is that how it really is? Stratton asked himself. Or are we simply a handful of men with nowhere to go and nothing to do, just looking for a place to create hell? They came to their feet as he entered the hallway.

Leading them to a locked doorway, he opened it and followed them through, shutting out questions he neither needed nor wanted to answer.

'I wonder how many of you have asked the question, "What would I do for a million pounds?" ' Fraser said, searching the faces with his eyes. 'Or perhaps someone has asked it of you?'

He stood, cast in shadow, for the only light in the room was hung by three chains and enclosed beneath a big oblong shade, like a softly glowing coffin-lid. Below was a full-size billiards table hiding its secret under a white cloth.

It seemed, as they faced him from around the table, that his amber eyes were on fire.

'Now!' he said, lowering his head to see them all. '*I* ask it of you.'

Fraser took hold of the white cloth, crushing a corner of the material in a tight fist.

'Under here is the possibility of a million pounds – and the way to get it. There are fourteen of you. Once the final object has been achieved, your loyalty to me will terminate. Any survivor will be free to make his way out – to disappear, with the certainty of his share of £1,000,000 sterling waiting for him if he succeeds. If any of you are not ready to gamble your lives, I give you one final chance now, before it is too late. The door is there.' His finger reached out under the light and indicated into darkness, but none of the men moved.

'Major Stratton said to me, when I told him what I planned to do – "Only the devil could succeed." Well, gentlemen, if that is the case, you have all just sold me your souls.' He pulled the cloth off, watching the bewildered faces.

Under the lights lay a perfect model of a tree-lined avenue with houses facing on to it. To one side, the surface of the table portrayed a large grassed area, with an elegant building beyond it, imprisoned by high walls. At each end of the avenue were black gates mounted in arches. Fraser picked up a billiards cue to use as a pointer.

'Some of you may have already recognized this area so, to put those minds at rest, we are not interested in Kensington

Palace!' The cue rested on the walled enclosure. 'Instead, gentlemen . . .' the pointer moved across the table and rested on the roof of a multi-aerialed building edging the green felt '. . . we are going to storm, capture and hold for as long as necessary this building, which houses secrets more deadly than any in Pandora's box!'

He let the billiards cue move across the roof, toppling one tall black aerial.

'Gentlemen, the communications and KGB building of the Soviet Embassy in London. The price for the release, unharmed, of the British prisoners? Simple. Our silence. The cost, if they are not released? Simple again. We break into the archives and transmit, uncoded, to Moscow the names of KGB deep-penetration agents, controllers, spy networks, secret codes . . . whatever, in fact, comes to hand. If, of course, the West has its monitoring stations listening in, then those secrets will no longer be secret.'

There was not a sound in the room. Stewart-Smith moved his haunted face into the light and broke the silence. His voice was flat.

'The very second we enter that building we will begin to die.'

'No!' Fraser roared. 'We will all begin to live!' He moved around the table and grasped the former intelligence officer's arm. 'On a precipice. Yes! On a knife edge. YES! But *by God* we will really be *living*. The world will sit forward in its communal bloody armchair and say – "*This is happening . . . now. Somebody is out there doing something. Something we dare not do ourselves because we're soft and we're feeble and we're rotten to the core*." ' He touched a fingertip to his temple to stop a jumping nerve. 'We can do it,' he breathed.

'I don't see how we can even get near the front door, Colonel. Never mind inside.' The voice belonged to James Dewey.

Stratton cut in.

'There is a way. Complex and dependent on strict timing, but there is a way.'

Fraser nodded and moved back to the top of the table.

'As Major Stratton says, there is a way, but for the moment that method must remain secret. You will have to have faith in me and take my word that we can get in there with minimal losses. More important now is for you to understand what is going to happen once we are inside, and to learn to counteract methods already proved successful by the authorities during other long-drawn-out hijackings and sieges.'

'But those were done by terrorists, sir!' the giant Murray protested. 'We're soldiers!'

Jonathan Fraser smiled as if to a child.

'Yes, Murray. We're soldiers but to the government we'll be terrorists.'

'And to the world?' Stewart-Smith asked.

'Ah, to the world. To the world we shall have our torch to hold high!' Fraser answered without looking at the questioner.

'Torch?' Murray was lost and trying hard to understand, bewildered by the turn of events. Soldier he understood. Terrorist was repugnant. Torch was beyond him.

It was Stewart-Smith's voice that soothed him but the empty blue eyes rested on Fraser not on Murray.

> ' "Take up our quarrel with the foe;
> To you from failing hands we throw
> The Torch; be yours to hold it high."

. . . John McCrae. Another war, another time, Colonel.'

Fraser gently shook his head.

'All wars are the same, Captain. It's the peace in between which changes.' He clasped his hands together with a crack. 'Gentlemen! We have work to do.'

Paul Stratton guided them through to an ante-room which had been set up with a large-screen colour television and a videotape machine. On a small table stood a pile of video cartridges containing every inch of filmed footage that Fraser had been able to amass on the subject of hijackings and armed sieges. These included a series of documentary films made by the BBC of the most publicized and recent of such incidents.

Although in the commercial films the parts were played by professional actors, these were of the utmost importance because they portrayed, as accurately as documentation allowed, the reactions and psychological deterioration of the terrorists and their hostages. There was also an invaluable collection of classified documents from a highly secret psychological warfare course run by the Ministry of Defence. Stewart-Smith, as a former intelligence operative, knew that the MOD didn't even acknowledge the existence of such a course, so was unable to prevent himself from raising questioning eyebrows. His shocked expression drew no answer from either Stratton or the colonel.

A 16 mm film projector and screen were ready to be set up when the videotapes had all been screened. Fraser explained that the events they would be seeing on videotape would illustrate the wearing-down methods used by the forces of law and order; and the films, with commentaries by a psychologist, would demonstrate the reasoning behind these methods and their affect. The films were produced by the American Psychological Operations Group in San Francisco.

Perhaps the single most important object in that room was a large percolator of black coffee, for none of the strike-force was to sleep that Wednesday night. The screens flickered unceasingly for hour after hour and Stratton surreptitiously added small doses of benzedrine to the coffee as it was passed around.

By morning the group was sagging visibly, with post-stimulant depression setting in fast. Fraser called a halt and had Stratton issue fast-acting sleeping pills. As dawn broke, the men slept where they had fallen, with just one small irritation tugging at the edges of their minds. On the table a recorder, with a circled loop of tape passing over its heads, droned continuously the same message.

'The Torch must burn.'

At noon on Thursday the men surfaced groggily. Fraser and Stratton were gone and Cornwell appeared looking fresh, having woken earlier, showered, shaved and prepared breakfast. Before allowing anyone to eat he punished the men with a cruel run around the grounds to get their circulation moving and clear their systems of any remaining traces of the drugs.

When they returned Fraser was sitting alone in the breakfast room. He nodded a greeting to them. Of Stratton there was still no sign.

Considerably refreshed by stinging hot and cold showers the men ate, then sat smoking, their eyes straying involuntarily to Fraser.

'Well, let's get on with it, gentlemen,' he said rising.

Paul Stratton was on the other side of London taking delivery of the newly purchased vehicles. Earlier that morning Fraser had dropped him off in Enfield and he had taken a mini-cab to Regent Street where he paid it off and picked up a taxi to a multi-storey car park at the Elephant and Castle. There, as had been arranged by telephone, he found the two olive-green vehicles on the top floor, the keys in an envelope hidden under a hub cap. He took the Range Rover first, reaching his destination around one o'clock. Opening the black door of the garage at the end of the Notting Hill mews, he drove the vehicle inside and locked up. Another cab, picked up in the street, took him back to the car park. He was glad to see that the Indian attendant had been relieved by a Jamaican so there was no danger of his being recognized. Nevertheless he pulled the brim of his cap down further. He was a very cautious man; if he escaped alive from the coming siege then he was going to make damn sure that nobody could link his face with it.

He brought the van to a halt on the forecourt of the manor at ten minutes to four that Thursday afternoon, went straight to his room, swallowed neat brandy from a silver hip flask and promptly fell asleep on the large double bed.

Downstairs in the video room Colonel Fraser began running the first reel of the film made by the PsyOp group in San Francisco. A Bostonian accent came through the speakers proclaiming their theories and findings.

'Psychology is the science of human behaviour. It aims to understand human behaviour, to predict human behaviour, and when necessary to change human behaviour.

'It is the last of these which concerns us in this study. The need to change human behaviour. To destroy, by the most subtle means, the protagonist in any plot or action against the state whether by direct attacks upon the morale or emotions or, failing that, to destroy the loyalty factor among his subordinates. It is safe to argue that in the case of this study, the protagonist may well be a cause rather than a person. However, when dealing with urban guerrillas and terrorists it could well be both. Remember then, that the element of loyalty will be way beyond the "normal pattern". There is no accurate measure of loyalty. It ranges from the small act of lending a friend your time or money to the "Grand Gesture" of stating, "I shall stand by

57

you till death", and actually doing it. This last fanatical form of loyalty, be it for cause or person, is almost impossible to undermine and destroy, for it carries with it a "fellow traveller" you have all heard of – the "death wish".

'If you have ever asked yourself how terrorists or even our own Special Action Groups succeed against all odds in reaching their objectives, the answer is clear : they do not fear death. They welcome it.'

On his bed in the upper reaches of the great house, Paul Stratton dreamed of a long straight dusty road along which he trudged, becoming more exhausted with each step. His companion was an aged man who pulled at his arm regularly, slowing his progress. With mounting horror he realized that as the miles passed he was beginning to see the road through the eyes of the old man and, at last, he was alone. He screamed in his sleep but there was no sound.

Awaking with a start he glanced quickly at the luminous dial of his watch in the darkened room. It was ten-thirty. He splashed cold water on his face and made his way down to the ground floor. Apart from the solitary figure of Fraser sitting on a chair staring at a blank television screen, the ideas room was deserted.

The glazed eyes hardly noticed him as he entered, with apologies for his tardiness, but Fraser dismissed them with a small hand movement and once again the empty feeling of being an outsider swept over Stratton.

Unable to sleep, he paced the corridors of the vast house. By the early hours of the morning his confidence in his ability to survive, whatever the odds, had all but deserted him; feeling defeated he gulped down two sleeping pills and lay on his bed again, staring at the darkened ceiling. Just as his body succumbed to the drug he had a sinking thought. The coming day heralded what was, in his opinion, the one mistake in Fraser's near-perfect plan. The colonel wanted the men to see the location of the strike for themselves, his argument being that for them to retain any contact with reality during the siege of the Embassy building they had to see the place in daylight, under normal conditions. The psychologist's filmed lecture maintained that there was less chance of disorientation with something familiar than something unknown when the pressure was on. In theory this was correct but Stratton felt deep down that, with so much attention already being focused on Kensington Palace Gardens, the exercise would be too dangerous. He'd pleaded with Fraser to discard that part of the operation but, as always, the colonel had his way. As Stratton fell asleep he recognized that it was his own anonymity he was afraid of losing.

Friday morning brought bright sunshine and the men were eager to get moving. Even Stratton felt his misgivings evaporate.

The men in the strike-force were made to understand that no more than two of them could be outside the Embassy at a given time. They were split into groups and given a time schedule. Fraser was confident that, as they had all worked undercover operations before, they would blend easily with the crowds of demonstrators.

They travelled to London in two vehicles, Cornwell in charge of the group in the van and Stratton, Stewart-Smith, Dewey and the colonel in the Jaguar. Upon arrival at Notting Hill Gate they split up and parked on meter bays, streets apart.

A vital aspect of the operation had to be carried out that day, in addition to the familiarization, and Fraser approached the Bayswater Road entrance alone.

Looking every inch the British Army colonel, he thrust his way through the chanting crowd and, ignoring the police, walked up to the Embassy gateman. He explained his appointment with the Nigerian High Commission and was ushered through.

His appointment was quite genuine so, with confident stride, he strolled half the length of the wide tree-lined avenue.

In one hand he carried a slim leather attaché case whilst the other he kept in the pocket of his overcoat.

He passed a guard box with a young uniformed policeman inside and gave a brief, 'Good morning.' The constable smiled a little nervously, never sure who might be visiting such hallowed ground.

Fraser passed the Nigerian High Commission by a few steps then, as if realizing his mistake, turned swiftly and released the lid of the attaché case which he'd held closed with one finger.

The contents emptied in a flurry of paper to the ground. Quickly he dropped to his haunches. The sound of footsteps made him look up to see the policeman running towards him.

'Let me help you, sir,' the young man offered, and began replacing the documents neatly.

'Damn nuisance,' Fraser muttered and opened a cigarette packet, his hand perfectly steady. 'Oh hell! Empty.' He patted his overcoat. 'Thank God for that. Another packet. Bad enough sitting through a meeting with the Nigerians without having to do without a smoke as well. Here, have one.'

'I'll get shot. Thanks all the same, sir.' The policeman smiled.

'Where's the wretched litter-bin? Never one when you want it,' Fraser snorted.

The young officer's smile turned into a wicked grin.

'Bung it in there, sir. It's only the bloody Russians,' he retorted, then coloured.

'Didn't hear a damn thing,' Fraser said, dropping the packet on to the earth and leaves accumulated behind the knee-high wall and the hedge above it.

'See that transmitter on top, sir – the big one – ' the constable indicated with his eyes, glad to talk with someone. 'I sit in my box, hours on end, wondering what they send to Moscow on that thing. Not the football results, that's for sure. Never know, I suppose.'

'No. I suppose we never shall,' Fraser said, smiling, then thanked him for his assistance and walked back to the Nigerian High Commission.

Under the hedge of the adjacent Russian communications building, the cigarette packet containing a slab of plastic explosive with a miniaturized electrode embedded in it was covered by a flurry of leaves.

Opposite the black-railinged gates a wine-bar called 'Ruskies' served as an observation point; with foreboding, Stratton watched for the men as they mingled one by one with the demonstrators. His attention was diverted by three figures coming out of the closed avenue, two men with a blonde girl between them. The gateman nodded to them as they passed through and crossed Bayswater Road to the wine-bar. The girl was beautiful, her hair long and un-styled, falling simply to her shoulders. Stratton felt an ache inside and drank from his glass of red wine.

They entered with the girl second, as though running a front and rear guard on her, then sat in an alcove where he could still see them. One of the men ordered wine and food for all three, but beyond that there was no conversation. The faces of the two men were hard and grim like a dense wall behind which their humanity was trapped. Their eyes never stopped moving. The entrance, the room, the people, were all taken in and filed. The girl had her head down as though committing some act of betrayal which shamed her terribly. Once, briefly, as she lifted her head Stratton locked her eyes with his and in them he saw stark terror. Very quickly she looked away, and one of her companions as if sensing some contact he had missed, gave him a hard stare of inquisition. A question was asked, sharp and quick, which Stratton could not hear and the girl shook her head mutely.

He knew that, outside, the day's work had been accomplished and that Fraser and the others would be waiting in the vehicles, but he was unable to tear himself away. Finally, putting his priorities in the right order he forced himself to leave, catching the girl's eye once more as he did so. He knew with certainty that she was screaming silently for help and there was nothing he could do.

Throughout the return journey her pleading eyes stayed with him, tormenting his already tangled emotions, but in the Jaguar, filled with animated conversation, no one noticed his silence. New arrivals to the officers' mess were always warned: Paul Stratton. The odd one. Watch him. You'll lose your woman to those dark eyes and your life if the sun set badly on him the night before. Leave him be, he's better alone.

He's better alone! Stratton remembered and sank into black depression. But Fraser drove at an easy pace, always keeping a number of vehicles between himself and the green van in front but never letting it get out of sight. And he was smiling.

5

At Special Branch Headquarters in New Scotland Yard, Chief Superintendent Colin Hammond was having a bad Friday. It was already three o'clock in the afternoon and he had received that morning's photographs of the demonstrators only minutes before. At last they were of better quality, now that they were being shot from a window in the gatekeeper's lodge, he thought, and not from the painfully obvious unmarked vans. Hammond had already handed a number of reports to the commander but they were no more than token summaries of days of negative work.

He was seething inside, angry that his other assignments were being neglected and milked of manpower to support the Under-Secretary's game of one-upmanship. The only way out of the nonsensical situation, he decided, was to file reports filled with such trivia that sooner or later someone (preferably the Minister, he wished savagely) would wake up to the fact that public money and police time were being needlessly squandered.

He exhaled noisily and began examining the photographs with a large magnifying glass.

'Elementary, my dear Watson,' he muttered inanely to himself. 'What do we have? Why! A sea of faces and every face tells a story. A hundred faces, a hundred stories. Ah now! There's an interesting one. Seen you before, my friend. Now where could that have been? Hard-looking bastard, aren't you . . . not very clear though in amongst all those other gawkers. Turtle-neck sweater, nice leather jacket, short hair, almost cropped, last of the skinheads, are you? Too old, I'm afraid. Kissing your thirties goodbye, aren't you, mate? KGB? Out in the crowd to do a bit of recruiting for the motherland, eh? Or maybe just watching us watching you? A spook's day out? No, my friend, you're one of us. Bloody British. Stands out a mile. Copper then? Not really. DI5? One of their hard-boys, are you? They're running something in tandem with us and we haven't been told? That would really be something for the

Minister, eh? All that lovely tax-payer's money being thrown away on a double-up that neither one knows the other is doing. All right, my friend! Let's pass your face around a bit just to satisfy my curiosity. Maybe you're our ticket for getting out of this can of worms!'

Hammond ringed the face on the photograph and took it along with a batch of others down to the lab personally.

'Give us some blow-ups of that handsome brute and some big ones of these crowd scenes. Saves destroying my eyesight with a magnifying glass.'

The supervisor objected that the cost would be high.

'Oh, but this is top priority, chum,' Hammond countered. 'Didn't you know?'

'Whatever you say, Chief Superintendent,' the man replied with resignation.

Hammond left the photo lab with its glum, cost-conscious overseer and decided he'd pop out for some refreshments – just for a change. He felt a little elated; perhaps he could now get rid of this stupid operation once and for all. Over a coffee he decided he'd call a friend at DI5, the security service, and get some inside information on whether they were running a team of watchers at the Embassy.

Back in his office ten minutes later he was reaching out for the telephone to make the call when his internal line buzzed. The voice of one of the lab assistants came on the line. He recognized it as belonging to Johnson, a young technician, very bright, with a compendious memory.

'Chief Superintendent Hammond? Look, sir . . . my boss gave me these prints of yours to blow up and . . . well, sir, I couldn't help but overhear him moaning about the cost and . . .'

Hammond raised his eyes to the ceiling as the voice continued, '. . . I've got a reasonable shot of this character on negative – it's a couple of years old but still better than any blow-up could be. Would you mind if I developed that?'

Puzzled, Hammond asked him what the shot on file had been taken for.

'Thought you might ask that, sir,' Johnson replied with the tone of someone who knew the answer to the question and had it prepared. '27 May 1975, the Regent Centre Hotel; like a spy and security convention that was!'

'Ah-ah!' Hammond exclaimed. 'So he is DI5. I thought as much!'

'Oh no, sir, I said spies and security because there were so many there watching the meeting.'

'What meeting?'

Johnson was not going to be rushed. He had his facts and he was going to trot them out at his own pace, Chief Super or no.

'As I said, sir, May 1975 the Devonshire Room at the Regent Centre. The initial recruitment for the so-called "African Assignment".'

'A mercenary! He's a bloody mercenary!'

'We photographed ninety at the meeting,' Johnson continued, completely ignoring Colin Hammond's outburst. 'This one, Roberts, Christian names Leslie Alan, walked out as soon as he heard what the target country was. He wasn't the only one either.'

Hammond was bitterly disappointed.

'OK. Go ahead and print one from the neg – not that it means anything now.'

'Sir?'

'Nothing. I thought this Roberts character was something else entirely.' He put down the phone and slumped back in his chair. 'Mercenary,' he said in exasperation. Nevertheless he telephoned his contact at DI5 and his depression grew. Nothing. No operation.

'Not really interested in residents' disputes,' his friend had jibed.

As he replaced the receiver his internal line buzzed again. He snatched at it angrily.

'Sir, it's me again – Johnson from the lab.'

'Yes, Johnson. What is it now – another cost-cutting brainwave?'

The technician ignored the remark.

'Well, sir . . . I don't want to appear as though I'm telling you how to do your job . . . but down here it can often be very boring and one finds oneself doing a bit of detective work – fantasizing if you like – looking for clues that real detectives like yourself might have missed.'

'Johnson,' Hammond sighed, 'right at this moment if you

want to be a detective I'll make you a deal. Take my job – with my best wishes.'

Once more the young man carried on talking as if there had been no interruption. '. . . rather like finding a speck of gold in a handful of sand. Now, when I began finding more mercenaries in the other blow-ups I thought to myself – Hello! What's this? . . . I've struck a vein. . . .'

Hammond cut in quickly.

'Mercenaries? There's more in that crowd scene?'

'Not in the same shot, no, sir, but I've found four known to us in different shots. That's a bit odd just on its own. Photographs are taken at intervals on this sort of spotting operation, as you know. So why are they all there separately? It's not logical. They've got to know each other or at least have met at some time. What's the attraction? A demo at the Soviet Embassy? Doesn't make any sense, does it?'

Hammond was beginning to ask himself the same question when a thought struck him.

'Johnson. How busy are you now?'

'Very slack, sir.'

'Right, do something for me. Check if any of the other faces were at the Regent Centre in '75 and whether they stayed or left the meeting.'

'Three were there and they all left,' the reply came promptly.

Hammond was starting to feel a growing admiration for the sharp mind at the end of the phone.

'The other two?'

'No. Definitely not.'

'Anything on them?'

'Only the usual in the records office – I checked, sir – passport details, visas issued. Typical spots, Africa and the Middle East.'

Hammond turned the information over in his mind. Mercenaries. But how could they be connected with the Embassy demo? Wasn't their scene at all. . . .

'Hope I've been able to help, sir,' Johnson said after a moment.

'Help? No – quite the opposite. I wanted to get rid of this job. Now it looks as though I'm well and truly stuck with it.'

'It could be a coincidence, sir,' the technician said.

'One mercenary, yes. Two, possibly, three unlikely . . . but five? Quite impossible. No. It smells. Thanks all the same, Johnson.'

'Sir!' The syllable blurted out as Hammond was placing the phone on the receiver. He raised it again to his ear. 'Yes?'

'You were interested before in the security side. You said you thought the first man might have been . . .'

'DI5,' Hammond cut him short.

'There's one in the photograph. Not civilian though – Military Intelligence – ex-SAS officer, so Records say, but they won't issue any details to me. But believe me, sir, I never ever forget a face.'

'How come you saw his face on a photograph?'

'Some rush job – couldn't tell you who asked for it. No one tells me anything down here. One thing I do remember – he was drinking heavily. Every photograph I printed showed him coming out of some club or pub. What jogged my memory was that I sent a new print to Records not so long ago.'

'Why?'

'They said they wanted one. I didn't ask the reason, sir. I only print the things.'

'You surprise me! I thought for a moment you were running the Special Branch from down there! Goodbye, Johnson, and thank you.'

Hammond replaced the receiver and smiled wryly. He dialled Commander Vere's secretary on the internal line and arranged a meeting.

With that done he set himself to the task of presenting a realistic report based, rather tenuously, on a series of possible coincidences. Johnson interrupted him with the promised prints and some hastily notated information on the reverse of each.

'You seem to know a lot about mercenaries, Johnson.'

'As I said, sir, it's my memory. I just don't seem to be able to forget what passes through my hands. Drives me mad sometimes. There again you don't get asked for prints of mercenaries every day, do you?'

Hammond made a sound of agreement.

'Look,' he said, 'I want to put in a report on this today. Can you spare me some of your valuable time?'

Johnson managed to raise a pleased grin to his serious freckled face.

'What exactly do you have in mind, Chief Superintendent?'

'Let's say that you have a brain I want to pick – no, not your brain – your prodigious memory and your obvious fascination for detail.'

'That's fine with me – makes a change.'

'Right. I'll start by getting some more detail on the men you've already identified, while you sit down with this magnifying glass and go through every crowd scene we've got from the area in the last couple of days.'

Hammond made the necessary calls to their own records office and also to the Criminal Records office, then on impulse called his friend in DI5 for the second time that day.

His contact was amused.

'Being leaned on for results, Colin? Never mind, we've all got our cross to bear.'

Hammond told him of the series of photographs showing the presence of five known mercenaries outside the Russian Embassy at different times of the day.

'Pretty unlikely coincidence, chum!' the security service officer retorted.

'Exactly!'

'Going to call the Gentlemen after you've spoken with us?'

'SIS! What for? They're not interested in a demo outside the Russian Embassy – except when it's in Moscow.'

'True enough. It rather depends on how seriously you're taking this mercenary business.'

Hammond paused a minute for thought.

'Mm – that's difficult to answer. When I called you before it was basically in the hope that you people were doubling up on the operation. If you had been, I could probably have persuaded the old man that the manpower we've diverted is more than just a burden – it's also redundant. Now? I don't know. I just can't bring myself to swallow five coincidences in a row. It's bloody queer.'

'That it is,' his friend agreed. 'Tell you what. I've got a line into "Six". Let me give her a call. Won't hurt to try. I'll call you back. OK?'

'You're on.'

'Right! 'Bye for now then.'

'Mr Hammond?' Johnson stood up, his brow furrowed. In his hand he held a print and a magnifying glass.

'What is it, Holmes?' Hammond joked.

The lab technician was unmoved.

'Now I'm not 100 per cent sure, but there is something here which could be interesting.'

'With your memory, you're not 100 per cent sure? That's the first time I've heard you admit to human fallibility. What's the problem?'

Johnson cocked his head to one side.

'Well! As far as I can see there are no faces in this batch of prints which belong to the category we're looking for. There's quite a few of your regulars of course: dissidents, Socialist Workers' lot and the National Front, but no mercs.'

'And?'

'And then I started looking at the fringes of some of these shots. Look here – this one shows the opposite side of the Bayswater Road in the background – see.'

'Yes, I can see that.'

'OK. Until a moment ago – still nothing – then I found this chappie.'

Hammond looked closely at a figure blending into the background of the photograph.

'Here. Try it with the glass, sir,' Johnson urged.

'So there's a passing pedestrian. So what?'

'Sir, if you – that is, if you weren't a policeman – if you were walking along opposite a place where there's a real old hurly-burly going on, wouldn't you, at the very least, turn your head and glance at it?'

Hammond drew down the corners of his mouth doubtfully but Johnson was insistent.

'Look at this lot. Just take a look!' He spread photograph after photograph on the desk. 'See! Not one face is turned away from the crowd. Every person that passes is looking directly in their direction!'

Hammond was still unconvinced.

'OK, maybe he's a villain casing the area or some bright lad who knows we take shots of crowds at demonstrations to keep on file – maybe he's screwing someone's wife down the road and doesn't want his face on the box. There *are* television cameras there you know, Johnson!'

'He's none of those, Mr Hammond.'

'You sound very sure.'

'The more I see that profile the more sure I am. All right he's wearing a cap and you can't see the hairline, but Jesus I'd recognize that profile anywhere.'

Hammond peered through the glass again.

'He's certainly blessed with good looks.'

'He's got those all right, my sister nearly wet her pants when she saw him on the box.'

'Did she now?' Hammond raised his eyebrows interested. 'On the box – when was this embarrassing incident?'

'About the time those mercenaries were on trial in Africa.'

'Well, he couldn't exactly be one of those, could he? They shot some and gave the others life – without time off for good behaviour.'

Johnson shook his head vigorously.

'No, sir – he wasn't out there. Remember the coverage of those events? TV news shots of mercenaries getting off planes – walking across the tarmac – boarding coaches – most of them covering their faces with papers or their hands – others turning away from the cameras. Well, our friend here wasn't with them but he was there by the coaches, just staring. Mad as hell he was, you could see that a mile off. That was when my sister had her momentary lapse.'

Hammond laughed but the earnest young technician remained his serious self. 'Don't worry about it, Johnson. She's your sister, not your girl-friend.'

'Whatever's going on – he's part of it,' he replied, ignoring the remark.

'Well, I think you're jumping at shadows, real police work is 99 per cent facts, one per cent inspiration and sometimes a little luck, but if it'll set your mind at ease, see if you can find a better print than this.'

'I don't have one.'

'Are you sure?'

'Absolutely.'

'I thought you said you'd done some work on these characters – the Regent Centre business?'

69

'He wasn't there – I'd remember.'

'Then blow up his face from this and we'll do a trace through criminal records computer.'

'Won't be easy. His features will distort badly. He's already a bit out of focus.'

Hammond pursed his lips.

'I think you're wasting time with him, to be quite frank – but you spotted the others, so do the best you can.'

'You'll get me the last batch of shots, sir?'

'Really interested, aren't you!'

Johnson allowed himself a grin.

'Well, you know this is . . .' He shrugged his narrow shoulders.

'I know,' Hammond said amused, 'exciting.'

'Not exciting really. It's just that I can follow up on a job myself instead of having to ask Who? What? Why? – and still never getting a straight answer.'

Hammond waved a hand at him.

'You go and print me a nice glossy ten by eight of lover-boy here. If it doesn't mean anything we can always let your sister have it. I'll make you a bargain though. If you're right about these mercenaries being involved in something I'll try and make your life more interesting in future.'

The technician made for the door, then hesitated and turned round.

'You don't think it could be more – bigger than another demo?'

'No, I don't. If it's anything at all they're just being used as a bit of muscle. Come on, Johnson, you don't think that four or five mercenaries are enough to attempt a coup and take over the country?'

'What about the Embassy?'

Hammond stared at him and then grinned.

'Sure. And the Kremlin too.'

'Friday the thirteenth!' Johnson said with a superior look. 'September 1974. The Japanese Red Army took over the French Embassy in The Hague – by force.'

Hammond sighed.

'Johnson, the Japanese Red Army are fanatical terrorists with a cause, not a band of ex-soldiers making a living out of other people's wars and misery. Go on with you, get to work.' The outside line made a mute croak. 'Hammond.'

'Colin?'

The chief superintendent recognized the voice of his friend at DI5.

'That was quick. Your lady couldn't have had any secrets to whisper in your large red ears.'

'No, nothing at all, I'm afraid,' the voice began, 'but she did hint that they've recruited a couple of mercenary officers. There's no other connection with mercenaries as far as SIS is concerned. She'll keep her ears to the ground though.'

'Listen,' Hammond said, 'I don't want to start up any minor wars between the intelligence organizations of this country. Perhaps you'd better leave it be.'

'No problem. We do each other the odd favour occasionally, you know. After all, we are on the same side!'

'Your lot and the SIS? Do me a favour!'

The voice at the end of the line chuckled.

'I'll leave you with your problems. See you, chum. Call me if you've got any more.'

Hammond surveyed his littered desk in annoyance and began clearing up the photographic debris that Johnson had left behind. He could not bear clutter. This done, he continued the report for the commander. 'Christ,' he thought, 'it's too sketchy. I could make myself look an idiot.' With these doubts running through his mind and without Johnson's enthusiasm to push him deeper without considerably more fact, he played down the presence of the mercenaries in the report. He did not mention the Military Intelligence officer, who he considered was just another gawker, nor the good-looking man in the background. Hammond believed that good-looking men rarely had the time or the desire to gawp around them – they were far too busy either looking at themselves in shop windows or at the passing talent.

Later, when he had his meeting with the commander, he was pleased that he had decided to treat the whole thing cautiously. Vere was not a man who took kindly to flamboyant streams of thought.

'Very thorough, Hammond,' the commander said. 'Very thorough.'

'The business about the mercenaries, sir – I felt it was better to mention them – another anti-Soviet group there could turn the whole thing into a general mêlée.'

Vere dismissed the explanation.

'It'll give the Foreign Office a bit of heartburn. They haven't quite got over the African fiasco yet. They still get petitions passed on to them for the release of the men held prisoner. Well, keep at it; shouldn't last much longer.'

'One of the photo lab assistants – Johnson – the one who recognized the mercenaries in the crowd, thinks they're going to hijack the Embassy!' Hammond said lightheartedly.

Vere's face froze.

'Chief Superintendent! You spread a story like that and I'll have your head mounted on my wall! Rumour like that would have the press baying at our door – immediately followed by the Under-Secretary and his master. I know you want to call this off, but if you think that spreading wild stories will achieve that, you're very wrong indeed! If that demonstration is suddenly banned we'll have the civil liberties union and God knows who else camped ten deep on the street outside. Do the job, Chief Superintendent, and make the best of it.'

Hammond sighed.

'Surely you don't take it seriously, sir?'

'I take everything seriously, Hammond. But in this case no, I bloody well don't. You just make sure you don't start any bush fires you can't control.'

Hammond nodded and made for the door.

'Hammond.'

He turned, surprised at the quietness of Vere's voice after the outburst.

'Double the number of uniformed men on the gates from tonight. I'll clear it. Tell them we think there could be a confrontation between the rival groups. And don't give me that look. It's a simple precaution, that's all. Now get out and tell your young friend Johnson to keep his nose well into his developing fluid!'

Colin Hammond spent the weekend in leisurely fashion enjoying the comfort of his flat in Horseferry Road. His private life was sacrosanct. He locked his door and shut out the devious world of the Special Branch whenever the opportunity arose, but the green telephone by his bed with its insistent shriek was a constant reminder that he was never really his own man.

Hammond had one secret which he protected to the point of paranoia. He loved a girl almost young enough to be his daughter. There was little hope that the relationship could survive a lifetime, so each private moment he had was jealously guarded as though it might be his last.

The flat contrasted utterly with his office. Deep carpets and fat overstuffed armchairs soaked up the sound of the rock music the girl played at excruciating volume through his expensive stereo system. Everything was for her and with each passing day he watched for signs that would let him know finally that she had realized twenty years separated them. He lived in mortal fear of younger, good-looking men.

Hammond watched her move, long-legged and fine; half a woman still, and only half his. He smiled at her distant eyes, lost somewhere in the music, the big head-phones clamped down over her wild hair, the long wire trailing as at random she fixed food, drinks, music and set table-places. The disorder she created caught at him like the gentle sharpness of a kitten kneading at clothing – a small pain, easy to bear for the love which was part of the movement.

They ate and she mocked him over forkfuls of food, the silver cutlery splayed between fingers which seemed uncontrollable. 'Don't look for for ever,' she whispered. 'I'm here *now*. You mustn't throw away now, working out what happens – whenever?'

'I love you,' Hammond said. 'I can't stop that. It isn't in me to stop it.'

'Don't then. Love me now. This is your home. I am in it. I sleep in your bed – you inhabit my body – and I love you at those times.' She lifted the loose top she wore, exposing her naked breasts. 'Take them – fill me whenever you want, I would never refuse you, but don't say tomorrow I will love you, tomorrow I will lay with you!'

She put her fingers lightly to the flame of the candle between them. 'I'm your candlelight. Hazy at the edges but I'm alight for you.' The flame faltered as she blew softly. 'When you want, or when I want, the flame will go out. No ground rules. No future. OK!'

The cold reality of her statement hit him. For a moment it seemed that she was already gone and that he was alone in an apartment fashioned for her. His emotions surfaced and, ashamed, he clamped his eyelids tight.

Horrified, she moved to him and held his head to her body. 'Oh no! Love, love – you mustn't trap me that way.' Pulling him down to the thick carpet she knelt above him, and threw her top aside which left her naked, for it was all she ever wore inside the apartment.

As he moved into her she spoke softly, her lips pressed against his ear. 'I need you all the time. Make time for me. Come to me. I'm always waiting, needing you. I want you more and more. You mustn't leave me here. Stay with me. Love me. More. More!' She fell on to him slowly, as though she had been hurt, her mouth open, ready for the cry which, when it came, was like an unbearable pain.

Hammond looked at the beautiful young body sprawled over him and with a cold shudder remembered the perfect profile of the uninterested man on the edge of the crowd in the photograph.

In Hertfordshire a mini-bus pulled to a stop outside the manor. Jonathan Fraser stood at the entrance himself, ready to greet the passengers. Earlier he had told the men that there would be a 'pleasant and welcome surprise' that evening.

Gravely, as though inspecting an intake of new recruits, he watched as a group of exceptionally pretty girls spilled from the vehicle and stood laughing delightedly as they took in the surroundings. The driver approached him and Fraser handed the man some notes as a tip, reminding him that he should return punctually on Sunday at noon to pick up his beautiful cargo.

The escort agency who had supplied the girls had been fed the story that an Arab sheikh, who would not be present, wanted to accommodate the needs of the British members of his security forces at a small private party in the English countryside. The girls, Fraser had insisted, had to be willing to stay till the Sunday and should be ready to cater to any reasonable demands by the sheikh's guests. For this 'special service' the agency charged a very large 'executive' fee. Even so, Fraser handed the girls envelopes containing £50 each as they trooped into the house and he noted that the agency had not merely been boasting when they said they had the most beautiful girls in the UK on their books.

As all the men had been taken straight from the recruiting party in Putney without being allowed to grab a change of clothes, they had been given the chance that afternoon to visit Enfield to buy outfits. Paul Stratton made quite sure that they all realized that they would not be spending that evening in all-male company. The comfortable recreation lounge of the manor had been opened up especially for the evening and once again echoed with the sound of female voices as it had when Spartan Leisure's wealthy clients used it.

Shrewdly, Fraser had made sure that Paul Stratton was out of the way when the girls first arrived, for he was aware of the man's appeal to women. Let the girls sort themselves out with the rest of the men, then Paul could work it out from there.

He met Stratton at the bottom of the great curving staircase and they went in together. A cold buffet, delivered and set up by the local hotel who normally catered for Spartan parties, was already being picked at and it was obvious that everything was going as planned.

'What's been troubling you?' Fraser asked as Stratton's eyes moved over the women. 'Forget the girls for a moment – there's plenty to go around.'

Stratton turned to meet Fraser's penetrating look.

'It's a feeling of not belonging any more – or perhaps belonging less. You know quite well that I'll go through to the end of this thing – and willingly. But the others! They've been bent – manipulated by techniques designed to make them stay the course. That places a barrier between them and me. A barrier between you and me if you like.'

'It was loyalty that brought them to that meeting, Paul. Loyalty and a desire to do something explosive again – not manipulation.'

'You remember you said to me : "It does no good to look over your shoulder at a road you've already walked along"?' Stratton asked.

'Yes.'

'That's what they're all about to do! You also said that a road never looks quite the same if you walk along it the second time. I interpret that as meaning the reasons aren't the same – well, none of these men will have the same reasons because you've virtually indoctrinated them with a new set.'

Fraser shook his head.

'That's not true. What they were subjected to was a test, as you well know. We were looking for – and found those most likely to stick it out. We're not going on a picnic. Or have you lost sight of that?'

'The test stopped being a test when you used the Torch tape – Christ, even Stewart-Smith, a very intelligent man, was triggered off to recite McCrae – I can tell you now, that gave me an unpleasant feeling.'

'I agree that the incident with Stewart-Smith was a triggered response but I refute the idea that any of the men are going in unwillingly,' Fraser protested.

'Of course they're not – they're all mad as hatters – so am I – but I'm going along because –'

'Because you don't give a damn?'

'Because I don't care. I lost direction in my life one hell of a long time ago and at the very least this decision – crazy as it is – is still a decision. I haven't made one of those for far too long.'

Fraser gestured round the room.

'Do you really believe that any one of them have any direction? They came – willingly – in answer to an ambiguous summons from me and have elected – willingly – to take their chances. Do you know the only way you differ from them? They all believe that they will survive. You, Paul, are beginning to believe you're dead already. Look at them, Paul. Look at their faces. They've never had women that look that good in their lives. They're not thinking of dying. That's the very last thing on their minds. In the '14–'18 war the generals gave the troops alcohol to make them go over the top; all I've done is give a bunch of losers something to win. They're tasting some of the victor's spoils now – in advance.' Fraser splashed brandy into a glass. 'Here. Drink this and join them. If anyone survives it should be you. Go on.'

Stratton lifted the drink to his lips and for a moment his dark eyes were sad.

'Somehow it was a finer thing when we started. There wasn't any need to manipulate the men.'

'You're a romantic, Paul. You're forgetting the money. Don't you count that as manipulation?'

'You must realize that it's not money that's taken them this far.'

'Agreed. But it's the money that'll take them through to the end.'

'Probably,' Stratton said, and lifting his glass once more in a small salute moved away.

As Fraser had said, there were plenty of women to go round and with almost insolent ease Stratton pulled two away from the main group. As the entire house had been thrown open for the evening there was no shortage of bedrooms or privacy and he noted that a couple of the men had already drifted out of the room. He shrugged. What was the use of standing around drinking and talking? Champagne stood in silver buckets on the table. He took two bottles and glasses and made for the door, the girls following him.

Upstairs, he unlocked his door and indicated with his eyes that they should go in. The curtains over the tall windows were open and moonlight spilled through. He lounged on the bed and uncorked one of the bottles, filling the glasses to the brim. One of the girls sat beside him while the other moved to the window to look down on the moonlit countryside. As he sipped the champagne, he watched her body, silhouetted by the moonlight which cut through her thin, flowing dress.

The girl sitting on the bed moved her hands over him.

'Undress her,' he said. Reluctantly she removed her hands and without protest went over to the window.

Gently she touched the shining halo of blonde hair that fell over the girl's shoulders, then let her hands stray underneath to her neck. The blonde arched her neck with the touch of the soft fingers and, easing her position, moved her legs apart, letting her body be taken over by the fine upper register of sensuality.

Stratton watched the two silhouetted figures blend into one as the thin film of material floated to the floor.

His expression changed perceptibly as the killing urge collided with hard sexual desire, and then, as always before, became one with it. Briefly the memory of the pleading eyes of the girl in the wine-bar stripped him of everything – then the moment was gone.

Stratton moved his hips and rose from the bed towards the two women.

The bell of the village church was the only sound that broke the stillness of the manor as it rang out for Sunday evensong.

The girls had gone and only the lingering scent of perfume on bedsheets was a reminder that they had ever been there. As every man on the strike-force had expected, Colonel Fraser announced that they would hit the Embassy the next day. He briefed them ruthlessly, leaving nothing to chance. Chance or luck, he told them, would be something only the survivors would need, to get out alive when it was all over. By nine-thirty that Sunday evening, every aspect of the strike and the holding of the Embassy building had been covered and committed to memory. Fraser declared himself satisfied and asked if there were any questions.

Stewart-Smith stood up.

'You do realize, Colonel, that the Russians are not going to stand there and let this happen?'

'As I said before, we must try to avoid bloodshed but not at the cost of our lives.'

The ex-intelligence officer shook his head. 'No, sir. What I meant was that the Russians will not leave this in the hands of the British police. They're not going to worry who is in that building. Any hostages we hold will be considered expendable. Their only concern will be to kill all of us before we start spilling secrets over the air-waves.'

Fraser nodded in agreement.

'Quite so. That is why the estimation of our losses was 100 per cent. I made a remark to Major Stratton last night and I'll repeat it now. We're not going on a picnic.'

'It had never crossed my mind that we are, Colonel. I'm merely stating a fact which perhaps you may have overlooked. I don't believe that we'll be the cause of World War Three but we will definitely be the cause of the biggest international incident this century. If you want to take this to an absurd but quite logical conclusion you could end up with the British security forces defending us against a Russian strike-force.'

'I don't think it would go to that extreme. The only counter-measure the Soviet government need to take to protect their secrets is apply pressure for the prisoners' release. That is the logical argument and I can't see such pressure being resisted in the given circumstances.'

There were no more questions so Fraser broke up the briefing, reminding everyone to ensure that all their civilian clothes, shoes and any personal items they had with them were placed in the army kit-bags that the RSM would provide.

Cornwell took over quartermaster's duties and kitted the men out with combat uniforms, boots and flak jackets. For headgear they were issued with peaked caps and the one item that cast an aura of mystery and a certain romanticism over SAS under-cover units – the black wrap-over scarf which concealed the lower half of the face. None of the uniforms issued to the men bore any insignia. Only Fraser, Paul Stratton and Cornwell had uniforms bearing lightly tacked-on flashes but none of the three men had ever served in the particular unit they indicated. The hardware needed for the strike would be issued next morning.

Paul Stratton wondered how many would sleep through the night and how many would live through the next day. All he could foresee was their bloody and shattered bodies laying in the building or grounds of the Soviet Embassy as mute testi-mony to one man's financial will and their own empty existence.

PART TWO

Strike

I

A bitter cold front swept across England that Monday, causing people to stay indoors and rely on television for entertainment. Garages put up chalkboards reminding motorists to check their anti-freeze and, throughout the day, the radio stations broadcast warnings of bad road conditions. Outside Kensington Palace Gardens, the crowd which had spent the day chanting slogans thinned with the onset of evening. A few hardy souls paced the pavement in orderly fashion holding placards aloft with numbed fingers. A line of overcoated policemen stamped their feet and cursed the Russians and their own overlords with equal venom, and wished silently for the comfort and warmth of their own beds and their women's bodies.

Across the wide road, a row of businesses had closed for the night, leaving only Ruskie's wine-bar and The Champion pub as harbour from the cold. The big employment agency to the far left of the block had one light burning in an upper window as someone worked late, but the hairdressing salon and the two antique shops were blacked out. Between the hairdresser's and the second antique shop, one shop front bore no markings excepting the poster stuck to the grimy windows proclaiming its vacancy. Above the shop the flat which came with the tenancy was dark and empty. Filthy net curtains were the only furnishings in the place. Back across the Bayswater Road the Embassy gateman's wife prepared supper and, charitably, cups of hot tea for the frozen policemen.

Less than half a mile away, in a locked mews garage, work was being completed on the fitting of a large metal reflective sign to the radiator of a dark green Range Rover.

Outside the garage Jonathan Fraser's Jaguar ticked intermittently like an unstable bomb as the engine block cooled. Fraser sat inside with his eyes fixed on the luminous dial of the steel Rolex around his wrist. His fingers tapped a rhythm on the dashboard, as an accompaniment to his steady thudding heart-beat.

He heard the big V8 engine of the Range Rover roar as it caught first time. Twisting his own key, he reversed the Jaguar to the end of the mews, got out and walked a short distance to a telephone box which he had ensured earlier was in working order. The number he dialled rang first time and he pushed the coin home.

'Police, can I help you?' a voice said as the pips stopped.

'Listen carefully,' he ordered, 'I'll say this once only. There are two bombs in Kensington Palace Gardens. You don't have very long.' He put the receiver down, then checked his watch; the time was exactly 8.45.

Further away, on the other side of the Bayswater Road a green van, low on its springs, pulled to a halt in the street running alongside Wellington Terrace. The tall angular figure of Leslie Roberts, the strike-force's most expert silent killer, stepped to the ground and surveyed the deserted street. He nodded to Cornwell, who gave him a quick sharp smile and pushed the compact pack of the field radio across the seat. Roberts lifted the webbing with one of his long slender hands and returned the smile. Moving fast, he made his way to the rear of Wellington Terrace and merged with the shadows.

Cornwell checked his watch. 8.45 to the second. Not a sound came from the heavily laden rear of the green van. Across the Bayswater Road and out of sight of the van, in the middle ground between the two sets of vehicles, a telephone rang insistently at the Embassy gatehouse. The policemen, gratefully accepting tea from the gateman's wife, turned towards it. One man detached himself and made for the instrument. He listened for a few seconds, then banged it down.

'Clear those people!' he yelled. The others turned, startled. 'Bomb – get them back!'

The police scattered, pushing the diehard demonstrators back; then stopped the traffic.

The Range Rover rolled out of the mews garage with its engine barely throbbing and its lights out. Fraser pulled in quickly to take its place, locked the garage doors with sure movements, seemingly unhurried and climbed into the Range Rover. Paul Stratton moved over from the driving seat. Fraser let in the clutch and quietly progressed to the end of the mews. At the corner he banged the accelerator to the floor and the big vehicle rocked on its springs as the pull of eight cylinders threw it forward.

Stratton rolled in his seat as he frantically reached through the open window to place the magnetic light and siren unit on the roof.

Cornwell heard the blaring of the double-tone siren before he saw the Range Rover blast out of a street the other side of the Bayswater Road. He threw the van into gear and drove full tilt for the end of the road, his own unit screaming in discordant unison. Both vehicles cut through the traffic with total disregard for safety and Cornwell neatly tucked in behind the speeding Range Rover.

The police held back the traffic at the gates entrance and pulled open the black railings. The barrier was still down. The reflective BOMB-DISPOSAL UNIT sign on the Range Rover shone in the lights of the halted traffic as Fraser turned in with tyres squealing.

'Get that barrier up !' he roared.

A policeman rushed to it.

'Christ, you were quick, sir. We only got the call a minute ago.'

'Out of the way !' Fraser shouted. 'And get those gates closed. Nobody comes in. Got it ? Move damn you, move !'

'You don't know where they are,' the policeman bawled. Inside the Range Rover Stratton pressed a red button on a small device and a blinding white flash preceded a muted bang. 'Jesus !' the policeman said, turning in the direction of the explosion. 'They've bombed the bloody Russians.'

'Get that barrier up, you idiot,' Fraser roared. The roof of the Range Rover screeched as the rising barrier was dragged along it, the policeman leaping out of the way as the two vehicles tore down the tree-lined avenue. 'Crazy buggers !' he yelled after them.

At the target building the front hedge and part of the low wall was scattered over the road. Fraser threw the Range Rover into a slide, the fat tyres scattering whole sections of brick over a wider area.

Cornwell rapped hard on the panel behind his head as soon as he saw the Range Rover twist and he felt the weight lighten as the strike-team rolled out of the rear doors. In the wing mirror he saw bodies bounce on the tarmac then rise up, moving fast. Pulling his left hand hard down he hit the brakes and the van slewed round, tilting on two wheels before settling.

Mclennan and Hubbard were already in flanking positions outside the building and the trio, Carter, Walters and Peterson, with the aid of Andy Fowler, had tucked themselves into the four corners of the space in front of the building.

A group of people stood in the centre of the driveway shocked and bewildered as Fraser, the only man with his face uncovered, approached them. Stratton and Cornwell stood to either side of him.

'Anyone speak English? Who's in charge here?'

A man with grey-flecked dark hair and cold, suspicious eyes pushed his way through.

'I am the Military Attaché – why are your men armed? You are a bomb-disposal unit.'

'Can you move these people back into the building,' Fraser said, ignoring the question. 'We need to check the grounds for other devices.'

The Russian's eyes came to rest on Fraser's shoulder.

'I don't understand what is going on here. Why is a full colonel in charge of this team? Why are your men's faces concealed?'

'These men are an SAS anti-terrorist team. Please move your people back into the building.'

The Russian flicked his eyes over the men, noting their positions were better suited to cover the crowd and the building than an outside attack. Suspicion grew in his eyes and Fraser saw it clearly. He gave a sharp nod of his head and, as though from nowhere, canisters belching smoke fell on the gravel. The Military Attaché reached inside his jacket and in the centre of the crowd another man made a quick movement.

Cornwell with precise shots from his silenced automatic shot the Attaché through the forearm, swinging straight-armed to take the man in the crowd with a bullet in the shoulder.

As the smoke rose, the men on the four corners of the crowd moved in with weapons ready, pushing the people back to the entrance door. Back at the gates the siren wailed to a stop.

'Johnny!' Cornwell shouted, and Hubbard, the man who loved explosives, readied a small package.

'Into the house,' Fraser ordered. 'We're setting another bomb.' This time the Embassy staff needed no violence to persuade them; they scrambled back through the doors, the strike-force on their heels.

Once inside, Fraser's men deployed to strategic positions around the building and on the roof. A burst of fire came from somewhere in the building and Stratton started for the stairs, but Cornwell stopped him.

'All right, sir, it was a Sterling.'

'Find a large room where we can keep these people,' Fraser ordered Stratton. 'And stand guard on them – I shall want to speak to them later. Take the RSM with you; his presence should stop any more heroics.'

The crowd of people moved nervously before the two men, one tall and the other diminutive in size but both with killer's eyes, the only visible feature on their faces.

Stratton found a spacious room, obviously some sort of recreation lounge, and indicated with the Sterling for them to go inside. He pulled a notebook from the pocket of his combat jacket.

'Fill this,' he ordered, having to speak loudly through the black scarf. 'Names and positions in the Embassy. Who speaks the best English?'

A girl raised her blonde head from her hands.

'I do,' she said quietly, and Stratton looked straight into the eyes of the girl he'd seen with the two men in the wine-bar days before. There was no doubt in his mind that as she looked at him she recognized him as well. A strange relief filled him first, then a feeling of confusion. She is part of the target, he thought savagely. No more – no less!

He looked away and saw that one of her guards, if that was what they were, was in the room. The other, he realized, had been the armed man in the centre of the crowd outside, whom Cornwell had shot with such merciless ease. He handed her the book.

'Names and positions as soon as possible. No one will be hurt if you don't resist. We mean you no harm personally. Tell them in Russian if they don't understand,' he said to the girl. She nodded, her eyes still fixed on his.

Fraser entered the room and the hostages stiffened perceptibly.

'I've made the necessary phone call but the real bomb-disposal unit is crawling up the road. It'll take time for word to reach them. I'm going out there. I won't have British troops shot.'

'I'm coming with you,' Stratton said.

'No need, there's enough cover from the men on the roof – they've got the night-sights on their weapons. You stay here and get me the information on these people. Oh, and tell them the injured men are being given medical attention.'

From the roof the men watched the slow process of the bomb-disposal unit vehicles as they cautiously edged nearer the Range Rover and the van. Along the avenue, people were coming out of the various buildings, and lights were being switched on everywhere.

Fraser moved out of the communications building with a bull-horn in one hand and a large box in the crook of his other arm. He set the box down on the entrance steps then walked out on to the wide road.

'I am Colonel Jonathan Fraser,' his voice echoed harshly through the bull-horn. 'Your attention, bomb-disposal unit. Go back to the gates. I repeat. Go back to the gates. There is a message waiting for you there from the highest level. Do not approach this building.'

The lead vehicle turned a spotlight on Fraser who flinched under the glare.

'What's going on, Colonel?' a voice blared through the vehicle's roof-mounted speakers. 'What unit are you?'

Fraser raised his bull-horn.

'Look to the roof of this building.' The light swung upwards and caught the black-hooded figures with weapons readied. A swathe of automatic fire stitched across the tarmac in front of the slowly moving vehicle. The driver braked violently, causing the light to fly wildly around.

'Go back,' Fraser repeated. 'I say again, a message from the highest level awaits you. I don't want bloodshed. Go back.'

With squealing tyres the vehicles reversed down the avenue.

On the roof of the communications building the men carried on with their preparations as Fraser stepped off the road and moved back into the house. At the entrance he stopped and looked around, then looked up to the small flat roof of the pillared doorway.

'Jimbo,' he said, knowing that the hulking figure of Murray was behind the double doors.

'Yessir!'

'It's all right. I'm in no danger. They're still bewildered out there.'

'I was covering you, sir.'

'I know but we're all right at this stage – come out here, I need your help.'

Murray stepped outside, his eyes swivelling over the road and the other buildings. Fraser calmly opened the carton he had placed on the steps and took out the big oil-flare.

'Where should it go, Jimbo?' he said almost conversationally.

'Sir?'

'The Torch! Where shall we place it?'

Murray's mind blanked for a split second and he heard, or he felt, he didn't know which, a drone so deep it could have come up from the bowels of the earth. Fraser was speaking to him but for a moment the words were only movements on his lips.

'Probably that's the best place – it'll burn on its own for a week at least,' Fraser continued coolly. He stepped down on to the gravel forecourt and pointed above the doorway. 'Can you get it up there?'

The man lifted the drum-shaped flare and found a foothold on one of the slim pillars. With one arm he raised it up and slid it on to the flat stone above. Fraser held a box of matches.

'Light it for me, Jimbo.'

Murray wrapped his big legs around the pillar, clambered on to the small roof and caught the matches. Carefully he struck two matches together and touched them to the thick wick. The flame grew slowly, gathering strength in the cold wind.

'Come on down,' Fraser called, but Murray's eyes were fascinated by the gusting flame. 'It's done. Come on down, Jimbo.'

Pulling himself away, the big man dropped to the gravel. 'That's the place, sir. Great that is. Burn for ever up there.' Fraser's amber eyes looked upwards and saw the strength of the flame.

'It might at that,' he said quietly. 'Let's go back in, shall we – this is just the beginning.'

Chief Superintendent Colin Hammond lay asleep, his arm around the young girl beside him, holding her breast, his body and mind relaxed after their lovemaking. The telephone shrilled and his eyes snapped open. He lay still for a couple of seconds, then pulled himself up. The light was still on. The bedside clock read seventeen minutes past nine. Hammond lifted the receiver.

'Hammond!'

Vere's voice! His tranquillity was dashed away immediately.

'Hammond here, sir.'

'There's a car on its way to you now. Get in it and get here! Don't stop for anything – you understand – nothing!'

'Commander what . . .?' but the phone had already gone down. As though in a dream he heard the police siren getting closer until the sound stabilized in the street outside. The doorbell buzzed and Hammond leapt for the intercom. 'Turn that bloody siren off,' he yelled.

'Can't do that, sir,' a tinny voice said from the earpiece. 'Siren all the way we were told – are you ready, sir?'

'Ready – I've only just got the call, you fool! I'll have to throw some clothes on.'

'Throw them on in the car, sir – our orders were to bring you in wearing a towel if you were in the bath.'

'Bloody hell!' Hammond swore savagely and slammed the instrument down. Quickly he pulled on trousers and a black roll-neck sweater, grabbing shoes, socks, jacket and overcoat. The girl sat up in bed her eyes wide.

'What's happening?' she said.

Hammond held her for the briefest moment.

'I love you. Go back to sleep.' He moved to the door as fast as he could go and took the stairs to the street five at a time. The siren reverberated against the houses as people came to their windows.

'Right – GO!' he shouted, but the car was already moving while his legs were still outside. 'Somebody shot the Queen? What the hell is going on?'

The policeman in the observer's seat half turned to the rear.

'Nothing's clear yet, sir, better wait till we get to the Yard.'

'What do you mean nothing's clear . . . what's not clear?' But the officer had turned to face the road, his hands clamped around the shoulder strap of the seat-belt.

'Better strap yourself in, sir,' the driver yelled. 'I've got orders to stop for nothing.'

Hammond dropped lower in the seat and clamped the belt across his body.

'This had better be good,' he thought murderously, and fleetingly longed for the girl in his bed.

When they screamed to a halt outside New Scotland Yard he was fully dressed. He leapt out of the car, made for the entrance doors, noting the increased activity on the ground floor of the building, and sprang for the closing doors of the lift.

Vere's door was open and he went straight in.

'Sit down. Listen to this. Don't say a word till it's finished.' The commander punched the play button on the tape recorder. A crackling began and Hammond knew the recording was made from the telephone.

'. . . Who is this?' a voice which Hammond knew but couldn't place. 'I was told this was an urgent call from the Soviet Embassy and we're to record a message – who am I speaking to please?' The annoyance was plainly obvious in the voice as it continued and suddenly Colin Hammond sat bolt upright.

'This *is* the Prime Minister and we are recording according to your instructions. Please speak now if you're ready.' The crackling noise diminished as a clear and distinctly British voice began to speak.

'Prime Minister. My name is Jonathan Fraser, Colonel, now retired, late of the Twenty-second Regiment, Special Air Service and formerly Fourth Hussars. You can establish my identity from the Army List.'

'Just one moment. I was told that this call was from the Soviet Embassy!'

'Please bear with me, Prime Minister. You have not been misled, this call is indeed from the Soviet Embassy – however, it is not from the Ambassador's residence but from the communications building. This building is now under the control of myself and my men.'

'I'm afraid I don't understand, Colonel Fraser – under your control – what does that mean?'

'It means, Prime Minister, that we have captured it – and of course all that it contains – think about that carefully, Prime Minister. I shall be calling again after you've ordered all police and security people away from Kensington Palace Gardens. Check on the situation, sir, and make the arrangements – you'll find that this is no hoax. I shall call again.' The recorder clunked to a stop.

Hammond sat stock still.

'That call was made at five minutes to nine,' Vere said.

'They did it!' Hammond said as though to himself. 'They went and bloody did it.'

'Apparently,' Vere muttered dryly, completely unruffled. 'The question, Hammond, is who are they and what are they after?'

'This is taking coincidence too far, sir – they have to be the men we photographed!'

'That's taken as read, although I'm afraid the PM is not going to be very pleased that nothing was done about it.'

Hammond felt his stomach churn. 'How much does he know, sir?'

'Nothing. That's why you were brought here in such a damn hurry.'

Hammond had the painful vision of his career falling in tatters around him. With a nervous gesture he touched his prematurely balding forehead.

'You'd like me to explain to the Prime Minister,' he said flatly.

Vere huffed impatiently.

'No one's looking for heads to lop off, Hammond. Just get every scrap of detail you've put together from those shots and be ready to leave in five minutes. We'll do our explaining at 10 Downing Street.' Hammond made for the door. 'You'll find you've got an assistant waiting in your office,' the commander called after him.

'Assistant, sir?'

'Johnson. He picked them out, didn't he? You'll need him for a while. Get a move on!'

As Colin Hammond opened his office door he was confronted

by an extremely pale-faced young man, whose hands trembled as he placed blow-ups of the crowd shots into a large buff envelope.

'I see you've had the kind of drive I've just had. Where did they bring you from?'

'Home, sir – Fulham. I was sick in the car.'

Hammond drew open a desk draw. 'Brandy – drink a little. It'll settle your stomach. And your nerves. Jesus wept!' he exclaimed. 'What a mess.'

'They *did it*, sir!'

'Don't you start. Come on, we've got a date with God.'

'Sir?'

'The Prime Minister.'

Johnson promptly heaved the brandy back up again.

The two policemen outside number 10 Downing Street saluted Vere as he, Hammond and Johnson clambered out of the police Rover and entered the world's best-known front door, to be ushered into an ante-chamber. The Prime Minster came in almost immediately and tersely bade them good evening, going straight through the double doors into the Cabinet room.

The great oblong table, covered with a green baize cloth, was surrounded by chairs, eight down one side, backing on to the fireplace; eleven on the other, facing it and the painting of Walpole. With a professional eye Hammond noted that there were six windows; one of these was a french window leading out to the garden.

The Prime Minster sat down at one corner, picking a chair at random.

'This is no time for ceremony. Sit down – all of you.'

Johnson took the seat which Hammond nudged towards him and sat down as if dreaming.

'You have something for me, Commander?' the PM said, his hand resting on a green telephone which was plugged into a wall socket.

'This is Chief Superintendent Hammond, sir, and his assistant, Johnson. I think if Hammond explains things it would save time.'

Hammond began lucidly, with the evidence of the blown-up

photographs, to explain that the Special Branch were aware on the Friday, that known mercenaries were outside the gates of Kensington Palace Gardens. He pointed out that it had been a bizarre series of coincidences and seemed to be no more than that yet. With the aid of Johnson's phenomenal memory he had put together a report forecasting a possible violent demonstration outside the Embassy. He added, with a certain amount of pleasure, that the Private Under-Secretary at the Home Office had been copied for his Minister's attention.

'Don't know anything about it,' the Prime Minister muttered.

Hammond placed a copy in front of him, but the PM didn't even glance at it.

'Go on.'

'That's it, sir.'

'What do you mean : that's it !'

'The gate detail was doubled, Prime Minister,' Vere interrupted.

'Was it now, Commander ! So you took it seriously?'

'Cautiously, sir. No more than that. There was no hard evidence that these mercenaries might . . .'

'Hijack the Russian Embassy? Is that what you were about to say, Commander?'

'Precisely, Prime Minister.'

'And have they? Do you have any "hard evidence" that they did?'

'We're working a line of coincidences here, sir – sometimes one has to believe in the inevitability of things.'

'That's an interesting turn of phrase.'

'We have to assume that part of Fraser's group are the men who were outside the gates on Friday.'

'I'll accept that as a reasonable assumption. Can I also assume that this Colonel Fraser does not know we had foreknowledge of the identity of some of his men?'

Hammond answered the Prime Minister's question.

'Every photograph was taken under cover from the gatehouse and the checking we've done on the men has been purely internal. We have not made any attempt to find them.'

The Prime Minister tapped the green telephone with his fingers.

'Then I suggest you do, Chief Superintendent !'

'I've got that in motion already, Prime Minister,' Vere interrupted again.

'Good, I'm glad about that.' The most powerful man in the country gazed stoically down at the table at them and the room fell silent. Under his hand the green telephone began to ring. There was a rap on the door and a man's head appeared.

'It's the call, sir. We're taping now.'

The Prime Minister lifted the receiver and placed it on the adjacent amplifier.

'You'd better hear this,' he said quietly.

A crisp voice filled the room.

'Prime Minister, this is Colonel Fraser.'

'Yes, Colonel, I can hear you.'

'I think by now you will have enough information to realize that this is not a hoax.'

'Yes. We do know that. The two army vehicles have been pulled back but the police will remain at the gates – to hold back the inevitable crowds.'

'That's acceptable, Prime Minister.'

'I think, Colonel, that you have some explaining to do. You realize that you have sparked off an international incident.'

'That was my aim, Prime Minister.'

The Prime Minister raised his eyebrows but his face was impassive, with only the hard set of his mouth giving away his feelings.

'Presumably then you have some sort of demand. Terrorists usually do. I have to assume, Colonel, that you and your men *are* terrorists as you are acting on your own behalf and not under government instruction.'

Fraser ignored the barbed words.

'It will take us some time to understand the radio and cryptography equipment here, sir, but when we do, I shall be transmitting a message to the President of the Soviet Union which I hope will receive a favourable reply.'

'I see.' The voice was still rock-steady, but the Prime Minister's eyes held their first trace of fear. 'Colonel Fraser! We are still unaware of your demands but if I might make a suggestion? You're an ex-army man as I am. Now you know quite well that holding a gun to the head of the enemy is no good unless you are prepared to pull the trigger. Listen to me, please. I have negotiated with the Russians – and their President – on many occasions, and I can tell you right now that any threats will not be well received. God knows what you might start, man! Either give up this madness or let me know what your demands are. I'll talk to the President.'

'No, sir.'

'Why not?'

'Because when the Russian President gets my message I'm afraid your motives will be suspect.'

'Fraser! What are you talking about?'

'I'll read you the wording of the message, Prime Minister – we'll be transmitting "*en clair*" so your Signals Intelligence unit will be able to pick it up clearly without having to decode. Message reads: To the President and First Secretary of the Union of Soviet Socialist Republics. Your London Embassy under my control, specifically the communications building housing Registry, Archives and Cryptography sections. Repeat. This building under my control by force of arms. I request your assistance in achieving the release of the British contract soldiers held prisoner in Africa at the present time. These men, upon release, are to be repatriated to the United Kingdom by aircraft without delay. In the event that you decide not to aid me in this cause, I regret that we will have to resort to extreme measures to enlist your aid. Although we hold as hostages some twenty of your fellow Russians in this building, I am no murderer and wish them no harm. Therefore as an alternative I shall begin broadcasting on an open channel to yourself the most sensitive information available in your extensive archives. As this information will not be passed through the cryptograph machines before transmission, I leave you to consider the resulting and quite irreversible damage to your intelligence networks and military plans within Europe. Neither I nor my men have any political affiliations whatsoever. We wish only for the release of the prisoners. Transmitted by Colonel Jonathan Fraser, CO, Strike-Force.'

The stunned silence was enough to tell Fraser that the enormity of his threat was not lost.

'You can't possibly do this thing, Fraser.' The Prime Minister's voice was gentle, almost a plea.

'I can, sir. And will. If necessary.'

'Look, man – the President is on holiday in the Crimea – he can't do a thing from there.'

'He'll get a message all the same, Prime Minister, and be flown back to Moscow without delay – I can assure you of that.'

'Fraser, give me time – let me speak to the Africans.'

'They'll laugh in your face, sir."

'Let me try at least.'

'Two hours – no more – and, Prime Minister, I do not want to kill British soldiers, but my men have orders to defend this position to the death and they will do just that. Our firepower is heavy enough to withstand an attack long enough for us to broadcast enough Russian secrets to damage their system immeasurably. Incidentally, I can now inform you that we are able to begin broadcasting at any time.'

The amplifier clicked and purred.

'Jesus Christ,' Hammond breathed, his fists tightly clenched on the table.

'We'll need a lot more than his help I'm afraid,' the Prime Minister exclaimed, rising fast. 'I want everything known on this man – every little detail – we have to make him change his mind or break him – before he breaks us all.'

'He's too lucid to be totally unbalanced, sir,' Hammond put in. 'I had the impression he was detached – as if he was listening to himself.'

The Prime Minister shrugged his big shoulders.

'God alone knows. Get medical information on him. There must be army records around still – and, Commander, I want that tame psychologist of yours here as soon as possible. Let him see what he can make of those recordings.'

The three policemen left quickly, leaving the nation's top minister resting his knuckles on the green baize table cover and shaking his head. Every other problem or crisis had suddenly become unimportant.

2

In the Embassy communications building Fraser was receiving his first report from Roberts, now safely settled in the empty flat on the first floor of Wellington Terrace. Fraser, with his usual meticulous planning, had ensured that the frequency used would not be picked up on police or military wavebands. But a radio 'ham' might stray inadvertently on to the transmission, so he insisted on the use of a scrambler all the time.

Roberts's voice was calm, giving a concise description of the activity at the Bayswater Road end of the avenue.

'Cub to Wolf-leader. I have entrance under observation. My position secure and vision good. Road blocks are up, traffic movement nil. Diversions must be operating. With NVD can see your vehicles. Heavy police strength here including marksmen and star-scopes – have counted sixteen. Gates closed – no one entering avenue. Is Torch all right? Not visible from here. Out.'

'Wolf-leader here. Pack in position. Torch lighted.'

'Suggest placing on roof.'

'Affirmative.'

'Will look for it.'

'Am blowing remainder of outside wall. Out.'

From his hidden position Roberts saw a flash, and the net-curtained window rattled lightly as the charge blew. The remainder of the wall and hedge spewed over the road, leaving a clear view of the entrance to the building. Two more flat explosions demolished the adjoining wall to the Nigerian High Commission and Palace Green.

'You have a killing ground, Wolf-leader . . . out.'

'Thank you. Hope you are not lonely.'

'Will look for Torch on skyline, Wolf-leader . . . out.'

At the sound of the explosions the police scattered, ducking behind their vehicles. Roberts watched them in amusement, then settled cross-legged on the bare wooden boards, munching a biscuit, his eyes level with the window-sill. The darkened room pulsed with the steady flash of a revolving blue light from a police car. For some reason this disquieted him but when he saw a naked flame flaring on a rooftop over the trees he smiled to himself and chewed happily.

Three storeys up, on the roof of the communications building, Jonathan Fraser pushed the aerial home into the set as the Torch was hoisted up and placed on the balustrade. Behind him the towering antennae of the powerful transmitter in the basement cast shadows in its glow.

'Colonel, you'd better see this.' Doc Peterson who, with his cohorts Walters and Carter plus Mclennan, was manning the roof, indicated the road below. Even without the use of the NVDs Fraser could see movement all along the avenue.

'Well, I don't think I'd stay in an area where bombs are being set off . . . I'd expected some sort of evacuation but this looks more like general exodus. Mind you, the Russians aren't leaving. Just keep an eye on those three buildings – five, thirteen, and fifteen. Bleep me if you need me. I'll be in the basement with Sammy.'

Fraser descended down the three floors, noting that for a building which served such a functional purpose the standard of décor and comfort was very high. But he realized that the KGB, under whose jurisdiction the building came, were powerful enough to feather their nest with a degree of luxury that might in another case be frowned on officially.

On the ground floor he dropped in on Cornwell who was baby-sitting the Russian staff. James Dewey was in one corner of the room checking the wounds of the Military Attaché and the second man – a security guard.

'How are they, James?' he enquired.

'Hurting, I should say. Still, that's what comes with fooling about with guns,' Dewey answered with twinkling eyes.

'Make sure their wounds don't get infected.'

'Nope. Very clean these little .22s. . . . Ah-ah hold still now, comrade!' If there was one thing Fraser could rely on it was James Dewey's constant good humour.

'Where's Paul?' Fraser asked, maintaining the use of first name only. Dewey pointed downstairs with his finger and Cornwell had to make a threatening movement with his little automatic in the direction of the Military Attaché.

Stratton's black notebook was open on the table; Fraser picked it up and noted the insertion for the Attaché. 'Colonel Davydov? Is that the correct pronunciation?' The man nodded, grey-faced. 'Colonel Davydov, I have no interest in your secrets nor have my men – we intend to use them only as a bargaining counter – if absolutely necessary.'

'This is a British trick,' the Attaché spat. 'A military operation. Your government is behind this. An imperialist attempt to provoke the Soviet Union.'

'Spare me the dogma, Colonel. We're both mature men and your party bosses aren't here to censure you for speaking without quoting Lenin. We have no political aims. All we want is to free some of *our* comrades from a lifetime in prison.'

'Inside Russia?' the Attaché asked more civilly.

'Africa.'

Davydov laughed. 'You think those stupid blacks will let white mercenary soldiers go? You speak of those held after the war, yes? They are butchers those men. Let them rot.'

'One can't cloak all men under the same coat of barbarism – it doesn't work. The men who were executed have paid the full price. They are merely extracting interest on the lives of others. Would the Cuban forces be jailed for life if they were on the losing side?'

The Military Attaché shook his head wearily.

'Colonel Fraser – I am told that is your name – they will never release those mercenaries – they are a symbol of victory – more than that they are a matter of pride to the rulers there. As long as those men are caged like animals, it proves that the white oppressor can be, and has been, beaten and degraded.'

Fraser smiled grimly.

'I hope you're wrong. Perhaps your President will persuade them to swallow their pride – because if he can't, Comrade Davydov, we shall begin broadcasting the secrets you hold down there, without the benefit of your very sophisticated electronic coding equipment!'

The Attaché sat paralysed.

'No! It's impossible – you cannot mean it!' he whispered.

'I'm sorry but there's no other way.'

Davydov dragged himself to his feet, pushing Dewey aside and ignoring Cornwell's automatic.

'Use us! Trade us as hostages – a life for a life – tell the President you'll kill us all if your comrades are not released! Don't, I beg you, tell him you will broadcast the secrets – don't even think of it!' The Attaché pulled at Fraser's combat jacket. 'Listen to me, please . . . if you hint at that we are all dead . . . you, your men . . . all of us. They will not allow us to live.'

Fraser shook him off.

'Rest assured, Comrade Davydov, that your President will make every effort to protect his secrets and the simplest way is to gain the release of the prisoners; he has the power – let him use it.'

Leaving the Military Attaché to digest his words, Jonathan Fraser made his way down to the basement where he had to negotiate two sets of doors before encountering Johnny Hubbard, Sammy Cohen and Stratton. The three of them stood before a grey-painted steel door which looked as though it would stop a Centurion tank in its tracks. He cast an enquiring look at Hubbard.

'You'd better do something soon, Johnny. I've told the powers that be that we are able to broadcast at any time we choose.'

Hubbard, who was happily placing plastic explosive into strategic points on the massive door, turned and grinned. 'Don't you worry about a thing, Colonel. Have this blown apart in a minute. Got to be real careful, see. All that sensitive equipment and stuff inside.'

For the first time Fraser was aware of a huddled form on the floor.

'Who the devil's that?'

'Security guard.' It was Cohen, the signals specialist, who answered. 'There's two of them, sir. This bastard who half-killed me with a throat chop and another who's dug himself in inside.'

'How bad is he?' Fraser asked, prodding the prone figure with his boot.

'Stone dead,' Stratton said, looking at Cohen.

'I had no choice, sir.'

Fraser glanced at Stratton who confirmed Cohen's words.

'Kyoei kick – under the armpit, fifth and sixth ribs punctured the heart. Sammy was going down from a mis-hit with a throat chop. He retaliated as he was trained to do. The man was going in for the kill.'

Fraser sighed.

'Unfortunate though.'

'What about the one inside?' Stratton said. 'When the door goes the concussion will fracture every bone in his body.'

Fraser searched around the walls with his eyes and found

what he was looking for. A communication device for emergencies.

'Who'd you use for the translation upstairs?'

'A girl – secretary to the Trade Attaché, she says.'

'And where's her boss?'

'East Germany – till Wednesday.'

'What's she doing in the communications building?' Fraser didn't wait for an answer to his question. 'Eyewash. She's KGB and he's the resident officer. Right – get her down here.'

Stratton moved past him out of the corridor. He found the girl along with the other hostages under the watchful eye of Cornwell. She was weeping.

'Colonel Fraser wants this one,' he told Cornwell, who nodded. Stratton took her arm gently but she held on to the chair she was sitting in. He dropped to his haunches and lifted her chin so that her eyes were in line with his.

'I mean you no harm. All we want you to do is talk to one of your people,' he said quietly. 'His life is in danger if you don't help us.'

The Military Attaché spoke rapidly in Russian to the girl and Stratton whipped round, producing as if from thin air a heavy Browning automatic fitted with a silencer. As he moved the KGB security guard whom Cornwell had shot leapt for the girl, his fist half curled with the middle knuckle extended. Stratton rolled, realising he was blocking Cornwell's line of fire and felt the snap of the small bullet as it flew past him, but it didn't stop the man. The big Browning came up double-handed in Stratton's grip and he squeezed off two shots.

There was a sound like a pillow being thumped twice and the security man cartwheeled backwards, shot twice through the heart. Cornwell's little .22 entry wound was high, above the lungs.

Stratton wrenched the Military Attaché to his feet and thrust the heavy silencer against the back of the man's lowered neck on the spinal column, in the classic execution position.

'He tried to kill her . . . what did you say? You're dead if you don't answer.'

The girl saved the colonel's life, for Paul Stratton was ready to kill again.

'He told me I am already a traitor and not to be a pig's

whore. . . .' She made a movement with her hand. 'He meant not to help you.'

Cornwell saw the finger on the trigger of the Browning whiten.

'Major, one's enough,' he said warily, knowing what Stratton was capable of when the blood was running.

'I'll do what you ask,' the girl said in an exhausted voice. 'Let him live.' Stratton thrust the man away and took the girl's arm, leading her out of the room. The Attaché roared after her in Russian. Cornwell pointed the small pistol at him.

'I wouldn't do that if I were you, sir! I have to tell you, you're lucky to be alive. That's the first time I've seen the major top only one man when his blood was up.'

'You're animals – all of you.'

'Maybe you're right, sir, but the same God made all of us.'

Out in the hallway, Stratton didn't hear any of this exchange. The holstered Browning might still have been in his hands, the hot barrel burning his palms. Pulling off his black scarf, he pinned the girl to the wall and pressed his lips hard down on hers. Her arms struggled with him yet she responded with her body, clinging to him instead of pushing him away. He stopped, looked into her eyes, then released her but stayed close.

'You are the one in the bar,' she whispered, her face almost touching his.

He nodded.

'Why did he call you a traitor? What have you done?'

'I was being forced – that day you saw me in the bar – to wait for someone. Those men were KGB.'

'I saw that.' He reached up and held her face with one hand. 'Wait for who? What have you done?' he repeated.

'They suspected me of passing secrets – to your Intelligence Service.'

'Were you?'

The girl dropped her eyes. Stratton jerked her head up forcing her to look at him.

'Were you?'

She closed her eyes slowly in affirmation.

'You're being paid by the British.'

The blue eyes flared.

'*Nyet!* No! It was the price for bringing my uncle out of

Russia. He is in Kaschenko – the KGB hospital for those who oppose the regime. He is nothing, not a scientist, not a great writer – just a man who said what he believed. They were destroying his mind. I wanted to save him. I have no one else.'

Stratton touched her hair.

'Come,' he said, and hesitatingly the girl followed him. In the basement Hubbard had completed his precautions and they stood waiting.

'I'm afraid I had to kill the wounded security guard,' he told Fraser, looking directly at him.

'Why?'

'He went for the girl – would have killed her. Cornwell put a round in him but he didn't go down. I finished him.'

Fraser moved his fiery eyes on to the girl.

'It's a bit of a mess,' Stratton continued. 'She's been passing classified information to the SIS, the KGB have got one of her family in a psychiatric ward. The SIS said they'd spring him for a price.'

'My only family,' the girl corrected. 'My mother's brother.'

'She could be a problem,' Fraser mused. 'Perhaps we'd better toss her out. I can't have the President thinking we're hand in glove with the Intelligence people – and it'll look that way if she's involved.'

'If you put me out on the street the KGB will kill me,' the girl murmured. 'I was to be flown back to Russia when Comrade Yukov returned from East Germany. I would be tried and executed.' She shrugged as though accepting the inevitable.

'She stays,' Stratton said.

Fraser studied him.

'For the moment – while she can be useful to us. After that we shall have to see.'

Stratton inclined his head in agreement. Fraser pointed to the door.

'Whoever is in there has sealed it from the inside.'

'Then you have no secrets left to broadcast,' the girl interrupted. 'His orders would be to destroy the microfilm bank and all classified files in the archives. There is a destruct mechanism.'

A deathly silence followed her words. Johnny Hubbard shook his tawny head vigorously.

'No. No bang! He's in there between here. . . .' He rapped on the steel door. 'And its brother along the way.'

'The second emergency door was closed?' the girl asked urgently.

'Yup!' Hubbard agreed. 'This one was dropping and the one behind it had already hit the floor. He couldn't have made it out of this one – well half of him might but the rest of him would be on the other side. Drop fast those buggers do!'

'There's no one for me to talk to then, Colonel. The man is dead. The space between the doors becomes filled with gas when the emergency shutters are dropped.'

'Christ!' Hubbard exclaimed. 'No wonder he looked like he'd shit himself.'

Fraser held her by the arm.

'But the archives would destruct automatically when the shutters came down?'

'No, that is not so. There could be a malfunction in the shutter mechanism causing them to drop by mistake – or when we do a security check. The archives will only self-destruct if you use explosive or cutting devices on the shutters. Heat or steady vibration will arm and trigger the destruction unit.'

The girl looked pointedly at the expertly placed explosive. Stratton pulled her face around.

'Can you open it? Is there an override switch in case of malfunction?'

She nodded.

'If you protect me. Yes, I will open both the doors and also direct you to the most sensitive material in the archives.'

'My dear, God knows we need your help, but we shall have enough trouble protecting ourselves in a few hours.'

Again she gave a resigned shrug of her shoulders.

'Then protect me now, I am to die anyway. In Moscow or in London. The KGB will kill me somewhere, sometime. I will stay.' It was her statement, her decision. Fraser had no choice.

'Open the door, young lady. You shall have our protection. For as long as we all live.'

There was a distinct bleep from the hand communicator in Fraser's pocket. He pulled it out.

'Doc here, sir. We're under fire. The flashes are coming from across the road. I'd say it was one of the Russian houses.'

'Police marksmen?'

'Roberts says no. Those guys are all sitting in a bus at the gate.'

'Heavy weapons?'

'Naw,' the Doc drawled. 'Couple of Kalashnikovs by the sound.'

'All right. Take them out. We have to show them we mean what we say.'

'All be over in a minute, Colonel,' the voice said gleefully.

Fraser turned to the girl.

'Your countrymen seem to be acting on their own initiative – I'm very sorry but we'll have to kill them.'

She stared dumbly at him, appalled by the certainty of his statements.

'They *have* to do *something* – there will be much trouble for the security people here over this.'

Fraser ignored her comment. 'I need that door open, young lady, as soon as possible; please see to it.'

Stratton took hold of her arm. 'I'll go with her.'

Fraser snapped a quick glance at both of them.

'Right. Do it then. I'll check the men around the building.'

'The release control is in Comrade Yukov's office,' she stated. 'His door has a heavy lock. I have no key.'

'That is no problem,' Fraser said, indicating Stratton's powerful automatic. 'Go now! I need every second of time.'

In his spy-nest opposite the gates, Les Roberts watched with interest the arrival of a BBC outside broadcast truck, followed only minutes later by a similar unit from the Independent Television network. He picked up his head-set and dropped the transmit switch on the radio, pressing the scrambler.

'Cub to Wolf-leader.'

'He's below, Les. What you need?'

It was Carter who had no regard for radio procedures.

'Tell him we're going to be on TV – they've just arrived. Both channels.'

'Yeah? Maybe they got a set here. Thanks, Les. You OK?'

'No problem. Out.'

'Cheers.'

From the roof of the KGB building Carter bleeped Fraser and passed on the message. The wind had dropped but the temperature had fallen with it and the four mercenaries on the top of the building were beginning to feel the effects of the cold. Apart from the dull glow of the street lights below the trees, and the flaring of Fraser's Torch, they were in darkness.

The houses along the avenue were cast into shadow as their occupants evacuated them. They stood against the night sky like empty castles. Like the KGB building, some of them even sported ramparts on their roofs.

Directly opposite the communications building, on another roof, the Security Forces' Anti-Terrorist squad were in the final phase of a very tricky operation, which had entailed man-handling heavy equipment silently and in almost total darkness from the rear of that building, at ground level, to the roof three storeys up. On the Park side of the communications building, identical equipment was being settled on to wet grass. Upon a whispered word of command to both units, two sets of switches were pulled.

The four battle-hardened mercenaries reacted as one man to a sound from their rear in the Park. A cough, followed by a full-throated mechanical growl. Walters, with amazing speed, rammed a Mecar rifle grenade into the muzzle of the Sterling and fired it a split second before they were blinded by the arc-lights. The truck-mounted generator threw sparks and flames over a wide area before it died with another flat cough. The crack of the grenade was lost in the blast of the four Sterlings on full automatic as the lights mounted on the roof opposite were extinguished in a shower of powdered glass. From the darkness of the Park someone was screaming.

Carter picked up a bull-horn.

'*You fucking bastards – you want to die?*'

Fraser burst through the roof exit.

'That's enough of that. What happened?'

'Those stupid bastards been creeping up on us – tried to blind us with searchlights!' Carter yelled.

'I doubt if it was an attack,' Fraser said calmly. 'They'd put lights on us to wear us down.'

'Stupid bastards,' Carter repeated.

'Anyone hurt?'

Carter pointed out towards the Park. 'Someone's copped it from the grenade, but we got the generator.'

Fraser stared out over the rooftops.

'At least it'll teach them that we know what we're doing,' he said.

Carter grinned.

'They're babies out there, Colonel. Still in their prams.'

'For the moment, yes. But if they decide to come at us you'll be surprised at what they'll throw in.'

The three self-styled Guns of August stood chuckling shoulder to shoulder with Jock Mclennan leaping up and down with the excitement of battle. 'Whoo-hee, whoo-hee,' he bawled at the top of his voice.

Across the way, a police special task force sergeant could just make out Mclennan's bouncing up and down to the accompaniment of his yelling.

'They're bloody nutters,' he breathed. 'Basket-cases, the lot of 'em!'

He didn't see Fraser's fiery eyes and flaring nostrils as he sniffed the cordite in the air, or there might have been more fear than contempt in the statement.

One hour of Fraser's two-hour deadline had passed and the Prime Minister of Great Britain had achieved nothing. To compound his failure, he had suffered the indignity of being fobbed off on to a minor government official who contemptuously informed him that no senior member of the governing council was available to speak to him. The Prime Minister had to hold his rage in check, almost having to beg the man to have the President call.

'If our President is available he will contact you,' was the last sentence he got out of the man.

The Prime Minister had decided to use the Cabinet room as an operational headquarters, for he had to be available at 10 Downing Street where the hot line to Moscow was situated.

Hammond and the still sick-looking Johnson had been installed in the small office adjacent to the Cabinet room, once a small private waiting-room for important guests of the Prime Minister.

The information Hammond had been getting from the uniformed police in London and the Home Counties all came down to one thing. The identified mercenaries had dropped out of sight on exactly the same day. All of them lived in lodging houses or had rooms in small hotels and, in each of the five cases, these rooms were like some suburban *Marie Celeste*. What personal belongings there were, and these were very few, were set out as if their owners would return at any minute. Hammond gave orders that every address was to be watched around the clock, although by now he was convinced that the five, with an unknown number of others, were inside the Russian communications building at Kensington Palace Gardens.

Inside the Cabinet room, the Prime Minister presided over an emergency meeting with the head of DI5, the internal security agency, and Commander Vere of the Special Branch. The Home Secretary joined the meeting, walking in at the same time as a distinguished looking grey-haired man who was unmistakably Jewish. Commander Vere introduced the man as Dr Marius Hoffman, an eminent psychologist who had assisted the Branch and the special anti-terrorist task force on many occasions.

Hoffman, tall and a little stooped, seemed totally unimpressed by the room or its high-powered occupants. His only interest was the situation under discussion and the mind of the man who had engineered it. He had little to work on. The file which he had read in the police car, driving at breakneck speed to Downing Street, had only supplied basic facts. Fraser's education, which had been the best available; army record – which was exemplary – and a medical report which described how a brilliant and distinguished career had been destroyed. On the available evidence, Colonel Jonathan Fraser was a fine man who had been cut down during his prime by injury. That in itself was not enough to explain his present actions. Hoffman needed more facts. What had Fraser been doing with himself for the last eight years or so? As far as anyone knew, he had been living on an army pension with a disablement allowance, plus a reasonable but not very substantial private income. How then was he financing mercenary soldiers? Why the overwhelming desire to obtain the release, by the most extraordinarily dangerous means, of the mercenary prisoners? Were any of them connected with him? Relatives? Friends?

'Where, Prime Minister,' he asked quietly, looking over lowered half-moon spectacles, 'are the answers to these questions?'

The head of DI5 coughed and looked up.

'Well, Colonel Fraser is something of a dark horse.'

'A dark horse!' Hoffman repeated, testing the phrase as if it were the first time he had heard it. 'It would seem so.' He raised his stooped shoulders. 'Perhaps someone would enlighten me . . . take the cover off the animal so to speak.' He smiled wanly.

'The difficulty is, Prime Minister,' said the security chief, 'I should prefer to have the Foreign Secretary present or the head of the FO.'

'If you've got something to say, say it. Don't pussyfoot with me.'

'Well – in the circumstances . . .'

'Spit it out, man!' the PM barked.

The head of 'Five' sighed.

'He has to be "The Colonel" they've been using for years to set up clandestine military operations overseas. We've been aware of him of course in a minor way – purchase of arms, movement of men, logistical things. None of this really concerns us because it's FO business. Everything he was involved in was overseas, nothing internal, not our pigeon.'

'Overseas where?'

'*You* know the form, Prime Minister.'

'Ah,' the psychologist exclaimed softly.

'Africa?' the Prime Minister asked the leading question.

The security chief nodded his bald head.

'And it was a disaster!' Hoffman said.

'It was meant to be, Doctor,' the Prime Minister stated. 'A question of policy more than anything. It's a case of the lesser evil – a Marxist regime or a government supported by the South Africans. It was decided that Marxism was more acceptable than apartheid.'

'I am not here to be convinced of the need for political expediencies,' Hoffman said. 'My purpose is to get into the mind of the man. Discover his motives, break them down and, eventually, reason with him – ' He placed his glasses on the green baize. ' – Or destroy him!'

The door from the private office opened after a discreet knock and Hammond leaned into the room.

'Prime Minister, I think this is important – it's for Dr Hoffman.'

As Hoffman took the outstretched paper the telephone rang.

'Yes,' barked the PM.

'Jonathan Fraser here, Prime Minister.'

The PM placed the receiver on the amplification unit. Hoffman casually read through the foolscap page of neat writing.

'Prime Minister. Your security people made an attempt either to attack or possibly only to spotlight this building – it was unsuccessful. I have to tell you now, regretfully, that your period of grace is curtailed. I shall be transmitting my message to Moscow without delay. I am sorry if any of your forces were hurt or killed in the incident. I should not try again if I were you – my men are expert at dealing with such attempts.'

'Colonel Fraser, I . . .'

As the Prime Minister began to speak, Hoffman pushed a clearly written note before him. The PM lowered his eyes. It read: 'DON'T ATTEMPT TO ARGUE OR NEGOTIATE. THE MAN HAS A CRITICAL BRAIN INJURY. HE IS CONVINCED HE WILL SOON BE DEAD – OR INSANE!'

'Oh my God,' thought the Premier. 'That's why he's so cool. He doesn't care.'

'Colonel Fraser,' he repeated. 'I give you my word that I had no idea that such an action had been taken.'

'Then as the commander of your forces, Prime Minister, you have a dangerous lack of information. Might I suggest you tighten up your chain of command before more deaths occur.'

The PM reddened. The gall of the man! He fumed inwardly, then recognizing that what Fraser said had been a fact and not an intended insult, controlled his temper.

'I will ensure that no more assaults of any kind are attempted.'

Another note was passed across the table. 'DON'T FEED HIM WITH POWER.'

The Premier glanced quickly at the psychologist, who made a fist and brought it down gently on to the table twice.

'But I have not lost sight of the fact,' he continued smoothly, 'that you and your men have perpetrated a violent act of terrorism which may require extreme measures on the part of this government.'

Fraser chuckled.

'You're testing me, Prime Minister. I congratulate you on your swiftness in getting your advisers together so promptly. Which analyst have you called in? Erwing – Lasky or Hoffman? I'd wager Hoffman! He's usually the one directing the anti-terrorist squad.'

The silence confirmed Fraser's words. The Premier stared helplessly at the doctor, who leaned forward resting his elbow on the green baize.

'Good evening, Colonel Fraser. You do still use the title, don't you? You'd win your bet. I am Dr Hoffman.'

'Dr Hoffman, it's a pleasure to talk with you. Yes, I still retain the rank – a little touch of vanity.'

'Well, Colonel, a title does set one apart from the mob, doesn't it? I've no doubt that when I retire I'll still call myself doctor.'

'Oh, I can live without it, Doctor, I don't need a title to set me apart from other men.'

Hoffman smiled.

'I am sure that you don't. However, for the sake of convenience I shall continue to address you as Colonel.'

'As you wish, Dr Hoffman.'

The doctor loosened his tie and undid his collar-button.

'Colonel, this is a very damaging situation – for the country. I wonder if we might have a reasonable discussion and perhaps come to some compromise. I am sure that your men – however expert they may be as soldiers – have no particular wish to die in a pitched battle – which unfortunately is quite often how these affairs end up.'

'Reasonable discussions in this particular case, Dr Hoffman, might just be for the purpose of gaining time – so therefore I regret that I cannot oblige you. As for my men, they all have their own reasons for being here with me. If they weren't prepared to die they wouldn't be here.'

'Flawless logic, Colonel. Mind you, men can often delude themselves that they are prepared – even willing – to die, but when it comes to it there are often so many things to live for.'

'I think, Dr Hoffman,' Fraser said coldly, 'that I am the best judge of my men. They have been well conditioned for this operation.'

Hoffman raised both eyebrows sharply.

'Conditioned, Colonel? What a peculiar choice of word.'

'I meant militarily.'

'Oh I see. But I understood them to be – experts – wasn't that the word you used to describe them?'

'They are experts at their job but they are also ready to give their lives for me. They are, I repeat, ready to see this through to the bitter end. Goodbye, Dr Hoffman, I hope your probing has given you the answer you are searching for, but I should warn you not to be too pleased with yourself – we know how to counteract your techniques.' The phone was put down at the other end of the line.

Hoffman eased himself back in the chair and placed one finger over his top lip.

'In my estimation he will carry out his threat and broadcast the secrets but he's hesitating at the moment. Possibly he's enjoying the feeling of total power, but it goes deeper than that. Once he begins to broadcast he will start to come down – like a drug addict after a shot of heroin – and that's what he wants to avoid. His mind could not take that sort of anti-climax, at the present time. There would be a reaction – probably irrational.'

Hoffman adjusted his glasses and read the detailed message from the Harley Street specialist.

'If necessary Fraser will bring everything crashing down around him,' he continued. 'You will note that at no time has he made any effort to conceal his identity, yet his men, so I have been told, have their faces covered. This man has made a thorough study of our techniques and knows that the prime object is manipulation of the mind and the emotions. By keeping the identity of his force secret he removes our prime card. We cannot attack the individual elements on a personal level here and here . . .' he tapped his head and his heart. 'But simply as a group – a mass if you like – controlled by his mind and will.' The psychologist frowned deeply. 'I should add that we are dealing with a very intelligent and forceful man. There is no way that we can treat this as a routine terrorist attack. As my American colleagues would say – it's a whole new ball game!'

Commander Vere leaned forward.

'He seems to know a great deal about how these things are handled by the authorities – my God, man, he even knew your name!'

Hoffman splayed his hands outwards.

'Commander, this is a democracy, if one really wants to know something and one is prepared to make the effort, there is not much that is truly hidden. Fraser is obviously a man with good connections – for him it would be relatively easy. The thing that perturbs me most is his confidence in the ability of his men to resist our techniques. He said "conditioned", not warned or taught. That presupposes that he has had them in seclusion for long enough to do a little manipulation of his own. He has the knowledge. The Special Air Service are not unaware of these methods.' He smiled a little grimly.

Vere checked a report before him.

'If our information is accurate, then the men we've identified have probably been with him for over a week.'

Hoffman laughed.

'Well, that's more than enough time. I've conditioned agents for the SIS in a day. I mean – ' he held a finger up ' – for one specific operation. The planting of false information in a man's mind so that he truly believes it is one example. If our friend had had a week or more then, with the right equipment, he could in theory burrow deep down in their subconscious minds.' Hoffman looked straight into the eyes of the Prime Minister. 'If this is the case, Prime Minister, then what you have in that building is the British equivalent of Kamikaze pilots.' He pondered for a moment. 'Fraser himself is a symbol – probably strong enough to keep them going subconsciously, even when their conscious minds and their bodies are so exhausted that they don't know what they are doing any more – or why they are doing it. But we know he may die. The specialist insisted that this could happen at any minute. A sudden movement of the steel imbedded in his brain and massive cerebral haemorrhage culminating in death is the result. Therefore, assuming the brilliance of his intelligence, he would manufacture some symbol to keep them going *even* if he died.'

'Would you explain that statement, Dr Hoffman?' the Prime Minister said. 'I'm a complete layman when it comes to your particular field – and frankly the little I do know about it makes me want to remain that way.'

Hoffman smiled.

'Oh there's nothing supernatural or sinister about the workings of the mind, Prime Minister. Mysterious, yes, and very challenging – but to answer your question I will give you an example. The Christian religion has the symbol of the cross. The name of Christ is invoked by this and kept alive. A more contemporary example, at the other end of the moral scale, is the swastika in Nazi Germany. No! Let's be more precise, remembering our particular problem – the swastika and Adolf Hitler.'

Vere shook his head.

'Their uniforms are unmarked. No badges, no symbols. Standard camouflage and those black scarves. There's not much light up there but with the glow from that bloody great flare they've got and with night-glasses we can make out the men on the roof reasonably clearly. Thought at first they were going to set the ruddy place alight.'

'What do you refer to, Commander?' Hoffman said.

'We thought they were going to burn the Embassy down. Fraser came out, cool as you please and got this fire burning over the door. Then I'll be blowed if they didn't haul the thing on to the roof.'

'I'm sorry,' Hoffman said, 'I'm still not clear. They actually set the door alight and then began on the roof?'

Vere shook his head.

'No, no. You misunderstand me. We *thought* they were setting the place alight but what looked like a petrol or oil drum at that distance was in fact one of those big all-weather flares – you know the type – doesn't blow out in wind or rain.'

The psychologist leaned slowly back in his chair.

'Brilliant,' he sighed. 'The eternal flame . . . the classic symbol of a cause . . . or of remembrance.'

'Well, let's put the damn thing out if it means that much to them!' Vere said, thumping the table with his fist.

Hoffman laughed but without humour.

'Commander, if you feel you'd like to commit suicide, I

suggest you try to extinguish that flame. But please don't send your men to certain death, it would be grossly unfair.'

'Now look here!' Vere snapped.

'Gentlemen!' the Prime Minister cut in. 'We have enough problems already.'

'I'm sorry,' Hoffman apologized. 'The commander couldn't begin to realize what that flame means to those men up there. If I'm right, they would kill without a second's hesitation if you showed any sign of trying to get near it – exactly the same as if you tried to kill Colonel Fraser. One is the same as the other. You cannot separate the flame from the man.'

'Then what are my options, Dr Hoffman?' the Premier asked. 'Up to now I've only had to deal with the Russian consul, but the Ambassador is flying back from East Germany on a special flight tonight – he may even have landed already! We have to do something – or at least make a show of action!'

'What has been done so far?'

The Premier shrugged. 'Both ends of the avenue are sealed as tight as a clam. The Park is just about trampled flat by the police. That's on the credit side! To upset all that and make the whole picture very untidy, we're getting no co-operation from the resident Russians. Quite the opposite in fact! They don't believe for one minute that those men in there are not ours. The last report we had was that shooting had begun from one of the Russian residences across the avenue and that Fraser's little army shut them up with no more than a few rounds. Now what the hell can I do to convince the Soviet President that I'm telling the truth?'

Hoffman studied the face of the man carefully before speaking.

'Prime Minister. May I ask you a very loaded question in front of these distinguished gentlemen?'

The Premier nodded warily, alerted by Hoffman's tone.

'You may, Doctor.'

'Then I must put this to you. Do you want to stop Fraser at all?'

Every eye turned and fixed squarely on the face of the Prime Minister. The silence was tangible. At last the Prime Minister answered.

'Dr Hoffman. I intend to stop Fraser broadcasting those

secrets if it costs lives to do it. If I fail, this government and I are politically dead.'

There was a discreet knock on the main door of the Cabinet room.

'The Soviet Ambassador has just arrived at Heathrow, sir,' the private secretary said. 'And the immigration people have informed us that he has brought in twenty-five men, all carrying diplomatic passports but none of them registered at the London Embassy. According to our people they don't look very much like diplomats.' He stood waiting.

'Can we hold them for an hour or so?'

'In normal circumstances we could,' the head of DI5 answered. 'But under the present conditions I dread to think what the repercussions might be.'

'Right. Tell the immigration people to let them through – but I want to know where they go. Arrange to have them followed with the utmost discretion.'

'I'll speak to the airport,' the head of DI5 said, and followed the private secretary out.

The telephone rang and a clipped voice spoke.

'Signals Intelligence, Brigadier Lyons-Weston here, Prime Minister. I have to report a top priority signal transmitted to the Kremlin from their London residency. It's uncoded, sir! I think you'd better hear the text of the message.'

'Is it signed Colonel Jonathan Fraser?'

'Yes, sir, that's correct.'

'In that case, Brigadier, I'm afraid I already know what the signal contained.'

'I see, sir. Any instructions?'

'Yes, Brigadier. I shall want to know of any further signals to the Soviet Union from that source. Anything, you understand?'

'Yes, sir.'

'And one final thing. I don't know when, but possibly quite soon, I may order you to shut down your establishment for an unspecified period. That will be obeyed to the letter!'

'Prime Minister!' the officer protested. 'Our monitoring systems? The early-warning information? We'll be totally reliant on radar.'

'Brigadier,' the Prime Minister cut in. 'I am not suggesting you cut down our defence capabilities. Your job as a listening post to coded signals from the Soviet bloc will remain unimpeded. But you will ensure that no signal between the Soviet Embassy in London and the USSR is either monitored or recorded by Signals Intelligence. Do I make myself perfectly clear?'

'Perfectly, sir.'

'Good. Let us hope it doesn't come to that.'

3

The Ka-25 'Hormone' Helicopter put down hard on the flat cobbles of the Red Square in Moscow. The big Zil 144 limousine was ready, engine running, to receive the person of the President of the Union of Soviet Socialist Republics.

The President hurried from the helicopter into the long car. The windows were curtained and the dark glass bullet-proofed. The deep upholstery and the fur-carpeted floor began to dispel the fatigue of the cramped, noisy flight in the helicopter. He closed his eyes briefly, readying himself for the ordeal.

The Zil arrived at the Lubianka, the central complex of KGB buildings backing on to Kirov Street, in less than two minutes. It was late and the streets were deserted. Security agents had already leapt from the preceding Mercedes to help the President to alight. He looked up and saw the light burning in the Chairman's office at the centre of the building. It was not the only one. Very few members of the state security organization were going to get any sleep at all that night.

He was rushed upstairs with heavy security, even inside the building. The Chairman greeted him briskly, indicating the standing officials in the conference room. At the emergency meeting were the First Deputy Chairman of the KGB, the Deputy Chairman, the Head of the First Directorate responsible for Foreign Operations, the Head of the Eighth Directorate, responsible for Communication Intelligence, and the Department Head for Registry and Archives. As the President sat down it was announced that all decisions could be made from that room and that whatever action was deemed necessary under the critical circumstances could be taken.

The Chairman of the KGB began straight away with a full report, slapping the flat of his hand on the table for emphasis. A green signal form lay on the polished wood, the name Jonathan Fraser standing out strangely at the end of the Russian translation.

The President sat heavily in his chair listening, head down, to every word, now and then nodding or making a movement with his mouth as certain statements were made. Finally the Chairman had finished.

'First,' the President said, heaving himself upright in the chair, 'the Africans. They will not release the men. Second, we would not bow to pressure even if they agreed. Third, I do not know if I believe this English colonel.' He reached for the signal. ' "Neither I nor my men have any political affiliations whatsoever!" ' he quoted in Russian. He tipped his palm one way and then the other. 'Political? Maybe not. What about national? He has trained soldiers – they have shot two of our comrades in darkness and in good cover. He has fine weapons, obviously fitted with night telescopes. He has expert radio officers who are able to use our equipment without much trouble, and he breaks through the British security with little problem. Cleverly yes! But it could not happen here. So, I think we should speak with the British Prime Minister, comrades, and see if we can talk some truths!' He turned to the KGB Chairman. 'Your men are ready in London?'

'Yes, comrade.'

'First I talk. After that, we shall see.' He lifted the red telephone. 'London,' he said.

In the basement of the besieged communications building, Colonel Fraser stood facing the banks of sophisticated electronic equipment; the transmitters, the cryptograph coders and decoders, the cipher machines and the recorders for the transmission of high-speed 'squirt' signals. The security doors had been raised and the gassed guard removed. As the girl had stated, the archives were intact. Stewart-Smith stood beside Fraser and the girl, with Sammy Cohen seated at the equipment. They were waiting for a signal from Moscow.

Stewart-Smith turned to the girl. 'Miss . . .?'

'Lashkova – Katrina. You have Catherine, it is the same.'

'Miss Lashkova, you say that the President will ignore our message.'

'I know it. He will never negotiate. How is it possible for the President of the Soviet Union to talk with the people who have taken over Soviet property? He will see it only as an insult to himself and the state.'

Stewart-Smith turned to Fraser.

'If he won't even talk to us, I think our position is extremely precarious.'

'He has to talk unless he wants the contents of these archives broadcast.'

'Never!' Katrina said. 'He will destroy this building before he allows this thing to happen.'

'How will he destroy it, Miss Lashkova?' Fraser asked.

The girl smiled.

'How? I cannot tell you this – but I know he will. Your police out there! He will push them aside like children. You are dealing with the might of Russia. *Russia!* You English! You still live in the time when you controlled the natives by social position. You drank your gins and tonics and kept your noses high and everyone walked softly for you. Where is it now? You are a nation making a smaller shadow with each sun. You are impotent and you will be destroyed.'

'Whatever they throw at us, no matter the cost, we are here to stay,' he said quietly. 'We came here prepared to die – well, so be it.'

As the clock chimed eleven in the Cabinet room, the last of the stream of Ministers departed, each one in possession of all the facts, but none of them bearing even a fraction of the load that the Prime Minister carried on his shoulders. In the end he was still left with his hopes resting on the psychologist who sat at the long table sipping interminable cups of unsweetened lemon tea.

The conversation with the Soviet President had been brief, to the point and laced with innuendo.

Yes, the British security forces were doing everything possible to ensure that the terrorists were stopped before they damaged for all time the relationship between Britain and the Soviet

Union. No, neither the British government nor the Secret Service had anything whatsoever to do with the takeover. Yes, the arms used by the terrorists were obtained illegally. No, the British government did not know how the arms were obtained. No, there was not the smallest possibility that the United States were involved in the attack. The American President had given his assurance on this. No, the British security forces could not attack the building whilst hostages were still inside. Yes, it was understood that Soviet citizens were prepared to give their lives for the good of the state but whilst the Embassy stood on British soil they were under the protection of the government . . .

Questions were parried with consummate skill by the Prime Minister, resulting inevitably in stalemate. Two of the most powerful men in the world were left, in diplomatic terms, completely impotent.

As the telephones went down, the Prime Minister was fearfully aware that, as ever, when the talking stops, violence would have its day. And at midnight, as Monday passed its chilly dark hours over to Tuesday, the gloves came off.

In a street in Highgate, a group of sombre men, grey with fatigue in the early morning, boarded a coach. The night rain fell in fine drizzle like a seeping net. The coach took a while to start. The East Germans checked the weapons concealed under their seats. The engine roared into life. They drove away and a dark car tagged on behind.

On the Bayswater Road, the police and anti-terrorist squad waited patiently for instructions which never came. The barriers were firmly across the wide road and the red lights flashed their ceaseless warning. By the gates of the Embassy, the gatekeeper's wife was passing around more cups of tea to the weary teams of marksmen and the ordinary bobbies. It seemed a night without end.

Roberts, concealed in his spy-hole, dozed like a soldier in the lull between battles but part of his mind remained alert and ready to act.

The coach made its way through the streets of London heading inexorably for the site of the siege. The watchers in the car radioed their headquarters to prepare for trouble.

At the barriers and the gates the police were informed of the approach of the coach, and tightened ranks, but no order was given for positive resistance. Police vehicles were driven up to block the road and the men at the gates stood stolidly, as British policemen do, barring entry to the avenue, but these were all futile gestures.

Behind the closed gates, and further along the rain-drenched avenue, in the communications building, the hostages had been bedded down for the night on the chairs, sofas and floor of the recreation room. Whilst Cornwell slept, James Dewey stood watch over them.

In the basement, Sammy Cohen slept fitfully, his head resting on his arms; the headphones still clamped over his ears. On a bench seat against the wall, Paul Stratton closed his eyes for a moment just to rest them, but he was far away from sleep. Beside him, her gold hair draped over his shoulder, Katrina Lashkova pressed her face against the coarse material of Stratton's combat jacket. Beneath her cheek she felt him stiffen, the muscles hardening.

'How do you come to be here?' she asked.

Stratton opened his eyes but said nothing.

'God help me, I am frightened.' Her voice was so quiet that the words were barely audible. 'None of you feels fear.' She lifted her head to look at him. 'You are dead. *You. You* more than all of them. Where did you die? *Why* did you die?'

Silence.

She lowered her eyes as though confessing. 'Women fear men like you but, in their stupidity, they desire you more than the safest or the kindest among all the rest. Who do you kill when you kill? Yourself? Is it yourself you are killing? And this madness to make love when you have killed?' She placed a hand on his rigid arm. 'Yes! I have seen it – felt it – you raped me with your kiss. Are you so lost that even the softest submission is rejected because it might be the way back from wherever you hide yourself?'

Turning, he held her face with one hand and kissed her full on the mouth. Then he released her. 'Don't begin a journey you have no hope of completing. You, nor I. None of us.'

Leaning back against the wall, he folded his arms, then crossed his long legs, one high boot over the other, the laces rasping. His eyes remained open, fixed dead ahead, unblinking.

She settled against him again, her eyes shut, but sleep did not come. Her own people had prejudged her as a traitor. She was, as far as they were concerned, already dead. The only reason she had been kept alive was that they did not know the extent of her treachery. She had not been tortured – and that in itself was proof that, as a living person, she no longer existed for them. She was simply a source of information which would be cut off – when a careful analysis had been made of any damage she had caused.

And I, she thought, with that sense of complete resignation which is the mind's anaesthetic for total fear, am clinging to a killer for the preservation of my life.

Stratton shifted position and the fingers of his hand touched the soft strands of her hair which fell across his folded arms. He did not move them.

Murray, Lippmann and Mclennan split the ground floor between themselves, patrolling at a regular interval, moving from front to rear of the house. Dewey, locked in with the hostages, could hear their quiet progress, like jungle animals padding the rim of a camp. On a chair in the hallway, Stewart-Smith seemed asleep, but his mind was in turmoil for he had seen some of the files in the archives and the information they contained deeply disturbed him.

Up on the roof Jonathan Fraser stayed with the remainder of his men. Fowler, Hubbard and Carter stood watch as Walters and Peterson slept under waterproof capes against the brickwork of the balustrade. The building was in darkness and with both ends of the avenue cut off to traffic by the police diversions, an unaccustomed stillness fell over that area of London.

The diesel clatter of the coach was quite audible to the men at the gates as it slowed at the first diversion, then quite deliberately gathered speed, brushing the barrier aside, sending it clattering along the tarmac, and thumped heavily into the rear ends of the two police Cortinas which were parked across the Bayswater Road.

The significance of the noise was quite clear to the police at the gate. They had no doubt whatsoever that the bus had crashed the road block, but there were still no orders as to the degree of resistance they could offer.

An inspector waved forward the blue bus which had carried the marksmen to the site, attempting to get it across the gates, but it was too late. The coach, filled with the KGB assault unit, swept into the entrance, forcing the iron gates back on their hinges and sending the drop barrier spinning down the avenue.

Roberts, in the observation post across from the gates, was already awake and had the microphone in his hand before the coach hit the gates. He used the night-glasses on the window of the coach and saw quite plainly the stubby Czech-made machine pistols and a vague shape resembling a long tube being lifted from the aisle.

He pressed the transmit button and shouted down the microphone. 'Wolf-leader – you're under attack! Rocket launcher – hit the coach – hit it! Hit it!'

Roberts noted two things in the same frozen second; the mangled bodies of three policemen on the ground and that he'd omitted to press his scramble button, but his attention was moving to other things. The police marksmen broke ranks and ran through the shattered gates, their scoped rifles cradled low on their chests, and rolled into cover.

The roof of the KGB building was a scene of disciplined urgency as every man took up a predetermined position for this very form of attack. Two of the Mecar rifle-launched grenades were loosed off like small mortar bombs, dropping almost too perfectly on the road before the oncoming coach and exploding upwards, killing the driver instantly and destroying the steering-linkage. Two more on a higher trajectory exploded eight feet from the ground to the left of the coach causing horrific injury to the occupants. The vehicle careered out of control and crunched into a low wall, mounting it before coming to rest. The searing white light of a flare crucified the men as they flung themselves from the coach, caught in a vicious cross-fire between Fraser's men and the incensed police marksmen. There seemed to be no escape from the glare and the hail of bullets which poured from the rooftop into the East Germans, and it was only a matter of moments and two more Mecar grenades before the force of twenty-five attackers was completely wiped out.

The Soviet President had used the men of a satellite state to test Fraser's strength. Now the battle would move nearer home.

At first light, the media were at the site of the siege in force. Cameramen using telescopic lenses like black gun-barrels homed in on the dreadful carnage in and around the coach. Fraser had refused to allow the police or ambulances any access to the avenue, but had instead sent out James Dewey, wearing a red-cross arm-band, to check for survivors. There had been none.

At eight-thirty he announced with his bull-horn that one ambulance at a time could enter the avenue to clear away the bodies of the dead men. The ambulance drivers were to reverse their vehicles towards the grenade-blasted coach with both rear doors open. His orders were carried out to the letter. Nobody now doubted the complete efficiency and ruthlessness of his force.

Inside the communications building, the hostages were fed with supplies taken from the night-shift clerks' store-room; it was basic fare, but sufficient to fill their stomachs. Fraser's men ate their iron rations and drank tea whilst standing guard on their designated positions.

After studying with his binoculars the avenue, the Park behind, the green between the building and Kensington Palace and the buildings opposite, Fraser left the rooftop. The men noticed that the tight skin of his face seemed to have softened and to glow with colour.

Colin Hammond lowered his own glasses as Fraser moved away from the rooftop balustrade and out of sight. It was his first sight of the fanatic whose name was now blazing across the world in banner headlines. Grimly he turned away from the gates aware, perhaps for the first time, that this particular siege was not going to fizzle out and die. 'Christ!' he thought, 'there's been a pitched battle with automatic weapons and grenades. Twenty-five dead, plus three coppers and it's happening here, on the streets of London!' He shook his head, trying to comprehend the mind of a man who could quite coldly wipe out twenty-five men with deadly precision and – more than that – have had a contingency plan for such an attack.

What nagged at the back of his mind was that the view from the captured building to the gates was obscured by trees, yet by all accounts, and from the evidence of the broken road surface, the first grenade had hit the coach before it could have come into the mercenaries' line of sight. Therefore they had been prepared, even at that hour of the morning, to repel an armed attack that had barely started; or perhaps Fraser was ready to hit anything that moved. But that was doubtful. The man had been far too precise in everything he had done.

All the eye-witness accounts were basically the same. The coach hit the line of the police, crashed the gates and the barrier, travelled about sixty yards and drove straight into the first grenade. What perturbed Hammond was not that they could lob grenades with incredible accuracy, but that they had *only* gone for the coach. What made them think that there was no other vehicle as a back-up? They were quite ready to fire grenades at random at a target they could hear but not see, but that did not mean that there were no others coming up behind. Yet to all intents and purposes, they totally ignored the possibility and concentrated solely on obliterating the coach and its occupants.

The answer to his question screamed at him as he entered the waiting police car, but Colin Hammond's face remained inscrutable as he gave the driver orders to return to number 10 Downing Street. He leant back against the cushions, forcing himself not to look up at Wellington Terrace and a strange excitement welled up in him as he remembered Frasers' erect figure on the rooftop. Mentally, he picked up the challenge that had been thrown down.

The emergency meeting in the Cabinet room at 10 Downing Street on Tuesday morning was a terrorist bomber's dream. There was enough power congregated in that one space to take a nation to war – or ease it back from the brink. But as Hammond entered, he thought he was walking in on a bar-room brawl.

Men were on their feet, Ministers and heads of services, hurling abuse at each other and no one noticed him for a full minute. Finally, he caught Vere's eye and the commander made a sign to the Prime Minister.

The rulers of the Establishment dropped back into their chairs.

'Yes, Chief Superintendent. You have something to report?'

The Prime Minister's voice was rough and edged with tension. Now every eye was on Hammond but still he felt the strange elation and even this gathering of power couldn't frighten him. When he answered his voice was smooth with no trace of nervousness and Hoffman, the psychologist, studied him keenly as he spoke.

'I think, sir, that we can take one, possibly two, of Colonel Fraser's men – alive.'

The Prime Minister smiled.

'And how do you propose we should do that, Chief Superintendent? They killed a total of twenty-eight men last night! What inducement have we to offer to make them even think of giving up?'

Hammond shook his head, his thinning hair falling forward.

'They have at least one man set up in a concealed position opposite the Embassy gates on the Bayswater Road – probably in one of the flats along Wellington Terrace.'

'You're certain of that?'

'No, sir, not certain. But it would explain how Fraser's men could react so quickly and efficiently to last night's attack. Also Fraser's a soldier, not a terrorist, so he would think along those lines – an observation post passing on intelligence and covering his flank.'

'Why not the other end as well then – the Kensington side?' The question came from a Minister Hammond couldn't place.

'Because, sir, they have a completely clear view from the Russian building to the Kensington gates – any movement at that end is visible to them – not so the Bayswater Road.'

'So what does it do for us if we manage to take one of these people alive?' the Premier asked Hammond.

'We have part of Fraser, sir!'

The Prime Minister frowned and Hoffman again gazed at Hammond with his shrewd eyes.

'I think the Chief Superintendent knows more about psychology than he has admitted,' he said. 'He's beginning to get the feel of the man. You see, Prime Minister, Jonathan Fraser is now committed – and every one of those men are part of him. If he loses one he'll bleed and if we can turn one or more against him, the hold he has over them might be broken.'

'Rubbish!' The retort came from the Minister of Defence.

'The man's a fanatical killer. Last night proved that. We're wasting time, Prime Minister, if I may say so. The press is already portraying him as some sort of legendary figure. All right, let's get his outside man alive or dead – at least that'll stop his flow of information – but we've also got to make up our minds to attack that building in force and the sooner the better!'

The Prime Minister sighed and smiled apologetically at Hoffman.

'We must not lose sight of the fact that there are some twenty Russian hostages in that building. I will not endanger those innocent lives until there is no other way open to us. The killing has already begun and the responsibility for that lies at the Kremlin's door. This government is not going to squander lives needlessly. We have yet to hear from Colonel Fraser this morning but I am sure he will use pressure as his main weapon and fire-power only under provocation. Up to now that has been the pattern.' The Premier turned again to Hoffman. 'What damage will be done if there is a look-out in Wellington Terrace and we have the luck to pull him in alive?'

'It'll hurt Fraser badly, but he'll still carry on. He has no choice. As I said before, the man is committed.'

'All right, Chief Superintendent,' the Prime Minister confirmed, 'do what you have to do.'

By early afternoon the clouds had cleared and a pale sun filtered through the damp atmosphere. Already the crowds were swarming to the scene, ignoring police loud-hailers requesting them to keep away. Residents of the immediate area stood in deep rows behind barriers set across the roads adjacent to Kensington Palace Gardens, gazing in amazement at the changing situation.

The most startling change was the arrival of two Saracen armoured cars parked directly in front of the entrance to the avenue, and the heavy presence of soldiers in full combat uniform, including flak-jackets, with heavy FN automatic rifles resting on their hips, barrels upwards. Every gate to Hyde Park and Kensington Gardens was sealed and guarded with troops backed up by armoured vehicles. Yet still the sightseers thronged towards the scene, cutting through Paddington, Kensington and Notting Hill Gate. It hardly seemed to matter to them that they could not actually see the building, the excitement of being near was enough.

By the time Colin Hammond's police driver had arrived at the Embassy gates, things were beginning to get out of hand. The police were in dispute with the television outside broadcast crews who, they felt, were whipping up crowd-emotions by their interviews seeking opinions on Fraser's act. Banners already proclaimed support for him or branded him a Fascist killer and scuffles broke out as their bearers clashed.

Hammond looked at Wellington Terrace from the interior of the Rover, noting figures leaning out of the windows of the flats above the shops. The offices, shops, Ruskies Wine Bar and The Champion had all been closed by the security forces – only the apartments were occupied. To Hammond the dark grubby window in the centre of the block with no gawking face at it was proof enough.

'They're here, sir,' the police driver said and Hammond turned around to see a grey Ford Granada, with four men inside, pull into Ossington Street.

'Right, wait here,' Hammond replied. He made his way over the Bayswater Road towards the small mews and got into the back of the Granada.

'Everyone armed?' he asked. The senior member of the four-man Special Task Force squad nodded. 'What about gas?' Hammond continued.

'We have it, sir.'

'Right, Sergeant. Alive if possible! He's no good to us on a mortuary slab. Now I don't have to repeat this to you. If I am right, there is a man, or men, in there. He or they will be very good – probably better than any of you. When you go in it has to be after the gas canisters – nobody is asking you to throw your lives away. Right?'

The sergeant nodded again.

'Let's go,' he ordered.

The team of four specially trained policemen walked unhurriedly from the car and made their way to the rear of Wellington Terrace. They wore raincoats over dark sweaters, denims and lace-up boots with thick, soft composition soles. Blue, padded flak vests protected their bodies from their chests to their genitals. Two soldiers patrolled the side road and the squad flashed their IDs at them, before turning down the same small lane that Les Roberts had taken himself. Further along, a plain-clothes officer stood against the brown brickwork. He pointed upwards.

'Green doorway. Twenty-three A.'

The four mounted the old-fashioned iron fire-steps. At the top they removed the raincoats, hung them over the railings and put on gas-masks. Outside the door of 23A they waited, two to either side. The sergeant looked at one of the team and pointed to the lock. The man dropped to his haunches and slipped a sliver of metal into the key-hole. The door swung open four inches, then scraped to a stop.

'Safety chain,' he breathed, and reached for the cutter in his back pocket. A thunderous roar blasted away the top half of the door as fifteen rounds of automatic fire was loosed off from inside the small flat. The crouching officer threw himself sideways, his hand feeling the top of his skull to make sure it was still intact.

Swiftly the sergeant tossed two gas canisters through the splintered panelling and another burst of fire cut the door to matchwood. Roberts came through the smashed woodwork left shoulder first, then swung upwards with a half-closed fist, felling the sergeant immediately. He couldn't swing his long legs in the narrow iron stairwell but his knees contacted the soft lower parts of a body and another of the men dropped clutching his groin.

The officer who had narrowly missed having his brains blown out reached for a fallen pistol, and Roberts broke his fingers with his boot before the flat barrel of an automatic hit him across the eyes and another three blows to the head knocked him cold.

'God almighty! I hope there's no more in there!' the man with the automatic exclaimed, looking down at the unconscious form of Les Roberts and the groaning or vomiting remainder of the Special Task Force. The sergeant shook his head and rose to his feet. They found the radio and Robert's pack, then signalled for Hammond.

The chief superintendent climbed the iron stairs and grimaced at the state of the door. Glancing at the unconscious mercenary and the vicious-looking Sterling, he was thankful that nothing had gone badly wrong.

'I want no problems out there,' Hammond told the sergeant. 'He's dressed pretty much the same as any of the soldiers, so get him into the car while he's still out. Pass him off as one of ours who's fainted and cracked his head. Right, get moving.' He smiled. 'You did well. Thanks.'

The team, nursing their own injuries, manhandled Roberts out of the flat. Hammond began checking through the contents of Roberts's pack and found a set of civilian clothes. Trousers, a roll-neck sweater, windcheater and a pair of black casual shoes. 'Why the hell didn't he wear this lot anyway?' he said aloud, but there was nobody to answer his question except his own shrewd mind. 'Fraser,' he mused. 'They were going into battle and the uniform made it honourable. Civvies makes them terrorists but the uniform keeps them as soldiers.'

At the bottom of the pack was a sealed envelope addressed simply to The Trustees, Werner Holdings. Hammond ripped it open. The document inside read: 'As per my instructions regarding the liquidation of all companies and assets owned by the undersigned on the agreed date. The bearer of this document shall be the beneficiary of the whole or part of the whole of the accrued sum. Any partition of this sum shall be by equal division of the estate between bearers of documents identical with this, presented within the instructed time limit.' The document bore a dark green wax seal with the letters WH one above the other. The signature was indecipherable and Hammond guessed it was no more than an agreed device for identification and validity.

'And that,' Hammond said, slapping the document against his thigh, 'is how you tied them to you, Colonel. A legacy.' He placed the letter in his pocket. 'Well, let's see how much you're worth.'

With care, he checked and noted the frequency on the compact transmitter receiver and gave orders to the uniformed policeman already on duty at the splintered door, that nothing was to be touched in the flat. Especially the radio. Hammond saw the look on the face of the young man. 'Don't worry,' he said. 'We'll have a new door put in today.'

4

Immediately after the stormy emergency meeting at 10 Downing Street that Tuesday morning, the head of British Secret Intelligence returned to Queen Anne's Gate and summoned the various department heads. He explained the situation and then, with a touch of theatre, dropped the bombshell of Fraser's threat to broadcast the KGB's secrets. The first stunned silence was followed by urgent discussion of the true implications and the advantages to be gained from the situation.

The SIS chief quelled them all with a raised hand.

'I spent most of the time with my mouth firmly shut,' he said. 'After all, if one hears that the Crown Jewels are going to be left unguarded with the doors unlocked, one does not inform the Commandant of the Tower that one is tempted to steal them!

'However, I had a most interesting conversation with a young man from the Special Branch who, it appears, was instrumental in identifying a number of this Colonel Fraser's group before the event. Purely by chance, I might add. A spot of luck from a routine surveillance of the Embassy extension demonstration. Now this young man is a photographic laboratory assistant – somewhat elevated since the crisis – and he allowed me to cast my eye over the photographs in question, and here, gentleman, comes the crunch!' He withdrew from a battered leather attaché case a blow-up of a man's face. The face belonged to Christopher Stewart-Smith.

'Now I know we've had our differences with the opposition but there does come a time when differences can be put aside for the common good. In a nutshell, this chap worked under cover in Ireland – both sides of the border – for Military Intelligence and was debriefed by DI5 after a particularly bad string of failures in the field. "Far too sensitive for the type of work" was the opinion of the inquisitors.' He paused to light his pipe and gestured to the others to smoke if they wished. When the pipe was drawing, he continued.

'Head of Five and I shared a car afterwards, strange as it may seem, but temptation sometimes puts the strangest people in the same bed. Now the rather clever young man I mentioned earlier had pointed out the face in the crowd to his super-whatever, but there was no follow-up because quite simply he was not a mercenary. Nevertheless, the young chap goes ahead on his own and blows up the face and – impertinent little devil – passes the print over to Five for a check, using his master's name as authority. Drums begin to roll and dark clouds form in the sky over Five. Why you ask? Answer – the man was under loose surveillance and Five lost him! Now, get the picture. Possible IRA double-agent drops out of sight and the populace is reeling once more from bomb-blasts – Five's sweating and top man is spitting blood. He and I sharing car – I flash my blow-up – he screams rape and we begin comparing notes. To wind it up, try this for a set of coincidences.

'Mercenaries photographed outside "little Russia" – same day as our friend. Mercenaries, identified by police, drop out of sight same day our friend flits. Colonel Jonathan Fraser ex-C-in-C SAS. Mercenaries identified as former SAS.' He dangled the photo between thumb and forefinger. 'Captain Christopher Stewart-Smith? That's right. Ex-SAS!' The blow-up fell to the antique desk. 'Now if Fraser broadcasts those secret files then every intelligence service in Europe and beyond will get their hands on information we would never divulge, even to our best friends. Things the Russians know about us that we don't want laundered in public. On the other side of the coin, any new secrets which are revealed would only depress the market – unless, gentlemen, we could have them for ourselves alone. Are we on the same wavelength?'

Quite suddenly the donnish figure behind the desk dropped the banter and became the ruthless head of what was arguably the best and toughest Secret Service in the world.

'I don't give a damn if Colonel Jonathan Fraser incites mass suicide in that store-house of secrets, but I want *our* share of them and I don't care if we have to turn, burn or use thumb-screws on Captain Stewart-Smith! He's going to pass them over and the Prime Minister won't know a damn thing about it! We'll put them on ice until after the General Election and trot them out just in time to influence the size of the secret vote. I have a feeling that the amount will be greatly increased when we show them that our cupboard is far from bare. And I think we have in our hands exactly the right weapon to soften-up the "sensitive" Stewart-Smith.'

In Moscow, the Russian President was far from being simply angry any more. He was in a thunderous rage.

'We are being led by the nose!' he roared. 'The mighty Russian people? We are cattle! Pulled by a ring through the snout to the slaughterhouse. A handful of bandits are beating our arses and the crowds are laughing till they choke. Imbeciles. "*Komitet Gosudarstvennoy Bezopasnosti*"? What State Security? You could not secure the locks on your lavatory door. Right! Facts. I want facts.'

'What is it you wish, Comrade President?' the KGB chairman asked calmly.

'An estimate of what is kept in the archives of your London building. Forget the rubbish. I want to know precisely what we are going to lose in top-level intelligence.'

'Comrade President, even if I gave you a complete breakdown it does not mean that this Colonel Fraser will know which is the most sensitive intelligence.'

The President sighed.

'He has top-class fighting men who slaughtered your "handpicked force"; he has radio technicians who can operate our most advanced equipment; and he is a man who can get into the cipher rooms without having micro-films and files exploding in his face. Don't you know by now, Comrade, that someone is helping him? Can't you face the fact that one of your people is betraying us?'

The Chairman stiffened visibly, for the dreaded suspicion he nursed deep inside had now been spewed up for all to see.

'It has troubled me but I could not believe this,' he replied.

'Then believe now, for I am certain that it is true,' the President said coldly.

The Chairman pulled himself up.

'There are two items which can harm us most. The rest is general intelligence which in time would be discovered or fed to the West for our own purpose.'

'The two items then, Comrade. The full truth,' the President warned. 'You are an old spy who might find it difficult to tell complete truths. This situation rises above our own personal ambition and protection.'

'Most important, because Great Britain is the target country, we shall lose a number of committed Comrades in very high and sensitive positions.' He wrote quickly on the flat pad before him and passed the result over. 'The names of our top agents within the British Establishment! Beyond this there are many well placed in industry and, naturally, the trade unions, but those are at the very highest level and their successful penetration of the government and civil service has taken them almost all of their lives. They could never be replaced and if they go, then many others who are under their protection will follow. Comrades in the highest echelons of the United States and West German Intelligence *apparat* would also be at risk.'

The President read the names and knew that the Chairman was right. They could never be replaced.

'The second item, Comrade?'

'A top-secret military document outlining our contingency plans for the Middle East and those countries which border our own. The document will reveal our already considerable preparations.'

The President leaned back heavily in his chair.

'I think then, that we must take some measures to destroy this British colonel. Where is our nearest aircraft-carrier to Great Britain?'

In the British Embassy a few miles away, the SIS Head of Moscow station received a message on a prearranged time and frequency 'on-line' transmission. The message was transmitted by 'burst' which meant that the group of ciphers was on the air for no more than two seconds.

He sat in the coding room of the British Embassy decoding the playback, for he operated under diplomatic cover. The message was from Head of SIS to him personally and gave his precise instructions regarding a further message he would have to transmit to London. The signal clearly stated that he would have to operate the equipment himself. In no circumstances should any other personnel be used. He made arrangements for the equipment to be clear for transmission at 8 p.m. Moscow time. There was a dryness in his mouth as he waited, having checked and set up the signal, using the Russian code of the day which the British Signal Intelligence Unit had broken months before, unbeknown to the Russians themselves.

In London, Katrina Lashkova and Christopher Stewart-Smith sorted through seemingly endless racks of files and material in the micro-film retrieval system. On Colonel Fraser's orders they were making a journey back through time to the middle of the 1930s and Stewart-Smith was becoming more and more stricken as they travelled through the documents. Finally Katrina produced a file which gave a detailed break-down of methods and results of recruitment used on those men and women who were the élite of the intellectual youth of the period. The SIS and the British Establishment had been aware for many years of the existence of such a file but no one dared voice the knowledge, for it would surely tear down the citadel of power. The KGB had named it the Cambridge File.

Stewart-Smith stood appalled as she read through the roll of those who had been approached, rejected, recruited or held in reserve. Some of them were now in positions of such power that his mind refused to accept the names which the black type threw at him. Of one thing he was quite certain. If Fraser broadcast the contents of this file, the damage to the nation would be irreparable. Britain would lose any credibility it still held in the world. But *something* should be done. . . .

'You are shocked?' Katrina said, seeing his face. He didn't answer but looked at her for a moment, his haunted face betraying his inner anguish.

'Is it so much of a surprise, Captain? You are of the aristocracy, you had the best that your system could offer, and sometimes you might have looked down below you and seen that there was need for change.' She thrust the file at him. 'These men and women did that – and also looked for an alternative. Perhaps the alternative was not the right one, but at the time it seemed so. The free society and the socialistic welfare state was a child yet to grow and some could not wait – something your colonel seems perfectly aware of.' She shrugged. 'You feel destroyed in the heart – come to Russia and they will destroy your soul.' Katrina turned and walked away, her eyes filling with tears.

'Captain!' Cohen shouted from the radio room. Stewart-

Smith ran through, followed by the girl. Cohen was taking down groups at an even pace, one hand to his headset, the other on the pad. Katrina frowned deeply, leaning over to watch the message build. Quickly she took a pencil from the radio desk and began decoding against the code-of-the-day pad. Halfway through her task, the signal died in Cohen's earphones and he glanced enquiringly at her. Her face was grey.

'What's the matter, love?' Cohen asked.

'It comes from Moscow,' she whispered. 'The KGB. The message is for me.'

'What does it say?' Stewart-Smith demanded and took the paper from her.

'Translate it.'

'The message reads to me personally. "We are . . . in full knowledge . . . aware is better I think. We are aware of your activities with the British SIS and must . . . presume . . . some co-operation exists between yourself and their agents now holding our comrades on diplomatically protected territory." ' She turned to Stewart-Smith. 'That is their way of saying you are bandits. There is more' – and now the tears were falling freely over her cheeks. ' "Nikolai Lashkov is to be executed for your crime against the state. Dawn tomorrow." That is all.'

Stewart-Smith led her aside and held her for a moment.

'Is there nothing that can be done?'

'Nothing. They will kill him. They kill very easily.'

'I thought the SIS were going to break him out from the hospital. That was the agreement, wasn't it?'

Katrina pulled away.

'Before, yes. But your colonel came, and it is over.'

Stewart-Smith turned away from her, his mind churning, his loyalties stretched to the limit. He realized, suddenly, that he was still clutching the Cambridge File. Turning his back, he slipped it under his combat jacket.

'I'm going upstairs,' he told Cohen. Katrina lifted her eyes to his face and he held them with his as though conveying a message. 'Come with me,' he said. Cohen watched them go, biting his lip. But he had only one loyalty.

Leading Katrina upstairs, Stewart-Smith directed her towards the KGB resident officer's room. They entered quietly but the room was empty. He switched on the shaded desk-lamp and laid the Cambridge File on the desk.

'Your SIS contact? What is your procedure?' he asked urgently.

'Normally the wine bar. Three contacts, two men, one woman. A different one each time. Fall-back was at the people's Speaking Corner in the Park.'

'Speakers' Corner?'

'Yes.'

'Emergency procedures? What about telephones? You must have been given a number – what if you were blown?'

'010-89467.'

Stewart-Smith dialled. The phone rang three times and when a voice gave the number he thrust the receiver at her.

'Speak.'

'I need an appointment,' she said. 'I am in severe pain.'

'Yes,' the voice in her ear said. 'Is it for an extraction?'

'Lashkov,' she said quickly. 'Please wait.'

Stewart-Smith took the phone from her.

'Listen to me,' he said. 'I am Christopher Stewart-Smith talking from the KGB communications building in London. I am part of Colonel Fraser's force. You must be fully aware of what is going on here and what this building contains. I want to speak with the Head of SIS.'

A cold voice came from behind him in the darkness.

'Replace the telephone, Captain,' Fraser said. Katrina turned and saw fury glazing in the man's eyes. Stewart-Smith replaced the receiver and leant forward on to the desk.

'Cohen?'

'Cohen,' Fraser affirmed.

Katrina moved towards Fraser. 'Stay exactly where you are, young lady!' he warned.

'He did it for me – he was helping to save my uncle – please, I beg you. . . .' The telephone cut into her plea with one sharp ring. Fraser moved forward and lifted it.

'Colonel Jonathan Fraser,' he said. The line echoed hollowly in his ear and the corners of his mouth lifted as he imagined the consternation at the other end. He put it down.

'How did you decode this?' he asked the girl, holding out a crushed ball of paper.

'Code of the day,' she answered, and even as she spoke her eyes showed her comprehension.

' "Code of the day!" ' Fraser repeated with heavy sarcasm. 'Transmitted on the machines? Or radio?'

'Radio.' Her voice was frightened now.

'High-speed transmission?'

She shook her head.

'At dictation speed then, so that Cohen could get the groups easily? And code of the day! No emergency code? After all, the building is occupied by enemies of the state. Oh no! The KGB would never think of anything quite as clever as that – they're such a very stupid organization. Don't you think, Miss Lashkova, knowing your masters as you do, that such a message would only be sent if it were followed by a threat? For example – unless you co-operated and destroyed the archives – then the execution would really be carried out? You did say that your activities with the SIS had been discovered?'

'They suspected this. They did not know.'

'So,' Fraser continued, 'they made no effort to warn you, by using emergency procedures, that you hold your uncle's life in your hand! No, they simply throw an immensely valuable advantage away. No attempt at coercion. Execution at dawn they say. Lord save me from fools!' he exploded. 'Who *knew* you were working for the SIS?'

'The KGB *thought* they knew!'

'You little idiot! I said who *knew*!'

'The SIS,' she screamed at him. '*They* knew. They had to know!'

Fraser glared at her angrily, but with grim satisfaction.

'The SIS. And they've blown you to the wide. Code of the day? They must have broken that sequence months ago but they could never break an emergency code because it's on a one-time pad. Right? Never used more than once. Message reads, "Execution. Dawn tomorrow." It might as well say, "Contact the SIS." Didn't you think? Are you completely stupid?' Throughout his tirade Fraser had completely ignored Stewart-Smith, but now he turned on him.

'And you!' he erupted. 'You were ready to destroy everything we have achieved. How can I bargain with any credibility if it is suspected we are dealing with an Intelligence agency? I told the Russians we have no political affiliation and you betray my word by going to the SIS!'

Stewart-Smith rose and thrust the file into Katrina's hands. 'Read it to him,' he said. 'Read it.'

Without opening it she recited. ' "British agents working for the Soviets on deep-penetration assignments . . ." ' And then the names.

Fraser did not even flinch.

'I'm not surprised,' he said flatly when she had finished. He took the file from her, then held it close to Stewart-Smith's face. 'You heard the names. How long before the passing over of this information would be relayed to the Russians? A week? A month? I'd give it twenty-four hours!' He gazed deep into the eyes of the man before him. 'I'm truly sorry, Christopher,' he said. 'Paul? Cornwell?'

Stratton and the RSM stepped out of the shadows by the door. The girl drew a quick breath, not realizing they had been there throughout the conversation. Fraser looked at them, noting the sudden concern in Stratton's eyes.

'Not the girl,' Stewart-Smith said quietly. 'She didn't know what I was going to do. Didn't know I had taken the file.'

'I accept that,' Fraser replied evenly. 'Take her out, Cornwell.' The RSM turned to him but Fraser shook his head.

'My responsibility,' he said. 'You too, Paul. Go.' His order to Stratton was hard and direct.

The girl struggled as she was led from the room, bewildered and frightened by what was happening.

'On the chair behind the desk, please,' Fraser said as he heard the door lock click.

Apart from a shaded lamp on the red leather-topped desk the room was in darkness. Stewart-Smith sat down in the comfortable chair. Fraser moved in the shadows behind him, and the captain dropped his arms to his side, forcing them backwards, so that his head was thrust forward and his neck taut, the vertebrae jutting out through the skin. He felt the cold circle of steel press lightly against the sixth vertebra, the metal warming briefly before searing flame scorched flesh and hair and the bullet severed the spinal column.

Outside the door, the noise of the silenced shot was inaudible but the thump of Stewart-Smith's body being thrown against the desk by the impact was quite clear.

Fraser pocketed the heavy Browning and moved away, noticing in a detached way that very little blood was visible against the red leather of the desk.

At 10 Downing Street, the Prime Minister was called from his private lounge to the Cabinet room. His private secretary stood at the long table, the receiver of the telephone held out. The Premier took it from him.

'Yes, Colonel Fraser?' he said. 'I thought we weren't going to hear from you again. I'm relieved that you are still being reasonable.'

For the first time that day the Cabinet room was empty, if only for a brief period, and he let his eyes move around, welcoming the fact. Yet solitude made the burden of responsibility seem greater than ever.

'I have some information, sir, which is going to displease you greatly,' Fraser said.

'Please go on,' the Premier replied.

'The Secret Intelligence Service has attempted to suborn one of the Russian hostages and one of my men into handing over details contained in one highly sensitive document from the archives in this building. Fortunately I was able to stop this.'

'The SIS? I know nothing of this.'

'I'm relieved to hear that, Prime Minister.'

'What document? What were they after?'

'That is no concern of yours, sir. I'm informing you simply because I do not want any government agency jeopardizing my operation. It seems that your own people are prepared to take action behind your back. As I believe I stated before.'

'Colonel Fraser, one second, please. How did you discover that this was going on?'

'By using my intelligence, Prime Minister.'

'What of the people involved – the hostage and your man?'

'The hostage is quite safe. My officer has been executed.'

The Premier stared at the telephone, stunned.

'Executed?'

'That is correct, sir. We are operating under the rules of war.

Aid to the enemy is punishable with death by shooting. That is what was done.'

'You executed one of your own men?'

'Yes.'

'God in heaven, what kind of man are you?'

At the other end of the line Fraser laughed, a harsh barking sound.

'You ask that of *me*! You and your people made me. I am a product of *your* policies – *your* mistakes – *your* obscene man-oeuvring and wastage of life. Pray that the Russians can make the Africans see sense, Prime Minister, because if they don't your disgusting Establishment will be torn apart by the biggest spy scandal of the century. Remember where I am and just try to imagine the secret information that is now available to me. I know that the Russians will try to destroy me, but believe me when I say I will not go down alone. A large number of very important people will be destroyed with me. Goodbye, sir.'

The private secretary took the telephone.

'Will you want a transcript made for Dr Hoffman, sir?' he asked coolly.

The Prime Minister fell heavily into a chair.

'I'm afraid that it's gone past the stage of trying to wear the man down. He's just killed – executed, he calls it – one of his own men! One of *his* men because some of *our* people couldn't resist temptation.'

Blazing with anger he slammed his fists on the table.

'Head of SIS! Here. Now!'

Within an hour the Prime Minister had on his desk the resig-nation of the Head of the British Secret Intelligence Service.

On the other side of the river Colin Hammond stared through grimy windows at the grey colossus of Battersea Power Station. The house he stood in was perfect for some of the less acceptable tasks the Special Branch had, on occasion, to undertake. It stood at the end of a row of derelict Victorian dwellings, all uninhabited and ready for demolition.

Les Roberts stood against a wall, his feet splayed and his body supported by his long slender fingers. Over his head and tied tightly at the neck, was a black bag of densely woven cloth. He was naked. Around the unkempt room were a few old wooden chairs which the interrogation team used between sessions. The officers had reached the point of exhaustion and were unable to understand how Roberts could have withstood the punishment they had dealt out through the afternoon and early evening. His resistance to physical and mental pain was phenomenal.

As a last resort Hammond had called Dr Hoffman and begged guidance. The psychologist had immediately suggested he should see Roberts himself and Hammond had warily agreed. He pulled his eyes away from the huge chimney stacks as he saw a black limousine pull up in front of the house.

Hoffman entered, grimacing with distaste at the spectacle. 'Any background on him?' he asked abruptly.

'No police record, not even parking offences,' Hammond replied, not missing the psychologist's disgust. 'It is necessary, Doctor – we don't have time for the niceties.'

'The world doesn't change much does it, Chief Superintendent? I seem to recall we had trials at the end of the war for those who allowed this sort of thing to go on.'

'No lectures, please, Doctor – I've a job to do and precious little time to do it in – nor much in the way of thanks if we're successful.'

Hoffman took a note-pad from Hammond's hand.

'Well, let's see what can be achieved with a little humanity. Remove the hood and dress him, please. Clean the blood off while you're at it.'

Hammond nodded to his team and Hoffman began reading through the handwritten notes.

'Parents?' he queried.

'Mother only, apparently. She's in Guy's Hospital. Terminal cancer.'

'Does he know you've checked that out?'

'He knows nothing.'

'What has he told you so far?'

Hammond laughed weakly.

'Told us? Nothing! Sweet bugger-all! He's been in that position for hours, with the headphones on and the sounds going at him without a let-up. The man has simply turned himself off. That's the only way I can describe it.'

Hoffman leaned over to pick up a pair of headphones and

placed them over his ears. He screwed up his eyes in pain and Hammond jerked the plug from the tape machine.

'Bad?' he asked.

'Worse than bad. That can do permanent damage over an extended period.'

'You haven't forgotten what's going on out there, have you, Doctor?'

Hoffman pierced him with his eyes. 'Not for a minute,' he replied coldly. 'Notice any sexual deviations?'

'What?' Hammond stared.

'Behaviour patterns out of the norm. Your men have beaten him up – did he react sexually – get an erection?'

'No.'

'Good, otherwise you might have been doing him a service – if he had masochistic tendencies.'

'For God's sake,' Hammond breathed.

'Time, Mr Hammond. You said it yourself – we don't have much of it and we have to find the weakness in him – and soon. No record of marriage here?'

'If there is one we can't trace it.'

'Homosexuality?'

'No convictions and no obviously feminine gestures.'

'That means nothing,' Hoffman cut in. 'So. Let's open him up. I need some things urgently.'

'Whatever you want. The entire Metropolitan police force is at our command if we want it.'

'Photographs. Pornographic. Hard core and soft. Heterosexual and homosexual. Another of his mother preferably taken tonight at the hospital – make her look as ill as possible – and some garment of hers. Shawl, nightdress, whatever, but something personal and if possible something he gave her. Check with the nurses. They always notice these things.'

Hammond picked the telephone off the bare wooden floorboards and began dialling, not relishing the thought of the comments which would be bandied about behind his back in the future. After he had given his directions he called his own number at Horseferry Road, but there was no answer. Frowning he checked his watch.

'Problem?' Hoffman inquired.

'Er – no. Thought I'd call home but there's no one there.'

144

'Hard life for a policeman's wife – perhaps she's with a friend.'

Hammond felt his stomach lurch.

'Not wife. Girl-friend. More than that . . .'

'Lover!'

A rueful smile broke across the policeman's face.

'Bad, is it?' Hoffman said. 'I'm sorry, I don't wish to pry.'

Hammond shrugged and then for no accountable reason pulled out a snapshot.

'Oh yes, I see. How much younger than you?'

'Too much.'

'It can work but it does take some doing. In your job though it could be difficult.'

Roberts was brought in and the exchange forgotten. The psychologist sat opposite the mercenary and for an interminable length of time said nothing. Roberts, now cleaned up and dressed in civilian clothes, ignored everyone.

Hoffman began. He talked quietly, as if he had Roberts's complete attention, discussing aspects of the man's life, from the meagre information gleaned from public records. Hammond sensed he was playing for time. A police car pulled up outside the house and two sealed packages were brought into the room by a uniformed officer.

'Do we have a small table of some sort, Chief Superintendent?' Hoffman asked. Hammond made a movement with his head to one of his own men who left the room and returned with a rickety card-table.

'That'll do quite well, thank you.' Hoffman smiled at the policeman. From one package he removed a set of photographs and placed them face down on the table, after glancing at them. He repeated the trick with a second set, then proceeded to turn them over one at a time moving from set to set alternatively. Roberts stared stonily ahead.

'Cigarette?' Hoffman asked.

Silence.

'I don't very often myself, but I do feel like one this evening. Do you have a light, Chief Superintendent?'

Hammond flicked the wheel on a heavy steel lighter and Hoffman dipped the tip of the cigarette into the full flame, but his eyes never left Robert's face. For the first time the mercenary's eyes reacted with a sudden movement towards the flame.

Hoffman undid the second package, withdrew a photograph in a heavy gilt frame and studied it for a moment before turning it towards Roberts and placing it upright on the table. Quickly he drew out a pale blue woollen scarf and lay it beside the picture.

Les Roberts came over the table so fast that everyone was caught flat-footed. Hammond went down with a blow delivered by the side of the hand to his shoulder, the psychologist threw himself sideways, landing heavily against the skirting board and the two Special Branch officers had to bawl for help as they reeled under Robert's expert unarmed attack. Finally four men subdued him and bound him, still struggling, to the heaviest chair.

'Your mother is very ill, Leslie,' Hoffman said, seating himself again.

'Bastards!' Roberts shouted. 'Bastards!'

'We are as concerned about her as you are, Leslie. And she is deeply concerned about you. Your name on the television, for instance, in connection with this business at the Embassy. She's an old lady, Leslie, and she is unable to take shocks like that. I'm a doctor and I know. Cancer is a terrible disease – excitement can cause the most excruciating pain – the cells become agitated. She asked for you, Leslie. She needs you. She is suffering even now as we talk.'

'Take me to the hospital.' They were the first reasonable words that the mercenary had uttered from his time of capture. Hoffman extracted another cigarette and glanced at Hammond. The lighter flared and the chief superintendent let it burn. Once again Roberts seemed mesmerized by the flame.

'The flame disturbs you, Leslie?' Hoffman asked gently, and with a voice that seemed not to belong to him Roberts said:

'The Torch must burn.' His eyes now were completely glazed.

'The Torch, Leslie?'

'The Torch must burn,' he repeated.

'Listen to me, Leslie,' Hoffman said in a smooth tone. 'You must remember your true loyalties. Your mother is dying. She may be dead by morning if you are not there to reassure her you are well. We will take you to her. I give you my solemn word. But first we must clear your mind of what has been put there to distort your true values. Your mother could die before you see her. Time is short. Cancer kills quickly and often unexpectedly. Where were you taken, Leslie? Take me there and then we can go directly to the hospital. Would you let her die knowing that you could have been at her side at the end? Ask yourself that. Could you live with that?'

'Untie me,' Roberts said in a cold voice. Then with a dry smile he took in the faces of all of them. 'You'll never beat him, you know. Whatever happens, he'll be ahead of you. When it ends it'll be on his terms. His way.'

The convoy of police vehicles tore along the London to Cambridge road at speeds well over the legal limit, flanked by motorcycle outriders who ruthlessly cleared the path for the flying column. Private cars and trucks were forced off the road as the speeding motorcyclists drew alongside them, emergency lamps flashing and sirens screaming. Then the ten vehicles thundered past in a blast of white paintwork and swirling light.

Colin Hammond sat in the rear of the leading Jaguar, with Hoffman at his side. Leslie Roberts was doubled up, sitting knees to chin, on Hammond's left, his wrists manacled to his ankles with two sets of cuffs. To the left of the police driver and strapped backwards in his seat, was a member of D11, the police specialist firearms squad. He wore a blue beret and battledress, and rested a Smith and Wesson .357 Combat Magnum along the top of his seat. The barrel never wavered from the mercenary's chest. As the column ripped apart the evening tranquillity Roberts said, 'Left, here.'

The police driver swore under his breath and passed the wheel expertly through his hands, using the brakes and accelerator together to preserve the momentum and keep the Jaguar flat on the road. The vehicles behind followed suit but Hammond heard a bang as one of them cracked into the rear of another on the severe hump-back bridge.

'Shit!' Hammond swore, spinning around in his seat. Roberts gave a quick half-smile. Hammond glared at him.

'The big gates up ahead – take a left,' Roberts said to the driver. 'You'd better chop the speed or you won't make it.'

The driver let the rear of the Jaguar slide, flicking the nose neatly between the pillars. Behind the Jag, the police motor-cyclists who had overshot the left-hand turn-off, skidded around on the gravel drive.

'The colonel knew you'd come,' Roberts laughed. 'He even left the gates open for you – he's really got you poor sods running all over the countryside.'

'I'm afraid he's right,' Hoffman said to Hammond over the noise of the spitting gravel. 'Fraser's buying time so that the Russians can work on the Africans and he's avoiding killing British police by diverting your energies elsewhere.'

'Well, perhaps he's *too* damn clever!' Hammond shouted as the Jaguar slid to a halt in front of the great house. Men dropped from the following vehicles, clutching automatic weapons, one or two losing their blue berets as they slipped on the loose gravel.

'It's empty,' the mercenary said.

'I'll think hard about that!' Hammond retorted, angry now. He waved in a group of eight men who split into two sticks of four. One group blasted the lower windows with automatic fire and the other shot away the locks on the heavy double doors. All eight rushed in, rolling as they hit the floor of the hallway. The great house mocked them with silence.

'Make sure nothing's been booby-trapped,' Hammond shouted after them. Roberts snorted at his side.

Hoffman shook his grey head.

'I don't think your men will be harmed. Let's go in, shall we?'

Everything in the manor was exactly as Fraser had left it. The model of Kensington Palace Gardens was still set up on the billiards table, its dust sheet folded on one side. The tape machines and video recorder were on their tables with tapes and cartridges neatly stacked beside them. The written notes for the lectures and the Psychological Warfare Study were placed carefully in full view. Of all the documents and records of the training procedure that Fraser had used, only one set was missing – the personal selection files and the results of the colonel's tests on his men. Hoffman guessed that such records had existed but knew that no matter how long the police searched they would never find any material identifying the men who had occupied the house.

148

'The cellars,' he said to Hammond.

As they opened the door leading on to the descending stone stairway a faintly nauseating odour hovered in the air.

'What's that?' Hammond said.

One of the D11 firearms specialists tilted his nose upwards.

'Cordite, sir – they've been firing live ammunition down here.'

'No. There's something else, I'm afraid,' Hoffman said quietly. 'Will you bring Roberts from the car, Mr Hammond.'

Hammond dispatched the officer to fetch the mercenary, then descended the stairs in the slow wake of the cautious psychologist. His fingers found a light switch. Behind the shredded sandbags the whitewashed walls were bullet-scarred.

'Makeshift firing range,' Hammond said, but he'd lost the attention of the doctor.

'Bloodstains,' Hoffman called from a crouching position on the floor. He pointed at the wall and the floor. Hammond placed his fingers in the holes in the wall, touching gently the flaking rusty stains around them.

Les Roberts entered the cellar, manhandled by two officers. Once again his eyes appeared glazed.

'What happened here?' Hammond demanded, but the psychologist placed a restraining hand on his arm. By now the unpleasant odour was beginning to turn their stomachs. Placing a silk handkerchief to his nose, Hoffman made unerringly for the doors of the two stress cells. The handles turned easily and the first door opened. Hoffman doubled over and vomited on the stone floor, dragging himself away from the aperture.

Colin Hammond rushed towards him but the doctor waved him back. He ignored the man, held his breath and thrust his lighter into the darkened cell. 'Dear God!' he exclaimed, sickened by the sight and turned away, his stomach contracting in spasms.

The bodies of the shot mercenaries had begun to putrify and the flesh had burst, revealing the mass of white maggots which filled the fly-covered corpses.

'They failed to protect us!' Roberts intoned with that strange distant voice. 'The safety of the greater number.'

'What's he saying?' Hammond asked, head down between his knees in an attempt to recover.

Hoffman stood leaning against the brickwork, his face tinged green.

'Fraser's words, not his.' He pushed himself off the wall and entered the small cellar Fraser and Stratton had used to control the equipment. With his handkerchief still over his face, he studied it and switched on the power circuits. The cameras picked up the other two bodies in the other cell immediately and he turned his face away momentarily, then began with furious speed using every control on the desk. On the screens the strobes flashed and the projectors swirled their surreal patterns. He punched the play button on the tape recorder and the low grumbling began. Carefully, to avoid snapping the tape, he moved the speed control upwards. Fraser's litany of loyalty and death boomed out, filling the whole cellar with resonant sound. Over and over it repeated the words: 'The Torch must burn. . . . The Torch must burn . . .' Hoffman put his head out of the control room and saw Roberts' face wearing a mask of enchantment. He switched off all the controls and returned to Hammond's side.

The chief superintendent stood staring at the mercenary, his scalp prickling.

'What in heaven's name was that!'

Hoffman shook his head sadly.

'God, if you like – to Roberts anyway.' He faced Hammond and looked directly into the police officer's eyes. 'I don't have the time or the means to undo all that Fraser has done to these men. I'm afraid there is only one way now. You'll have to kill them all and pray that the cost is not going to be too high in human lives. I'm sorry.' He climbed the steps out of the cellars and to Colin Hammond his stooped shoulders seemed even more bowed.

PART THREE

Storm

I

The Russian 39,000-ton aircraft-carrier *Kiev* battered its way through the chilly waters of the North Sea, a flat wedge of steel and sheer power. Above it, low and circling, an RAF Nimrod kept pace, buffeted constantly by the high wind. On the carrier's bridge, the lookout held the aircraft in sight at all times even though the radar operator never took his eyes off the blip on the screen.

Below decks, Alexei Grechko sat in the captain's quarters. Grechko was a naval commander (air) past his prime and expendable. He knew it, and so did all the younger men clawing their way through the rankings. There are no more wars, he thought, for the young to burn up their insatiable appetite for glory and power. A good flyer – even the very best – had to wait for someone to retire or die before he could begin to rise to where he would be noticed. Unless, of course, he had friends in the right places.

Ah! Alexei, he consoled himself, why worry yourself? You're not an old man yet – not young – but certainly not old! But for a flyer forty is old, he admitted as he sipped his hot lemon tea. The eyes of the Soviet President stared down at him from a portrait. Communism? He was too old to believe in politics – and anyway what is the difference between the so-called capitalists and us? They have more television sets and more automobiles. They are no more and no less free than we. Jobs, families, rents, problems as one grew older, all the same frustrations and disillusionments. Thank God! he had no ties, no dependants, his marriage was to the service and even that in peacetime had lost its sting, the stimulation which kept his love alive. Bah! let's get the damn thing over. If we're going to have a war – then let's have it. Let's not sit around on our fat arses boring each other to death.

'Alexei.' The captain greeted him as he entered, and Grechko rose to his feet. 'No, sit. Drink your tea.' The *Kiev*'s commanding officer moved around the desk and dropped heavily into his high-backed chair. Behind the façade of the uniforms the two men were good friends and, informality was common between them.

'They have gone mad, Alexei,' the captain murmured softly. 'Quite mad! And now they ask me – order me – to pass on their insanity. They need a volunteer. You are considered suitable.'

'Do I have the choice?'

'You could refuse – then I would have to make it an order.'

Grechko lifted the hot glass to his lips, waiting.

The captain placed a signal on the desk between them, his hands covering the contents.

'They say that you are a courageous man, a flyer of great ability who has seen combat and survived. A man able to discard rigid training procedures and press on to destroy a target under the most adverse conditions.'

Grechko smiled.

'What it really says, then, is that Alexei Nikolai Grechko is fool enough to carry out their task.'

'It also states that you are to be made a Hero of the Soviet Union.'

Grechko laughed.

'What must be done as payment for this honour?'

The captain uncovered the signal and passed it over. Grechko's eyes flicked through it quickly, then stopped, hesitated, read one line again and moved upwards to stare directly into the other man's face.

'They have taken leave of their senses. Do they realize the consequences of such a thing?' His finger stabbed at the flimsy.

'Our Comrade President seems prepared to take that risk.'

The flyer's eyes returned to the signal.

'This building – the target – what is it? What does it contain? What could be of such importance?'

'Alexei, all I know is what is written there. The aircraft's navigation computer will be programmed with the target coordinates. How you reach that point is up to you. Your countermeasures should be minimal but you *must* reach the target. You must be *certain* that the building is completely destroyed.'

Grechko thrust out his jaw.

'What do they wish? That I should go down and check?'

'They have ordered the use of the Yakovlev 36.'

'Then they really do want to be sure.'

'You must make a visual check. Do whatever is necessary. Take any risks, but you must succeed. Those are the orders.'

'And the Yakovlev?'

'Destroy it if you are forced down.'

Grechko gave a great laugh.

'I shall try to stay in one piece long enough to press the button, Comrade!'

The captain looked down at his desk. 'Alexei. You are politically suspect – ideologically unsound – yet they know from your record that you are a loyal Russian, a highly decorated flyer. It would be difficult for them to act against you, but not impossible. They are offering their hand to you. Take it, and return. Past mistakes are easily forgotten.'

'Is that written in the signal?'

'Not written, but it is there.'

'Come,' Grechko said, rising. 'There is no more time.'

'They've brought a YAK on to the flight-deck, boss!' the observer said in the Nimrod.

'Putting one up in this breeze, Ned? I doubt it. Keep an eye on it, though. Remember those things can go straight up. Don't want to catch one between the cheeks, eh!'

'Righty-ho. I'll watch the bugger. You drive the bus.'

Grechko stood on the bridge; his flying overalls drawn from the ship's stores were new and without insignia of any sort. He felt shorn of all his many accomplishments; a man reduced. Yet as he saw the red stars being blacked out on the Yakovlev he felt a strong, pleasurable thrill. He was being stripped of all recognizable ties with the State. He was no longer part of the huge grinding machine. He was Alexei Grechko, a man alone. A complete individual.

'The Nimrod will report as soon as my wheels leave the deck!' he commented.

'I know,' the captain replied. 'I too have my orders.'

Grechko shook his head in disbelief as the captain picked up a hand microphone.

'Missile launch,' he said coolly.

Twin streaks of red flashed for a moment in the sky, followed almost immediately by a great ball of flame and a deep thud, as the blast hit the thick windows of the bridge.

'Now you have no one to see you go. Goodbye, my friend. Go well.' The captain turned away from Grechko, his face, in profile, becoming a death-mask without expression.

Grechko, still shaking his head, made his way down the companionway and across the flight deck to the aircraft. He began the pre-flight checks. Below him on the flight deck the crew were removing the chocks from the wheels and the flight controller murmured in his earphones that he was readied for take-off.

Grechko ignited the two lift engines immediately behind his cockpit and the large single turbo-jet.

'Bitch!' he muttered aloud, for the YAK 36 was a difficult machine to fly. Pushed into production early by the Soviets to combat the British Harrier and the West German VAK-1918, there were still pitch–roll coupling difficulties in the vertical/short-take-off-and-landing assault aircraft. The new and highly refined flight-control system, however, had succeeded in making the aircraft very steady in the hover.

The YAK lifted cleanly from the planking of the deck, the two lift engines capable of producing 7000 pounds of thrust each. Grechko raised a hand to the figure on the bridge, hung there for a moment, then pushed the throttles forward and flashed away from the *Kiev*.

He was flying and he was free. The falling night closed around him like a black tunnel as he headed straight for London.

At the Ministry of Defence establishment, which houses the headquarters of the Royal Air Force Fighter Command, the controller sat in his chair overlooking the great display board upon which the dispositions of all RAF patrols were laid out. Around the balcony, computer tapes chattered happily and, directly before him, the pictures from the coastal radar stations blipped and pinged in counterpoint. A female voice came through the head-set.

'Nimrod off the screen. Sector four. No radio contact. Presumed down.'

The controller pushed buttons and the computer ejected its answer on the read-out tapes.

'That's a visual run on the *Kiev*. What's her position?'

'Dogger Bank, sir.'

'Got a signal from the homing beacon?'

'Negative, sir.'

'Odd! If the aircraft was in trouble and went down fast we'd still get the beacon. Check the coastal stations for mayday calls. They could have gone off the frequency in an emergency.' The head-set hissed in his ears and he gazed down at the position of the Soviet aircraft-carrier. 'The *Kiev* has turned!' he said. 'Why didn't you tell me?'

The girl's voice came back confidently.

'It *is* on the board, sir – I thought you'd noticed.'

'Perhaps the *Kiev* saw the aircraft go down. She may be going about for survivors.' Again the hiss in the phones and the controller checked the machines feeding data in rapidly. 'She's certainly making sea-way out there. The computer gives her maximum power as she's running now! Air-sea rescue already gone?'

'Soon as we lost the signal, sir.'

'Right, go to alert. Status yellow. Don't like aircraft carriers on the doorstep – 'specially when they go about and run after we lose a tracker.'

'Confirmed, sir. Moving to status yellow.'

Over the Norfolk coast a B-52 tanker aircraft of the United States Air Force flew straight down the beam of the radio beacon at the USAF base at Mildenhall.

'Hey, skipper! We've got a UFO!' the engineer bawled. 'Down at ground zero – to starboard. Jeeze, look at that sonofabitch go!' The captain tilted the huge aircraft to his right so that it was virtually standing on its starboard wing-tip.

'Hell! It sure is moving along.'

'Get on down there, skipper, let's see the sonofabitch close.'

'In this rig – you crazy, Jackson?' a voice shouted through the phones, its owner at the extreme rear of the plane.

The captain smiled and let the aircraft slip sideways, like an enormous silver cross falling out of the sky.

'We have a visual on a UFO,' he transmitted to the air-base. 'Am going down for identification.'

Alexei Grechko had crossed the Norfolk coast at a point between Sheringham and Cley. He knew that to penetrate the highly sophisticated radar and missile defences the most effective technique was to fly very fast and very low. Ground features, and interference, make it difficult for radar to pick up and track the aircraft at sufficient range to allow time for the defensive systems to react. It is also difficult to intercept at that level.

The terrain below flashed by so fast that the effect was almost hypnotic. He sat back and relaxed, for the plane was flying itself, the onboard computer making the adjustments as each obstacle reared before him. Grechko's dark warm cocoon was suddenly obliterated, as the trailing blast from the huge engines of the strato-tanker rocked the YAK violently in its wake. He increased his speed to get out from under the line of the tanker. Suddenly he realized that the monster airplane was coming down to him and that the line of descent would match his own course.

The strato-tanker's landing lights came on and he knew that within seconds he would be identified and the elements of speed, secrecy and surprise would be gone. Below him and very close there were only marshes but somewhere there had to be trees – a small copse or a wood would do. There was no more time. The tanker seemed to plummet down beside the YAK, dwarfing it, shaking the air-frame madly in the turbulence and roar of the enormous engines. Grechko yanked the throttles back, dropping full flaps. The YAK seemed to be jerked backwards and away from the tanker, then slowed further and hovered a few feet above the ground as Grechko switched to the wing nozzles.

The great aircraft before him seemed to raise itself up, the tail section being forced downwards as the captain fought for height. But the ground was too close and the sky too far away.

The tail-section was the first to break off, followed by the starboard wing and engine pods. By then the fires had begun inside the wiring of the plane as the systems short-circuited.

Grechko moved forward behind the rise and saw the sky brighten before the blast.

'Well, Alexei,' he said aloud, 'two airplanes down in less than one hour. I think you must go to ground before the hounds get your scent.' But inside his head a question smouldered, threatening to burn him up if it were not answered soon. What was happening in London that had made the Kremlin issue such an insane order?

Gently he gained a few more feet in height and hopped over the rise, then with minimum power to keep the noise level down, he skirted the wreckage of the strato-tanker and began his search for cover.

The controller at Fighter Command Headquarters leaned forward in the chair with his teeth clamped hard into the stem of his pipe.

'Mildenhall are reporting a B-52 crash, sir. An air-to-air refuelling plane, thank heaven – not a SAC bomber. No weapons aboard.' The girl's voice remained steady even though she was aware that the aircraft could easily have been one carrying nuclear devices, whether armed or not. It was a fear they lived with daily.

'Got a fix on the crash site?'

'Not on our screen, sir, but Mildenhall tell us it was approaching down the radio beacon – last words were, "Have visual on a UFO – am going down for identification," then they lost it.'

'Was that "going *down* for identification"?'

'That's correct, sir.'

'Hm. Don't like the sound of that. If he was flying down the beam he couldn't have had much height himself. Could have been chasing his own shadow. How's the weather up there?'

'A clear night, sir, but no moon to speak of.'

The controller bit harder on his pipe stem, his mind ticking off the possibilities. The girl interrupted the process.

'They've found the Nimrod, sir.'

'Survivors?'

'There's very little left, sir – multiple explosion, so they say.'

'I see. Pass along our thanks to Air-sea rescue.'

'Already done, sir.'

'Looks like *Kiev* is running for home.'

'Second tracker has moved into position over her – do you want to hold?'

'For the moment, yes. I'm rather unhappy about all this.' Beside him a green telephone rang. He listened intently, moving one earphone aside. 'Thank you, I'm very grateful.' He replaced the phone and spoke into the slim microphone fitted to the headset, flicking a switch on his control-panel.

'Listen carefully, please. We have a report that the Norfolk Police are receiving complaints of a low-flying jet aircraft. Going too fast for visual identification but probably a fighter. Any of you got a tearaway flying tonight?'

The upturned faces shook their heads negatively.

'Right. Move up to status blue. We may have something under the net. Let's kick this one upstairs.' He lifted the red telephone.

The Prime Minister stood looking out through the french windows of the Cabinet room into the darkness of the garden beyond. Colin Hammond sat at the long table with a sheaf of notes before him, writing furiously. They were alone in the room.

'And Hoffman has given up?' the Premier asked.

'Completely, sir. He said we will have to kill them all now. They've been conditioned too well.'

'But you think you can find a way to save the hostages?'

'Surely that is all that matters, sir.'

'In the final audit, yes, I suppose it is.'

Hammond continued writing, occasionally glancing up at the hands of the Premier as he clenched them tightly behind his back. Somehow the complete expression of frustration was visible in the interlocked flesh and bone.

'It's time that's the problem, Prime Minister – you'll have to buy me some time with the Russians. There's no way it can be done otherwise.'

'Are you ready to explain it to me?'

Hammond shuffled his notes into a neat pile.

'Yes, sir, I am now.'

The Premier turned around to face him for the first time since the policeman had entered the Cabinet room and Hammond was appalled at the exhausted face, and thankful that he would never have to shoulder responsibilities such as the man before him was facing.

'I'm ready to listen to anything, Hammond, at this moment.' He lowered himself into a chair, wearily. 'Go on.'

'There's only one way to stop Fraser broadcasting those secrets, and to get him, his men and the hostages, out of that building. And that, Prime Minister, is to give the man what he wants. Wait, sir! Please let me finish.'

The Premier settled again impatiently.

'When a man wants something badly enough – to the point of insanity – I don't believe that he will be thinking very clearly when the object of his desire is placed in front of him. I asked myself a question today while standing at the Embassy gates. Why did the police let Fraser's force through the security barriers so easily?'

'That's obvious,' the Premier interrupted. 'Because they were dressed and equipped as a bomb-disposal unit.'

'Exactly, sir! But more than that – the police *wanted* a bomb-disposal unit to arrive, they wanted one urgently and they were so relieved that one arrived quickly that they didn't question the authenticity of it. Do you see, sir?'

The Prime Minister let the beginnings of a smile touch his lips.

'Oh I see, Chief Superintendent, I see very clearly indeed!'

'Of course,' Hammond continued, 'we will need the complete co-operation of the media – well, certainly the television people and the radio and naturally all the countries involved. There must be no way that any statement made by us can be denied. If that happens we are finished before we start.'

'I think that can be arranged. The Russians are bound to agree and they can lean on the Africans. Who will you want to use?'

'Shouldn't we fight fire with fire, sir?'

'The Special Air Service! My God, that's *playing* with fire. Fraser's a living legend in that regiment.'

Hammond's eyes narrowed.

'And I mean to make them see that the man is deranged – that he is destroying everything he stood for. We'll never destroy the man if we don't destroy the legend.'

'You sound as if you're taking this whole business personally, Chief Superintendent.'

'No, sir,' Hammond lied, remembering the imagined challenge at the Embassy gates. 'Nothing personal.'

The Prime Minister rose from his chair and moved over to the heavy-based red phone at the far end of the table.

'I think we had better speak to the Soviet President.'

The Soviet President was called from his bed to take the call from London. He listened intently to every word and inflection in the British Premier's voice, measuring the degree of truth in the statement of intent the man was urgently placing before him. It is always difficult to know when a man is lying, if that lie is at the end of thousands of miles of cable. The eyes, he thought. They are the true mirror. The voice is the tool of the liar. Yet, somehow, he found himself believing. Finally he spoke.

'Prime Minister, here in Moscow it is past two o'clock in the morning. I feel that we are two old Grand Masters playing a game of chess and both very tired. We would like the game over so that we can enjoy the warmth and comfort of our beds. I am going to place you in an impossible position and, if you are a realist, you will accept the inevitable. This Colonel Fraser and his men have knowledge of Soviet secrets and I cannot allow them to walk free. You understand? A short while ago I gave the order for one of our aircraft to penetrate British defences and destroy the Embassy Communications building in London. You have two options. You may shoot down the aircraft and escalate this situation between our two countries, or you can agree to let a team of our marksmen liquidate this Colonel Fraser and his men once you have them out in the open.'

In London, the Prime Minister put his hand over the mouthpiece and asked Hammond to leave the room for a moment.

'Mr President,' he began, after he was sure the door was closed, 'I cannot sanction the death of these men in cold blood. Also there is the question of the hostages and the men who would volunteer for this operation.'

The Russian's voice was merciless at the end of the hollow line.

'That is a risk they must take. But only you should know of this plan, for afterwards many questions will be asked and it is better for you as a statesman that you can show clean hands. Blame anyone, but do not admit you knew. Mr Prime Minister, I give you a way out from an impossible situation – my suggestion is that you take it. What are the lives of these people when weighed against the possible circumstances?'

'And your aircraft, Mr President? What am I to do about that?'

'You may destroy it. Without fear of retaliation. It should be over London at any moment now.'

'I agree to the conditions. There seems to be no other way.'

Immediately the receiver of the hot line went down in the Cabinet room, the Prime Minister's defence priority telephone shrilled at him, its light flashing.

'Prime Minister. Ah! Air Marshal. I was expecting to hear from you.'

'You were, Prime Minister?'

'I'd have been worried if I hadn't! You've a Soviet aircraft below our radar defences. Correct?'

'Did Signals Intelligence pick up its radio, sir? I have no clear indication that it is a Russian plane.'

'You may take it that it is, Air Marshal. And you may give the order to shoot it down and dispense with the alert.'

'But, Prime Minister . . .'

'Shoot it down, Air Marshal. We have the authority. The plane should be approaching London soon.' There was a moment's hesitation. 'Well?'

'I'm sorry, Prime Minister, but the fighter is nowhere near London.'

'Well, where is it then?'

'We have absolutely no idea, sir.'

For a brief second the Premier was touched by panic. Then he took a grip on his already mangled nerves. His voice was rock hard.

'Find that plane, Air Marshal. I don't care what it takes. Find it and destroy it!'

Alexei Grechko switched on his landing lights and dropped below the level of the hummocks into the dip, virtually taxi-ing the YAK in mid air.

'Oh yes!' he exclaimed softly. 'This will be just fine.'

The copse was like a natural hangar, with dense undergrowth right up to the arch of the trees. In its centre was a small clearing but the entrance to it was overhung by drooping branches. It was going to be very tight.

'Think of it as a woman, Alexei!' he murmured to himself. 'And you'll slip in there like a dream.'

The grass looked firm, but he didn't dare risk being trapped, so before entering he settled the plane carefully on the ground.

Increasing downward thrust, he lifted off again feeling the YAK unstick itself easily from the soft earth. He blew out hard.

With his lower lip gripped in his teeth, he concentrated on flying through the trees, holding tons of airplane less than three feet off the ground. His eyes switched quickly from wing-tip to wing-tip and sweat broke out over his body. It was too tight! The wings were too wide!

'So! Too much man for the lady, eh! Be polite, Alexei,' he joked aloud, but he was conscious of his fear.

The YAK eased backwards in the air and Grechko let it drop. He sat staring through the glass at the haven denied him by a few feet of space. Suddenly, he smacked his helmet with an open hand. 'Idiot! Fool!' he shouted and punched a button. The wing-tips folded upwards.

Grinning widely, he pushed the throttle a fraction, letting the wheels roll but still maintaining enough lift to keep the massive weight off the ground.

The YAK slipped easily between the trees, overhanging branches brushed along the top of the fuselage, then dropped behind the exhausts, the leaves burned into charred curls and blasted into the night.

Grechko looked around him, and lifted the plane again, swinging it slowly on its axis until the nose faced the entrance to the copse. The wheels touched and he cut the turbine.

The silence was numbing and he knew that the squeal of the jet, even at absolute minimum power, must have pierced the still night. He shrugged, and pulled the cockpit cover back, and dropped to the grass, kissing it and drawing in the smell of the rich earth.

'God give me soil! I am sick of steel and plastic and freezing salt water.'

Dawn was breaking over the marshes as Grechko completed his work. Gentle sunshine filtered through the early mist and the colours of the rough countryside lifted the grey from the landscape.

There was no way that he could completely conceal the entrance to the copse, but hard labour with the heavy-bladed knife from his survival kit established a green curtain of foliage from the low overhanging branches to the earth. Exhausted, he walked back along the shallow valley of the dip and surveyed his efforts. Satisfied, he studied the ground for any trace of wheel tracks from his brief touch-down, but the spongy soil revealed nothing.

'Just like a feather, Alexei!' he congratulated himself, and climbed to the top of the hummock on his right. The sight of sweeping marshlands, marred only by a line of pylons, filled him with pleasure but he did not forget he was a hostile intruder perpetrating an undeclared act of war. This was enemy territory.

Grechko knew that he would have to remain hidden until the inevitable search was called off. The hunters would begin in the wreckage of the giant B-52 tanker, assuming the possibility of a mid-air collision, but they would also dispatch light aircraft and helicopters for a ground sweep of the surrounding area.

They will be looking for my remains, he thought; not for me. If I were in their place that is what I would do. If they find nothing, they will believe I have aborted and run for home. There is no reason for them to think that I am flying a vertical take-off fighter, for logic would dictate the use of the fastest strike aircraft possible, and the Yakovlev is certainly not that. 'If,' he said aloud, 'they know anything at all!'

With a tight grin on his face he scrambled down the hummock, brushing the coarse grass with his hands as he descended. A startled rabbit bolted down a hole and Grechko's face creased happily. 'Ha! my fine friend, now I shall enjoy something better than the tasteless slabs I am supposed to survive on.'

Dragging a branch behind, he made his way back to the concealed fighter and unclipped a small calibre automatic, fitted with a fixed silencer, from the survival pack. Patiently, he sat behind the curtain of green foliage and watched the dip.

Rabbits popped from the warren in twos and threes, sniffing uncertainly at the air, bewildered by the alien smell of aviation fuel. Grechko pumped five shots in rapid succession into the nearest group. One died instantly, another, its spine damaged, spun in circles. Swiftly he dispatched the stricken animal.

Once again he covered his tracks and, back in his green shelter, skinned one rabbit and hung the other. Disjointing the carcass, he placed the pieces in one of the chemically heated containers from the survival kit, topped it up with water from the emergency flask and began to boil his breakfast.

With some surprise, he realized that he felt more content than he had done for years. All he needed now were answers to his questions : what was so important about one building in the heart of the British capital that the Kremlin was prepared to risk a dangerous international incident and an expensive warplane and pilot on its destruction? He knew now that they had chosen the wrong man. One of the young eagles, fired with zeal for the ultimate victory of the Worker State, would do the job without asking the questions – and probably die in the attempt with the name of Lenin on his lips.

Grechko barked a short sharp laugh. 'But you are the one who is here!' he said aloud, pulling roughly at the rabbit meat before tossing the bones down and climbing up into the aircraft. Settling himself into the seat, he strapped on his harness, and slept.

The hunters came at noon. A Wessex air-sea-rescue helicopter clattered directly over the copse coming in from the direction of the coast.

Grechko woke instantly, his pulse and heart-rate accelerating with the harsh clatter of the revolving blades. The downthrust of displaced air rocked the trees covering his refuge and he watched impotently as part of of his fabricated curtain of foliage fell to the ground. His hand rested momentarily on the ignition control for the engine but the Wessex clattered away. He breathed deeply. 'Go safely, my friends,' he muttered, steadier now.

His survival pack contained fifty cigarettes. Grechko waited ten minutes then lit one, feeling the tingle as the nicotine filtered through his body. They will come again, he thought. Once more at least – depending how much they know or suspect – but without signs of wreckage, or a crash landing, they will give up.

'One day, Alexei,' he said aloud, 'patience for one day.'

Throughout the afternoon, as he dozed lightly, he heard the telltale clatter of helicopters in the distance as they covered their search patterns and, once, a small aircraft circled high above, but there seemed to be no urgency now and finally, in the failing light, they were gone. Stiff-legged he heaved himself from the cockpit and dropped to the ground.

He had asked himself the questions – now it was time to find the answers.

2

Colin Hammond had left Number 10 in the early hours of the Wednesday morning, unaware of the penetration of British defences by the Russian fighter. He returned to his flat to find a letter pinned to his pillow. Before opening the envelope he checked the wardrobe and saw that the girl's clothes had gone. He breathed deeply, as if to get warmth to the cold pit of his stomach. For a while he sat staring at the envelope, debating if it were better to pretend she had never been there, or to know the reason for her leaving. At last he tore it open. There was a key taped to the notepaper and a single line of writing. 'You knew it would end this way,' was all it said. He stood up, placed the key in his pocket, and flushed the note down the lavatory.

In the living room he poured himself a stiff whisky and sipped it while he checked every detail of his plan to deceive Colonel Jonathan Fraser. Then he went around the flat and destroyed all evidence that the girl had ever existed, wiping her from his mind like chalk from a blackboard.

The police driver rang his door-bell at 8.45. Hammond was dressed and ready. They drove to the London headquarters of the Special Air Service in Chelsea where his warrant card gave him immediate access to a young colonel, who, although only medium height and almost bone-thin, exuded a frightening physical and mental self-assurance.

Colonel Grenville seemed mildly impressed by the letter, bearing the signature of the Prime Minister, but halfway through his reading his cold eyes looked up with frank hostility at the policeman. Hammond knew that he had reached Fraser's name. The letter which ordered every help to be given in the destruction of the mercenaries and their leader was placed on the desk and the SAS man looked at Hammond without expression.

'I wonder,' Hammond said forthrightly, 'whether I have come to the right place.'

Grenville placed both hands flat on the desk, his fingers square ended and calloused on the edges.

'Right place. Wrong man!' he said flatly. 'However! If this has to be done – and I suppose someone will be found to do it – we would prefer the job came to us.'

'What is it about Fraser that makes him so bloody special?' Hammond exclaimed, his anger suddenly rising.

The officer turned a hand palm upwards.

'A man is only "special" because other men make him so. With Colonel Fraser that was all too easy. He is a leader of men.' He picked up the letter, then tossed it down again. 'If he had gone into politics, it would be his signature on that letter. I am not exaggerating.'

'But you will help me?'

'You?'

'The authorities.'

'As I said. If the job has to be done, we would prefer to do it.'

'He's sick. You know that, don't you? There's shrapnel in his brain and it is bound to have affected the mind.'

'In other men perhaps. Not Colonel Fraser.'

'Why not! Why not Fraser?' Hammond was exasperated.

'You cannot judge one man by another. He is Fraser. He *is*. He *exists*. Look! How can a man, whom you maintain is demented, plan an operation like that? How can he recruit men to perform it successfully, against all the odds, and have worked out a bargaining counter that has the Prime Minister of Great Britain jumping around like a rabbit in a bag? Or are you going to tell me that it really is the lives of the hostages that's causing this furore!'

'How much do you know?' Hammond asked.

'I read the papers.'

'Then you'd better know the truth. But it stays in this room. I want your assurance on that.'

The SAS officer nodded.

'You have it.'

Hammond explained exactly what he had heard that first night in the Cabinet room; then went on to describe the equipment and the decomposing bodies in the cellars of the manor, Dr Hoffman's assessment of the depth to which the men had been brainwashed and his opinion that a fight to the death was the only possible outcome, unless the African government gave in.

'But *you* think there is another way,' the officer said, obviously disturbed.

'I'm convinced there is.' Hammond took out his sheaf of notes and moved around the desk. 'This is what we have to do,' he said urgently. 'And we don't have much time!'

The newspaper which carried the headline 'The Wolf in the Russian Lair' that morning was one of the tabloids, but the other national dailies were no less dramatic. The editors had no choice but to make the Fraser legend and the location of the siege the main angle to the story, for the Soviet government refused bluntly to release any details on the hostages. Reporters badgered their diplomatic contacts ceaselessly but met with nervous silence. It was obvious to Fleet Street that there was a cover-up operation. Sources inside the British government claimed they knew nothing and Number 10 simply repeated the original statement. 'Colonel Fraser's demands remain the same. The lives of the Russian hostages for the release of the British mercenaries imprisoned in Africa.'

Then BBC radio released the news that the Soviet Foreign Minister had arrived in Africa and that a statement by the Kremlin was expected within the next twenty-four hours.

At Kensington Palace Gardens, Jonathan Fraser heard the broadcast and went immediately to the room where the hostages were held.

'I have some news for you,' he told the Military Attaché. 'Your government have sent its Foreign Minister to Africa. It seems they are finally taking me seriously.'

'I do not believe this. They would not negotiate with the Africans,' Davydov retorted.

'The news was on the radio. Why should the BBC lie?'

The Military Attaché dismissed the question with an angry

wave of his hand, wincing with pain from his gunshot wound.

'They will do nothing! You are a fool to believe otherwise. Colonel, we are dead – all of us. The archives have been broken into – correct? The traitor Lashkova has helped you and you have studied the files. That is enough.' He paused. 'Is it true you shot one of your own men? I overheard some talk between the others.'

'Yes. The man attempted to contact the British Secret Service. That was directly against my orders and it would have broken my word to your President.'

'I admire you. You have integrity. There is little left these days. But it does not matter, they will kill us anyway.'

Fraser smiled.

'Who? Your people or mine?'

Davydov settled himself back in the chair with a sigh, rubbing his wound.

'Colonel Fraser. You are a military man not a politician. You understand problems of a strategic and logistical nature but you cannot begin to understand how the mind of a politican works. A politician has no loyalties – except to himself. I have known some who, in their madness to stay in power, have bitten their own limbs off – metaphorically speaking. What you have done is unforgivable. You have challenged their power – made them appear stupid and incompetent.'

'Which they usually are!' Fraser interrupted.

'Granted. But they are powerful and they are not afraid of using that power. You know how politicians survive? I shall tell you. They rely on secrets! Without secrets there are no problems. Without problems no need for power cliques. You have stolen secrets – you have the knowledge that gives them their power. Ergo, you must be destroyed. We too, because we are tainted by your wolf's breath.' Davydov smiled and pointed to a chair. 'Sit down for one moment, Colonel, and I will give you a story. I heard your men call you the Wolf. This I believe is a device you cold English use when you wish to show affection or bestow honour. A special name singled out for one person. Am I right?'

Fraser nodded.

'Then this story will interest you particularly,' the Russian continued. 'I am what the Party calls "rehabilitated". In the sixties I was purged along with numerous other officers, and was sent to Siberia. You have heard all the stories about Siberia, Colonel, so I shall say no more, except that they are true, but that memory dulls. Hence the experience was far worse than recollection allows. The one thing you are not told is that there is widespread collaboration between prisoners and guards. This is logical because, although there for different reasons, both are inside the same perimeter fence and suffer the same weather conditions. In short, they have all been sent to Siberia. Of course, prisoners don't eat as well as their guards, nor do they stay quite as warm but that is merely a matter of privilege – the fact remains the same – Siberia is the common environment. So! You have the more privileged and the less privileged all thrown in together. In such a close environment, Colonel, things are known by both groups. Weakness, political standpoints, things like this. Because of this, certain concessions are made and certain secrets remain secret. In Siberia, food cannot always get through so, inevitably, hoarding took place by the guards and a sizeable secret store was built up. Unfortunately for them we found out and could have given them away to a visiting Commissar – food hoarding is a capital offence against the State, especially when that food is State food. But we said nothing, we merely let the guards know we were aware of their secret. A compromise ensured that a percentage of the food would be given to us when times got really bad.

'One day, in the grip of winter, a Siberian grey wolf, driven by hunger, penetrated the camp and discovered the food in an outhouse. Shall I tell you what happened, Colonel? Prisoners and guards hounded that animal to the death, following its tracks across the wastes of snow until it was finally killed. Only then did we realize that we were miles away from the camp! The barriers had been thrown down in the chase after the common enemy. Be very careful, Colonel, that certain barriers are not going down at this moment to ensure your destruction. I tell you this because I, and all of us here, wish to live. Use your judgement very carefully because our lives may depend on it.'

Fraser rose from the chair.

'Don't worry. I'm a very careful man. Rest now. I'll keep you informed of developments.'

Johnson Cornwell stood guard over the hostages and as Fraser passed on the way out he stopped him.

'They're getting a bit short in the pantry, sir. It wasn't stocked for anything like this.'

Fraser frowned.

'Doesn't matter to us, because of the iron rations, but I really wasn't expecting to hold this many hostages. If there hadn't been that trouble out in the forecourt, two-thirds of these people could have got away. All right. Go easy on what's left and I'll see what we can do.'

There had been no change in the defensive positions around the building since the strike on the Monday. The small force had its standing orders and stuck to them. Every contingency, even an assault by helicopter-borne troops, had been taken into account. Fall-back positions were settled and barricaded and every man was primed to act singly or as part of the unit in the defence of the building.

Fraser completed his tour and descended to the basement to check for signals from Moscow. As he entered Sammy Cohen glanced up and shook his head. Wearily he pulled the head-phones off.

'Nothing, sir. I've got the direct link from Moscow hooked up through the print-out so I won't miss anything but the whole lot might just as well be switched off for all the action we're getting.'

'Then we'd better give them a little taste of what to expect if they don't move a little faster. Where's Major Stratton?'

'Resting, sir,' said Cohen without expression.

Fraser checked his watch.

'Well, he's entitled to his break the same as the rest of us. If he comes in, ask him to wait here for me. I'm going up to the roof to see if there's any word from Roberts.' He knew better than to ask where the Russian girl was but, as long as it suited his purpose, Stratton could have her.

In a tiny room at the top of the house that was usually used by the night-staff between shifts, Stratton sat on the edge of a narrow metal bed, head bowed, his dark hair falling over his face. The room had no windows. It might have been night or day or, to him, some period in between which has no normal measurement in time. The loneliness of the dream he had experienced at the manor had returned to him. It was, he knew, a turning point; he was beginning to come face to face with himself.

'Are you cold?' Katrina said, touching the skin of his back.

He shook his head. She lay naked on the bed, her body spreadeagled, her legs stretched out to the bottom corners, one hand still gripping the iron bed-rail behind her head. A fine sheen of perspiration covered her body.

'You have taken what you wanted – I have given all that is possible for me to give. It was as never before. Do you want more than this? I am not debased by your lust, or your power over me.'

She pulled herself up, her breasts pressed against him as she placed both hands on his shoulders. Stratton closed his eyes, lifting his head slightly in response to her touch.

Without turning, he put his hands on hers. 'If it were that – and only that – then I would be the animal you believe I am.'

Gently she put her lips to his skin. 'Look at me,' she whispered. 'Turn around and look at me. Where you are now is cold, find your warmth in me. But don't spend yourself inside me with the heat of your body only. I want you, but I want you to see beyond another empty face.'

Turning, he released her hands slowly and put his on her breasts, cupping them, his eyes lowered to her. Then, without raising his eyes, he lifted his face so that the brush of their lips became a kiss, as if the motive had never been there – an accident and yet a purposeful action.

She stared at his face as he moved into her. Then, as he felt the soft scream working its way through her body, his eyes suddenly opened and he clamped a hand over her mouth. Gently at first, and then harder, she bit into the flesh of his palm but the sound remained locked inside. His dark eyes widened as if in shock or pain, and his entire body shuddered. Then, still staring down at her, he collapsed.

With her arms clasped tight around him Katrina held his body, bearing the weight without a murmur of protest.

From somewhere in the building – it could have come from anywhere – Fraser's voice called.

173

'Paul! Come down to the radio room and bring Miss Lashkova with you. I need her advice.' He called again but this time from outside the door. His voice was flat. 'Roberts's channel has gone dead. We'll have to write him off.'

'You asked for our protection, Miss Lashkova,' Fraser said, 'and the time has come when you must confirm your position in all this. I intend to broadcast selected information which will put pressure on the Kremlin but will not harm them to any great degree.'

'Domestic intelligence?' she asked, looking him straight in the eye.

'International. Not policy though, that could be harmful in the future. How about military strengths in an area not directly concerned with Europe?'

Katrina thought for a moment, then went into the archives. Fraser raised his grey eyebrows at Stratton who gave a quick nod and followed her. Five minutes later he returned holding a thick sealed file and followed by Katrina.

'Soviet military strength, Far East,' he said.

'Is this up to date?' Fraser asked the girl as she came in behind Stratton.

She shrugged.

'It is possible that the Americans have some of it from the satellite pictures or their field agents but if it is put over the air, then it will confirm their own reports. It may not damage, but it will frighten.'

Fraser agreed.

'Put together a selection of facts under the headings. Strategic. Army and navy. Time it so that we transmit no longer than fifteen minutes. Understood?'

'I understand, Colonel.'

She began processing the documents through the Telekrypt machine using the key-code for deciphering the latest material. Fraser stood at her shoulder as the displays came up on the small screen.

'Some of this is domestic,' he interrupted.

'Strategically yes!' she said, turning her face up to him. 'But classed as Far Eastern. If you wish to frighten the Kremlin you must work from the Soviet borders.'

Fraser tugged at his moustache.

'Are you sure that this information is already known to the Americans?'

'I cannot swear to it, but a threat that has no teeth to it will make them believe you do not know which is the primary material. Then they will feel safe. If you mean to make them fear you then your first shot should be heard around the world. That is a Western saying I think.'

Fraser gave his crooked smile.

'It is also a Western saying that it is excellent to have a giant's strength, but it is tyrannous to use it like a giant!'

Her eyes became serious.

'How long will you stay a giant, Colonel? Another day? Two? Time is your enemy.'

'We'll use it,' Fraser said firmly, then turned to Sammy Cohen.

'Transmit when she's finished and make sure it goes out slow enough for the listening posts to get the full text.' He looked into Stratton's dark eyes, then closed his own as pain lanced through his head.

Karamurzel US Air Force base in Turkey is a sprawling complex covering four square miles. Its most prominent feature is an enormous circular construction of steel girders and interlocking struts, known as the Elephant Cage. Underground, below this structure, are some of the most powerful radio receivers in the world. This CIA monitoring station is primarily for the interception of Soviet military signals concerning the status and operation of their missile and nuclear-strike bomber bases and is a vital link in the chain of distant Early Warning stations feeding information back to the US from agents within the Soviet Union and monitoring radio traffic into Russia. That Wednesday, an uncoded message was received direct from London, the signal was strong enough for the complete text to be recorded clearly:

REPORT. AZ/4116ST   MOST SECRET.
DATA ORIGIN. MARSHAL KARASHIMOV.
   COMMANDER FAR EASTERN SECTOR
DISTRIBUTION. COLONEL NIKOLAI DAVYDOV.

SUBJECT. ARMED FORCES STRENGTH (FAR EAST)
STRATEGIC

IRBM sites near Vladivostok, Chita and Karaganda. SS-X-20s on Kamachatka peninsula.

Ballistic missile submarines currently based in Far East include; 8 Yankee, 3 Hotel 11, 12 Echo 11. 8 Golf 1 and 11. 5 Juliet and 4 W Twin Cylinder.

Nuclear hardened command, control and communications headquarters in Mongolia. References Grid JYT/C23 Command Schedule.

Movement to Far-Eastern sector MiG squadrons 84 and 76 (Vladivostok) Aircraft type MiG 23 Flogger. 16 Backfire Bombers.

ARMY

45 Divisions (7 armoured). 3 armoured and 6 mechanized infantry divisions in Mongolia. Deployment also on rivers : Ussuri and Amur. Modernization imminent. Equipment standard below Eastern Europe. Only 15 Divisions at Category 1, full strength full equipment. Remainder at Category 2, three-quarter strength, complete combat vehicle establishment.

NAVY

750 vessels based on Vladivostok. 200 Nakhodka. 543 Sovetskaya, 120 Gavan. 320 Magadan and Petropavlovsk. New bases open; Korakor. Sakhalin Island. Pacific Fleet current complement 10 Cruisers. 80 Destroyers. 120 Submarines. 100 Minesweepers. 35 Osas. 40 River Patrol craft. 38 Amphibious. 15 Intelligence.
MESSAGE ENDS

The two CIA operatives on duty looked at each other unable to believe what they had in their hands.

'Too rich for our blood!' one said, and lifted the telephone.

3

From 10 a.m. that morning, men had been hard at work transforming the Cabinet room at 10 Downing Street. The complete model of Kensington Palace Gardens was transported from Hertfordshire to Westminster and set up again on the green baize table cover.

The Prime Minister walked in, smiling briefly at the workers

– policemen under their overalls. Two older men, wearing over-coats, were checking the model against Polaroid shots taken at the manor. Satisfied, they placed the photographs on the table and left, nodding deferentially as they passed.

'Everything as it was, sir,' one said.

'My thanks,' he replied.

As they disappeared, an RAF officer put his head around the door and rapped the panelling.

'Come in,' the Premer said, turning. 'Ah! The aerial shots. Would they have any idea these were being taken?'

'Absolutely none, sir. Far too high. Lucky there was a break in the weather for a few hours.'

'Yes. Let's hope the luck continues that way. Thank you for these. Goodbye.'

The officer saluted, leaving the Prime Minister gazing at the model and shaking his head.

'What a man,' he murmured. 'What a mind!' Then sadly, 'And what a tragedy we have to destroy both.'

He walked out through the french windows into the garden and sat on a bench, lighting his pipe slowly and deliberately, leaning back and savouring tranquillity amidst all the bustle and the shuffling for power.

'Prime Minister,' a voice said, and he broke from his musings to look into the face of Colin Hammond.

'Sorry to disturb you, sir. This is Colonel Grenville of the SAS.'

The Prime Minister rose to his feet, taking in the man as he did so. My God! he thought, the fellow frightens *me*. How on earth do we create these people? Where do we find such extra-ordinary men? Do they have this aura about them before we get hold of them or do we put it there with the training?

'Colonel Grenville,' he said. 'Tragic situation. I wish we could have met in happier circumstances, but we must do what has to be done.'

The Cabinet sat in their usual chairs, but the Prime Minister stood by the fireplace, ready to explain to the men who ruled the country the realities behind what they were going to see on their television screens and read in their newspapers.

'I feel it is better that what is said in here today is not noted down, gentlemen. Only a very few of you know the full facts behind the siege at the Soviet Embassy and I shall not apologize for that. Until now there has been no need for the entire Cabinet to be informed.'

There was an outburst of protest.

'I understand your feelings, but protests must wait. In a moment I shall be bringing two men into this room. One a policeman, the other a soldier, a rather special kind of soldier. We will treat this as a briefing rather than a formal Cabinet meeting. I realize all this is very unusual, but then so are the present circumstances.' He pressed a button on the mantelpiece, the doors opened and Hammond entered with Grenville.

'Chief Superintendent Hammond of the Special Branch and Colonel Grenville of the Special Air Service. Gentlemen, Her Majesty's Cabinet. Please begin, Chief Superintendent, and let's have it all – from the start. Some of us here are not aware of the full facts.'

Hammond moved to one end of the room where a large easel and board were covered by a white cloth. He removed this and revealed a number of blown-up photographs pinned to the wood. A lamp had been fixed to the top of the board illuminating the faces clearly. Hammond cleared his throat.

'Last week,' he began, 'it came to our notice that a number of known mercenaries – British mercenaries – were showing an interest in the Soviet Embassy.'

'*Last week!*' a minister interrupted angrily. 'You mean you knew this was going to happen? By God, we deserve to lose the election if this is the sort of cover-up that's going on !'

'*I will not have talk like that!*' the Premier erupted. 'This officer had the very leanest shred of suspicion as his only basis for action and *no evidence*. No evidence at all ! Go on, Chief Superintendent, and my apologies on behalf of my colleagues.'

'As the Prime Minister says,' Hammond continued unperturbed by the outburst, 'we had no evidence whatsoever. If it had not been for the sharp eye and the phenomenal memory of one young man we would not have identified any of Fraser's force. Certainly we would not have been able to put together the facts we now have on their rather special training.' He nodded to Grenville, who walked to the opposite end of the

Cabinet table and together they removed the cover from the model.

'This is what we found set up on a billiards table in a house in Hertfordshire.' He passed down the table a set of large colour prints taken at the manor. 'You will see from these photographs that this scale model of the Embassy location was not the only thing we found. There were also four bodies in an advanced state of decomposition. I hope you gentlemen have strong stomachs, otherwise I suggest you avoid looking at those particular shots.'

Hammond waited for the noise to ebb.

'In the house we found two rooms set up for a mind-conditioning process. Brainwashing if you prefer.'

'You mean that Fraser's men are brainwashed?'

'That's correct,' the Prime Minister cut in. 'Those cells were inspected by an eminent psychologist whom we've used to set up these very techniques for our own ends. He not only confirms that Fraser's men are brainwashed, he has predicted the only way to get them out of the Embassy building. What were Dr Hoffman's words to you, Hammond?'

'He said, "We'll have to kill them all and pray that the cost is not too high in human lives." '

The Premier held his hand up.

'And here we come to the whole point of the meeting. Chief Superintendent Hammond has come up with a way to deceive Fraser into giving up the building and of course the hostages. But here, gentlemen, I have to reveal something to you which will make you understand why so much secrecy has been employed and why you have not all been fully informed. Colonel Fraser has threatened the Kremlin that he will begin broadcasting, uncoded, the contents of the intelligence archives in the KGB building which he is holding. Now some of you knew what was going on and I thank you for your confidence on this matter, but what none of you know is that Colonel Fraser began broadcasting that intelligence this morning. The transmission was picked up by Signals Intelligence who, in turn, informed me. I ordered them to shut down.'

He waited patiently for the uproar to settle.

'I can understand your protests. Free intelligence for the grabbing and we don't take advantage, but we're a responsible government dealing in *international* matters and it could be dangerous to exploit an incident such as this. The American President called me and told me that the CIA have also monitored the transmission and that they have recorded it. The information was military and quite potent, but no real damage has been done to the Soviets by its revelation. It stands to reason that Fraser will make sure that the next transmission will contain stronger meat. It is imperative that he is stopped – and soon.' He paused to relight his pipe. 'I have been in close contact with the Soviet President. He has approved Chief Superintendent Hammond's plan and has promised full and complete co-operation. He has also spoken with the American President and certain strategic arms concessions are to be made by the Russians at the next SALT talks in return for a full clamp-down on CIA and NATO monitoring of signals originating from this source in London. So perhaps Colonel Fraser has done some good after all. Now, Chief Superintendent, show us how you intend to solve this problem.'

Hammond, using a pointer, indicated the twelve photographs pinned to the board.

'These men are the mercenaries currently imprisoned in Africa. You must remember that this is what they looked like before they were imprisoned. According to our information their physical appearance has considerably deteriorated.' He put down the pointer and moved to the head of the Cabinet table. 'Immediately after this meeting, the press and television services will be informed that tomorrow evening these men will arrive at Heathrow Airport on board a Russian airliner. This is what will happen afterwards.'

Colonel Wesley Grenville moved forward from the shadow behind the bright light on the board and began speaking.

At the Special Branch safe-house in Battersea, Les Roberts was under heavy guard. He had been allowed to visit his mother in hospital and came away with the certain knowledge that she was on the verge of a cruelly painful death and that only drugs were keeping her alive. One thought filled his mind, until action became imperative. He was an intelligent man; he realized he was still being held at the house only because someone wanted his existence kept hidden.

Hammond was running a four-man guard on him, two in the room with him, and the others on the ground floor of the house. Roberts looked down from the window to the small patch of garden at the rear of the house. The earth was still waterlogged from the rain, the sun never touching it.

'I've been up all night,' he said to the two policemen. 'I want some sleep.'

The younger of the two nodded towards the bare floorboards. 'Go ahead. Nobody's stopping you.'

'My circulation's bad enough already with these chains on. If I fall asleep I'll lose my hands and feet.'

'No chance, mate. They're staying on. We've heard all about you.'

'Well, give me a blanket then, or something to put over me.'

The older man opened the door. 'Frank, there's a rug in the boot of the car. Bring it up. Our friend wants to take a nap.'

Roberts heard the front door open, then, after a few moments, slam, followed by feet pounding up the stairs. Three in the room, he thought. One of them must have keys to the manacles. He turned and, taking two quick steps, launched his body through the air in a perfect double-footed drop-kick at the centre of the opening door. The policeman's rib cage smashed as the feet connected. Roberts fell to the ground with a crash, rolling to absorb the impact, then, from the floor, thrust hard with chained feet at the exposed groin of the older of the two guards. He twisted again as the man screamed, clutched at his genitals, then fainted with the pain, vomiting unconsciously on the boards. The young officer in abject fear of the unarmed killer scrabbled under his jacket for the .38 revolver they had all been issued with. Roberts threw a chair at him knocking him against the wall, then went at him with his head, butting him three times in rapid succession between the eyes and the bridge of the nose. He pushed the man, face first, to the wall, wrenching the pistol from under his coat, then turned and fired three rounds through the woodwork of the open door. There was a yell and a thump on the stairs. Holding the revolver two-handed, he burst through on to the landing to find the fourth man halfway down the stairs, holding his foot, his face contorted.

'My fucking ankle's busted,' he said, not looking up.

The mercenary hopped down the stairs towards him and stuck the gun into his groin, pulling the hammer back.

'I'll blow it right off,' he said quietly. 'Where's the keys for these monkey-chains?'

The policeman shook his head and Roberts brought the edge of his hand down on the broken limb.

'Don't play heroes, I haven't got the time.'

'DS Wilson, the balding one – on a chain – belt to back pocket, Jesus, I'm going to pass out.'

'I'll help you,' Roberts said, and hit him with very little force behind the ear. The figure slid down the stairs.

He shuffled back into the room and found the keys in the pocket of the vomiting detective sergeant. In two minutes he had the chains off and moved around all the men, hitting them with an identical blow. Checking his clothes for blood, he entered the bathroom and dabbed at himself until he was clean, then stepping over the unconscious man on the stairs, lifted a raincoat off a hook in the hallway. He opened the door, studied the car outside, changed his mind and rifled the pockets of the policeman on the stairs for money. Finding a wallet he pocketed it, and ripped out the telephone connection on the wall. The car was unlocked, so he smashed the radio and immobilized the engine.

At a steady pace he ran the length of the street of condemned houses and walked towards Battersea Bridge. A taxi pulled up at his signal.

'Guy's Hospital,' he said. 'Can you make it quick, chum, my mum's ill.'

The taxi pulled up in front of Guy's and Les Roberts paid him off, noticing at the same time a flower stall by the gates. He checked the money he had taken. There was enough.

He entered the hospital with an armful of flowers and the nurse on the reception desk stopped him.

'Visiting hours are over,' she told him.

He looked at her pleadingly.

'It's my mum, Mrs Roberts, Elsie Roberts, she's got cancer. My mum's dying, miss. I tried to get here at the right time but couldn't make it. Give us a couple of minutes, please. Just to give her these. I won't be more than a couple of minutes, honest.'

'What ward is she in, Mr Roberts?'

'They put her in a room on her own – I know the way.'

'A couple of minutes, no more. If you're longer I'll have to get the sister to bring you away.'

Roberts nodded thankfully and made his way to the second floor. His mother was laying raised against the pillow, her eyes closed and her skeletal face numbed by the drugs.

'Mum,' he whispered. 'It's me, Les. Brought you some flowers.' Gently he took her hand which was reduced to bones and tendons by the disease.

She opened her eyes and he turned away from the pain in them.

'They let you come back, son.'

'It wasn't anything bad, Mum. They thought I was someone else. No problem – really.'

'You should've stayed in the real army, Les; your dad did.'

'I'm in a real army, Mum. You mustn't worry about me.'

The thin face fell slowly to the side, the dry lips curling inwards.

'Can't they take the pain away, Mum?' Roberts said, tears starting to his eyes. She shook her head with a tiny weak movement.

'Here, smell these flowers, they're beautiful.'

Roberts placed the flowers against her face and with a quick chopping stroke snapped the frail neck. He adjusted the shawl around her and stood up weeping.

'Goodbye, Mum,' he whispered through the tears.

He took the Underground as far as Marble Arch and from there he jogged steadily towards Notting Hill Gate, until he was forced to a halt by the sheer mass of people. With determination he forced his way through their seemingly endless ranks and eventually stood staring at the black railings guarding Kensington Palace Gardens.

Soldiers stood beside a Saracen armoured car, sipping from mugs, whilst the police held the crowds back behind wooden barriers. Roberts eased his way through to the front until his hard hands came to rest on the thick wooden rails. He stood for an hour, patiently watching for one thing he knew would happen. The gates would open and the gatekeeper's wife would come through to collect the cups from the soldiers and give others to the policemen. He had watched that same process many times from his spy-nest.

Then it happened. Les Roberts vaulted the barrier and charged at the gates, felling two policemen and the woman as he threw it open. He ran as he'd never run in his life, zigzagging across the wide avenue and stumbling once in a pile of wet leaves.

A young lieutenant yelled at him to stop, but he heard nothing except the sound of his lungs and thudding heart. Above him, against the afternoon skyline, he saw the yellow flame and to him it was all that existed in the universe. Something snatched at his body, spinning him in a full circle and with surprise he found his face against cold stone. He moved his body, searching for the Torch, but the world had turned upside down and the sky was below him with the road above. Some huge irresistible force slammed into him, pushing him further along the road and he thought it was raining because the ground was wet and he could hear the pattering against the black tarmac.

'No good lying down,' he said aloud, but, although he had got to his feet, his body was still stretched on the road spraying blood from a severed artery. In his mind he began walking, slowly at first but then faster as he saw, on the rooftop, men waving, their mouths opening and closing silently. Next to the Torch he saw Jonathan Fraser, an immovable figure against the sky, raise one arm in an impeccable salute.

'It's a real army,' Les Roberts said, and died.

4

The Prime Minister sat with Colonel Grenville in the private dining room at 10 Downing Street. In silence they completed their meal, Hammond's half-eaten food a testimony to his hurried exit.

'Why would a man throw his life away like that?' the Premier asked sipping coffee.

Grenville put sugar in his cup before answering.

'He wouldn't consider he was throwing it away, sir. In effect the brainwashing technique was an order he was unable to disobey. What Roberts did was to follow it through to the end.'

'And to kill his own mother? Hammond told me that every penny he had was put into her treatment. The bank records confirm it. So why kill her and then get himself shot, dammit?'

'I think he realized that no amount of money was going to cure her, which left him with nothing. Except the one final pull – Jonathan Fraser. You've never met the man, sir; if you had I think you might be more aware of the motivation behind all of this.'

'Yet he still had to buy them with a paper promise – and condition them to carry out his commands.'

Grenville picked up Fraser's legacy document from the table. 'He didn't buy them, he was willing it to them. There is a difference. Hammond didn't say if he'd traced the money, did he, sir?'

The Prime Minister shook his head.

'We know that Werner Holdings is based in the Channel Islands where company laws do not require directors to be named. My guess is that Werner have registered offices in Switzerland – or some other place equally impossible to get information from when you're talking about large sums of money. How wealthy was Fraser?'

'I know he had some directorships in the city and made a bit out of Oman and the Gulf. Otherwise . . .' Grenville shrugged.

'No, we've checked all that thoroughly. There's a few thousands of course, but if there's big money it's not in the United Kingdom, or anywhere we can get our hands on it. Your Wolf is far too canny for that.'

'But your people are still digging?'

The Prime Minister stood up and eased his back with his hands.

'Oh they're digging all right, but don't think I'm counting on it. No! I'm afraid everything is in your hands, Grenville and I'd like to ask you a very direct question.'

Grenville nodded.

'Fraser is something more than an ordinary man in your eyes

– that is very plain. I'll ask my question once only. Your word will do. Colonel, do you have any doubt whatever in your mind that your regiment is the right one for this very personal task?'

Grenville stared him out.

'This is family, sir; we will take care of our own problems – no matter how deep it cuts. Personal loyalties must sometimes be sacrificed to circumstance.'

'Good. That is what I hoped to hear.' He checked his watch. 'Now, Grenville, you must excuse me. I'm afraid I have a rather important call waiting for me.'

'We'll do the job, sir,' Grenville said. 'But don't expect us to enjoy it.'

'I don't expect that for one minute.'

They walked together to the lobby, then the Prime Minister entered his office alone and lifted the heavy red telephone.

'Moscow,' he said.

In the Kremlin the Soviet President took the receiver off the hot-line telephone.

'It seems we are both working late, Prime Minister,' he said. 'What news do you have of our aircraft?'

'None, I'm afraid,' the answer echoed along the line. 'Our tracking stations had him but lost him shortly afterwards.'

'It is an interesting thought, don't you think?'

'What is, Mr President?'

'Why, that we are able to penetrate your defences with so small an effort!'

'Mr President. We would appreciate having the name of the pilot. It is possible the aircraft has crashed in some remote area. Perhaps the man is injured and is being given aid by people who are unaware of who or what he is.'

'In a tiny island such as yours?' The Soviet President laughed. 'One of your men could easily do this in the Ukraine or some other area of Russia, but not the reverse I think!' His humour evaporated as he considered for a moment whether the giving of a name could have any ill-effects. He spoke again.

'Commander Alexei Grechko is the pilot. If you do find him somewhere, Prime Minister, please return him to us. He is a valued officer and very experienced.' Again he broke into laughter at the thought.

'What of the Africans, Mr President?' the British Premier said, ignoring the harsh laugh.

'That is already arranged. An Ilyushin will deliver your cut-throats to London but, I must warn you, the Soviets will not look with favour upon any change in the agreement.'

'There will be no change. You have my word on that.'

'And our own private agreement?' The President's voice become hard. 'I hope you have not forgotten.'

'No,' the Premier replied curtly.

'That is good. I shall expect that certain men travelling in the Ilyushin will not be impeded in any way when they enter your country. Please ensure full diplomatic status.'

'It will be done.'

'Goodbye then, Prime Minister, I hope that tomorrow we will sleep more easily in our beds.'

Hammond was shown into the room where the Prime Minister sat gloomily pondering over his brandy.

'Ah, Hammond,' he said wearily. 'Sit down, tell me what happened.'

The policeman removed his raincoat and dropped heavily into a chair. 'Thank you, sir,' he breathed, gratefully accepting the offered drink. 'Shouldn't be drinking really, I'm still on call.'

'Nonsense,' the Premier replied. 'You've done your bit for the day. Let's make this a short discussion, then we can both get some sleep.'

'Jesus, they're good!' Hammond exclaimed. 'Roberts's body was still on the road when I arrived – they came out of the building in a stick of four men with one giant character to lift the body. We had one warning from the man on the roof – no announcement, just a burst of automatic fire across the road and the four dived out of the house using the cover available as if God had put it there for them. Then the big man came out and took the body inside.'

'There's nothing you could have done,' the Premier said.

'No, not while they have the hostages, but it makes me worry about tomorrow because they're still so damn sharp.'

'I suppose the cameramen took pictures?'

'Well, they got parts of it but it happened so quickly.'

'Another drink?' the Prime Minister asked, but Hammond

shook his head. 'What have you done with that young man –
the one who identified the mercenaries?'

The policeman smiled.

'Johnson? Oh he's fully employed at the moment, back at
the Yard, closeted with stacks of photographs being doctored
for press release in the morning. Glad to be away from here, sir;
the corridors of power had a habit of making him throw up.'

The Premier grinned. 'I know the feeling well, Chief Superintendent. Very well indeed.' He paused in contemplation, the
crushing weight of his secret deal with the Soviet President
resting heavily on his mind. 'You still insist on going up that
road yourself? I really don't see that it is necessary.'

Hammond nodded firmly.

'I'll use Fraser's radio-link to set up the exchange and tell
him that I shall personally administer our side. It is imperative
that the man believes we are ready to go through with it.'

'Then you must ensure that you are not caught in the middle
if something goes wrong. You're a policeman and not a trained
combat soldier. I would prefer you to withdraw after you have
established the basis of the exchange with Colonel Fraser.'

Hammond studied the politician for a moment in silence.

'I'll withdraw when my presence is no longer required, sir.'

The Premier looked up.

'I'm not implying that you are afraid of the risks, Hammond.
Far from it. But I feel that specialist tasks are best left to those
who are the specialists. You are a specialist in deduction and
I'd like to add that without your brain we'd still be in the throes
of this mess with little likelihood of a solution. Incidentally, the
part you've played will not go unrecognized, I can assure you of
that.'

Hammond rose from the chair.

'Thank you very much, sir, but let's leave the plaudits till
afterwards if you don't mind. Tomorrow is very much another
day.'

The Prime Minister shook his hand warmly, and Hammond
felt a wave of uneasiness break between them. The pronounced
warmth of the gesture had a distinct finality. 'I'm dying,' he
thought irrationally, 'and this is the last goodbye.'

He left 10 Downing Street but couldn't face the empty flat,
so found a restaurant and ate a solitary meal with too much

wine. In the background a guitarist sang quietly and he thought of the girl. Tomorrow seemed a future he had already lived through.

With that singleness of purpose which often precludes logic, Alexei Grechko struck out across the Norfolk marshes.

The nature of his mission suggested that its true purpose was either so secret that he could never hope to uncover it, or that it was linked to an event so public that he could not fail to see it. Censorship of the media was not common practice in Britain as it was in the Soviet Union, this he knew. If a critical situation existed and was being reported on, he could get the facts.

The night was his protection and he had to use the next few hours to their best advantage. Once again the survival kit had proved invaluable. A hand compass and a rubber-framed torch with a back-up set of batteries gave him direction and light. The skeletal pylons planted across the darkened countryside acted as signposts for his safe return to the aircraft and as indication of population areas beyond the marshes.

Within an hour of tramping, sodden-footed, through the wastelands, the high-voltage cables whining in the dark above him, he came to an unexpected halt. A square black shape at the base of one of the huge pylons made him switch off his torch instantly. Approaching carefully, he found a concrete blockhouse with a locked, metal reinforced door. For ten minutes he moved cautiously around the structure, searching for any sign of life inside. The blockhouse seemed empty.

Grechko moved away and tossed a handful of stones at the small metal-framed window, then waited once more.

'Wake!' he whispered impatiently, forcing himself to remain crouched in the wet grass as the cold seeped into him. Exasperated, he crunched across gravel chippings and placed his torch against the window. Inside, caught in the beam, were a series of dials and switches fixed to the far wall. Moving the beam, he saw a metal table and two folding chairs. Two more chairs, folded flat, leant against the right-hand wall. He unzipped one flying boot and, using it to protect his fist, he punched solidly at the window. The glass burst inwards, spraying gleaming needles over the floor.

Replacing his boot, he reached up to the low roof, his fingers gripping the rough-cast concrete, then swung legs first through the tight frame. The blockhouse was deserted but on the table was evidence that it was in daily use. Two enamelled mugs, one unwashed, stood on an open newspaper, brown circles across the print marking the passage of the tea drinker.

Grechko checked the paper with his torch, not daring to use the main lights in such an open area. It was dated the previous day. Sweeping the mugs to the floor he folded the paper over to the front page. Banner headlines screamed his answer.

'The Wolf in the Russian Lair.' Below it, less dramatically, 'The Siege Continues,' and 'Soviet President To Put Pressure On Africa.' Grechko read on, astounded.

My God! he thought. The Codes; the political information; the secrets! Archives full of them, built up through the years! Trained men, able to decipher and use what lay in those vaults, would be in a position of enormous and deadly power. Soviet spies all over the world could be in jeopardy. It must be the secrets they were after – why else hit the KGB building? Now he knew why the Kremlin were prepared to make an air-strike in the heart of the United Kingdom. No survivors could be allowed from that building.

He knew, too, that the *Kiev* would not return for him. A live victorious flyer would be an embarrassing diplomatic liability – a dead lunatic could be apologized for or simply denied. 'Commander Grechko . . . the strain of constant vigilance against imperialist aggression . . . the responsibility for his actions must lie with the West.' He was being used and discarded, but he was still a Russian.

He studied the photograph of Jonathan Fraser's lean face.

'Wolf?' he said. 'You certainly are that!'

In the last trailing hours of Wednesday night, the name of Alexei Grechko was being passed through computer banks for positive identification. Shortly after 2 a.m. on Thursday morning a full dossier had been compiled, listing Grechko as a Soviet naval commander (air) with meritorious active service in Korea, and both combat and training duties in the Vietnam conflict. By a stroke of luck a photograph was available, taking during an SIS trawl for Russian defectors at the height of the Soviet naval build-up in the Indian Ocean.

The dossier would be on the Prime Minister's desk by nine

o'clock that morning, but the essential information was put on the wire to police and army units still engaged in the search for the missing flyer. The information was also distributed to the Ministry of Defence. A loose security net began to form through the passing hours of darkness but the authorities were convinced that they were searching for a crashed plane and a dead or injured pilot. It would take too long before someone remembered that the *Kiev* had been equipped with YAK 36 vertical take-off aircraft as well as its full complement of MiGs.

The Torch burned brightly next to the tower of the radio antennae as Jonathan Fraser stood watching dawn break.

'I have almost won,' he thought, then smiled, knowing that there is no such thing as near victory. Victory was like death. Absolute.

Feeling weary for the first time since the conception of his plan, he left the rooftop and made his way down through the building to the office of the KGB Resident.

Stewart-Smith's body had been removed and now lay next to Roberts's in another room, but, as Fraser sat down, traces of dried blood were still there on the desk.

With a quick movement, he swallowed more painkillers to ease the burning fire at the back of his brain, laid out the copies of his legacy and meticulously added the agreed signature to each. He blotted the papers carefully, leant back on the chair and placed them in envelopes.

As light filtered through the windows, he slept, his hands stretched out on the desk.

Around the building, his strike force changed watches quietly, while in the small bedroom Paul Stratton and Katrina Lashkova lay together with that awareness of each other which comes with the inception of love.

It was a new day, heralding a beginning or an end.

5

Colin Hammond awoke before Thursday's sun rose behind heavy grey clouds. He had slept badly, the wine upsetting his stomach and causing his head to ache. Gingerly he got out of bed and walked through to the kitchen, pouring himself a glass of orange juice from the fridge.

'Oh hell,' he moaned, leaning against the refrigerator, 'all I need is a bloody hangover.'

Forcing himself into action, he ran a bath, making the water as hot as his body could bear, to try and sweat the alcohol out. After pulling the plug he let the shower unit turn his muscles rigid as they reacted to the ice-cold spray.

In the bedroom he dressed meticulously, taking particular care that his underwear was clean and his socks without holes. The sensation of living his childhood again filled him with a strange haunted feeling like an old dream with details forgotten but still retaining its aura of reality.

In the kitchen the kettle shrilled and he absently made himself a mug of coffee to charge his system for the cold start to the day. The toaster threw bread, burnt dark brown, up at him and he buttered the slices, eating them as he put on his overcoat.

Outside in the street, he threw a crust to an early rising pigeon, then began walking along the Horseferry Road, ready to cross London without the aid of a police car, and within minutes a drifting taxi pulled over to the kerb as he hailed it. The driver raised his brows over tired eyes.

'Where'll it be, mate? Not too far, eh? I'm on me way 'ome.'

Hammond told him the address and ignored the protest as he got into the back. They arrived at the Embassy gates just as Colonel Fraser left the rooftop.

Evidence of the crowds was still on the street; litter, dropped wherever people had been standing, had blown in drifts against the Park railings.

Hammond walked up to the soldiers guarding the rear entrance to Wellington Terrace and produced his warrant card.

'Anything happen overnight?' he asked and received a morose shake of the head as an answer. 'Right. I'll be up there, in the flat, if I'm needed.'

Mounting the iron steps, he repeated the routine with his warrant card for the benefit of a middle-aged constable who barred his way. Inside the flat he sat down as he imagined Roberts had done and sighted along the avenue with the night-vision glasses. For a while he toyed with these, then checked the radio, using the instruction-booklet he had obtained from the Ministry of Defence. In five minutes he had contacted the rooftop.

'My name is Hammond,' he said slowly, unsure of the signal strength. 'Chief Superintendent, Special Branch. I want to you to bring Colonel Fraser to the radio. I have a message regarding the African mercenaries.'

He waited, watching the rooftop through the trees, then saw an erect figure step out from a small doorway and crouch down.

'Fraser here,' a voice came through. 'What have you to say to me?'

The policeman could feel the animosity over the air-waves.

'Colonel Fraser? Chief Superintendent Colin Hammond. I need to talk to you. Can we arrange a meeting? I will come alone and unarmed.'

'Any talking can be done over this radio-link.'

'I suggest that this is not secure, Colonel,' Hammond replied.

'There is a red scrambler button on the set. Hold it while you are speaking.'

'Right. I have it.'

'What have you to say to me?' Fraser repeated coldly.

'Colonel,' Hammond protested. 'I did not kill your man.'

'He'd been tortured, Hammond. I saw the marks on his body.'

Hammond's anger boiled over.

'But I didn't tamper with his mind, Colonel!'

'Ah! So Dr Hoffman deduced that?'

'He didn't have to. Roberts took us down to the manor. You didn't bother to cover any evidence.'

'I wondered what had happened to Hoffman,' Fraser said with satisfaction. 'Of course if he came with you, he'd know that there is nothing he can do. Correct?'

Hammond remained silent.

'Correct,' Fraser said. 'Come on, Hammond, I'm becoming bored with this. Out with it. What about the exchange?'

Hammond set his notebook before him on the floor.

'Do you have a television set there, Colonel?'

'Two.'

'Good. We have an ETA on the Soviet airliner carrying the

mercenaries from Africa – seven o'clock this evening.'

'I know; the Kremlin swallowed their pride and sent me a signal containing that information.'

'Hardly their pride, Colonel, they simply want to stop you producing another programme of their secrets.'

'But they're putting on a television show for me, am I right?' Fraser asked with acid humour.

'We have arranged complete coverage of the landing and the transfer of the twelve men through immigration to a coach, then straight to you here. There will be a BBC-TV camera crew inside the coach, transmitting pictures throughout the journey.'

'One moment, Hammond! I would prefer that the men get straight into the coach from the aircraft.'

'So would I, Colonel; it would make the security aspect much easier, but those men might be carrying all kinds of disease and the health people insist that they go through a check-up.'

'How long?' Fraser demanded, his voice heavy with suspicion.

'They're putting on a special team to give them the jabs and whatever else so that we can get the men through quickly.'

'How long, Hammond?'

'I can't say for sure. Perhaps half an hour.'

Fraser was silent for a moment and Hammond lifted the glasses to the rooftop but the colonel was hidden behind the balustrade.

'You could do anything in half an hour,' he came on again. 'I shall need a guarantee that the men who go in are the same as those who come out. Put television cameras in the medical unit.'

Hammond protested.

'I can't order the TV people about!'

'If you're running this operation, Chief Superintendent, then at this moment you've got as much power as you want – and you know it. Cameras inside the unit, and no curtains to be drawn over the examination cubicles. I don't give a damn if the populace is shocked at the sight of naked men. Those are my conditions.'

'I'll try.'

'You'll do more than try. You'll do it.'

Hammond agreed reluctantly.

'And, Hammond,' Fraser continued, 'pass this message on to your masters. One hint of a trick and a specially prepared recording of the most secret documents in the archives will be put on the air. A recording, mark you. This will continue to spill out highly classified material until you have killed everyone in the building. Then you will have the problem of getting past the sealed security doors to turn the tape off. If the Russians let you get through the front door, that is. Remember one thing, Hammond, anyone who enters this building is a threat to them.'

'I'm sure we can overcome that problem if it arises, Colonel, but I see no need to worry. We have no intention of tricking you. The Soviet Ambassador will officially take charge of the building once the exchange between the mercenaries and the hostages is over. The same coach that brings the mercenaries from the airport will take your men back there to board their flight out of the country.'

Again Fraser fell silent.

'I presume you accept the South African offer of sanctuary,' Hammond asked.

'I have discussed it with the Prime Minister. We accept,' Fraser said coldly.

'Good,' Hammond said. 'Well, it seems you've won, Colonel.'

'No, Chief Superintendent, I doubt if I have won, but your people have certainly lost. Goodbye.'

With that enigmatic statement the radio went dead.

'No, we haven't,' Hammond said to the tall figure on the rooftop as Fraser stood up and stared directly at the grubby window.

The policeman smiled and went in search of a telephone.

Grechko traced his way back across the marshes to his aircraft. As he topped the last rise he saw the copse which hid the YAK. The plane dripped with dew as he climbed to the cockpit and settled himself into the seat, strapping on the harness. He began a dummy run of flight and weapons checks; then, with these completed, plotted his course using the Thames as a mean guide.

He pictured the fighter above the river and his face broke

into a broad grin. 'Well, Alexei,' he said aloud, 'there's always a first time for everything!'

Setting the alarm on his wrist-watch, he dozed as the first birds of the morning began their chirping.

In London the Prime Minister was in conference with the Director General of the BBC and the Chairman of the Independent Broadcasting Authority. On his desk lay two typed letters signed by him. Below his signature on both, was a space for the name of the man before him.

The Premier explained exactly what had to be done, stressed its confidentiality and, after confirming that there were no forseeable problems, the letters were signed and the two men left.

The Prime Minister sat at his desk, unable to concentrate on the mundane day-to-day problems of government. Again and again the image of a rooftop manned by marksmen with high-powered rifles sprang to the front of his mind and he shook his head fiercely as if to rid himself of that knowledge and of the certainty of carnage to come.

Almost before he realized what he was doing he had drafted his letter of resignation. Perhaps he would never use it, but in some strange way, the very act of drafting it eased his conscience.

'*Mea culpa*,' he said aloud and locked the letter away.

An hour later, Colin Hammond, armed with the two letters signed that morning at Downing Street, met with the technical directors of the television authorities and laid out the second phase of his intricate plan of deception. He emphasized that no one should know what was to happen until the last moment. The strictest security had to be maintained, for any leak could end in disaster. The technical aspects had been hammered out and the split-second timing which would be required had been fixed, when he left the men to buy himself lunch.

The buzz of the crowded restaurant seemed like a distant and quite unreal noise inside his head. He noticed as he sipped his coffee that his hand was shaking madly. A woman at the adjacent table stared at him with disdain. Hammond smiled – she probably thought he was an alcoholic.

He paid his bill and walked out into the throng of Oxford Street, letting bodies thump into him as he strolled against the flow of people, fighting the tide of humanity which seemed to be going everywhere and nowhere at the same time.

A newstand caught his eye and he stopped to buy a paper. *'Imprisoned mercenaries freed'* ran the headline. 'Home Tonight.' Lower down and to the right, a smaller section ran a story titled, 'TV Coverage.'

'At last,' it began, 'the siege at the Soviet Embassy may be over. At this time details of the arrangements for the newly freed British prisoners are not available, but it has been confirmed that the entire operation is to be covered live on both BBC and ITV tonight. However sources say that if violence begins, as in the 1980 SAS operation at the Iranian Embassy in London, live transmission may be stopped to protect new counter-terror techniques. Whatever happens one thing is certain. Colonel Jonathan Fraser, the legendary ex-SAS commander who seems to have taken over from Carlos "The Jackal" Ramirez as the most wanted man of our time, is going to give the television companies their largest viewing figures this year.'

Hammond folded the paper and turned down Lower Regent Street, to where his driver waited in the police Rover.

'Heathrow bloody Airport,' he said. 'And use the siren.'

'All the way, sir?' the driver turned in surprise.

'That's right! Just to prove that we exist.'

The driver made a face in the mirror, switched the klaxon on and whipped the car into the traffic, leaving scorched rubber on the road.

High in the stratosphere, an Ilyushin jetliner streaked like a silver arrow leaving four contrails – and Africa – behind it.

Inside the pressurized cabin the freed mercenaries sat, each manacled to a Russian guard and restricted in even the smallest movements.

All twelve were underweight, with hair shaved to stubble and skin turned grey from prolonged incarceration. They were attended on the plane by a Russian physician who had done his best to improve their physical condition with vitamin injections, but in the time available the task was impossible. Nevertheless his orders were that the men should arrive in London looking reasonably fit. The only option left to him was cosmetics.

As the flight continued, two make-up artists set to work. Each

197

man left his seat in turn, shackled to his guard, and sat at the rear of the plane, whilst skilful hands worked him over.

As the work was completed, and the men were issued with new blue denim shirts and trousers, a definite pattern began to emerge. They became almost indistinguishable one from another. The same thin frames and neatly cropped hair, the same lightly tanned skin colour from the make-up and the identical clothing. All of this produced a uniformity which, given men of the same slim build, could be reproduced time and time again. Height alone was the difference between them and, when seated even this ceased to exist.

The Soviet jetliner thundered high above the clouds and the prisoners inside ached for their first taste of freedom in many years.

At five o'clock Jonathan Fraser received a telephone call from the Prime Minister. The exchange arrangements were confirmed.

Fraser made his way down to where the hostages were being held and informed them that their ordeal would soon be over. As he had expected, this news was received with mixed feelings by the Russian staff.

An unmistakable air of fear and apprehension hung over them.

'There is nothing to fear,' he told them. 'My object has been achieved. I wish no harm to any of you. My information from the Prime Minister is that your Ambassador will take charge of this building as soon as the exchange has been made between yourselves and the twelve men being brought here from Africa. We will all move out of this building on to the road and you will be allowed to walk towards the gates. You need fear nothing.'

'What of the girl Lashkova?' Davydov, the Military Attaché, asked.

'I'm afraid at this stage I cannot answer that,' Fraser replied. 'It will need some consideration. I am sure that, left behind, she is as good as dead.'

'She is a traitor,' Davydov said evenly.

'Possibly she is, but that is of no importance to me. I must make my decision without prejudice.'

'You will give her to the SIS,' the Attaché stated.

Fraser studied him wearily.

'How many times must I repeat myself? I have no connection with the British or any other secret service. I am not here to hand over defectors to anyone. I really don't wish to discuss this further.'

Davydov eased himself up from the couch and stood close to Fraser, their faces almost touching.

'Remember my warning, Colonel! Let me speak to Moscow. I will try and ensure that there is no action taken against you after this.'

'In exchange for the girl?' Fraser asked.

'There is always a price. If I could convince them that it was she who gave you the information from the archives – that you and your men were unable to use the equipment without her help, it is possible they might believe this.'

'No,' Fraser said emphatically. 'They would not believe you, and I do not sell people's lives. Whatever happens is meant to be. Let it go on.'

'You are a fatalist, Colonel Fraser. I did not expect that from a man with the strength of will you possess. I am surprised – disappointed.'

Fraser shook his head.

'The future is predetermined by the events of the present. Otherwise we wouldn't expend so much energy trying to shape life.' He placed a hand on the Russian's shoulder. 'I regret any action that may be taken against you or any of your people by what I have done. But if your system is so devoid of trust, then I am afraid for the future of your country.'

The Attaché spread his palms then sat back on the couch watching Fraser as he left.

'So am I, Colonel,' he said quietly and turned to take in the strained faces of his staff. 'So am I.'

Heathrow Airport became a fortress as darkness fell. Around its perimeter, the army took position in an operation that had been successfully carried out on many occasions during the seventies.

Scout cars moved cautiously along the outer ring road, checking vehicles and vulnerable areas for any possible attack on the

Russian airliner, and troops, on full scale alert, patrolled openly between the buildings.

The Prime Minister was determined that nothing should go wrong and had decided that he trusted no one. The possibility of some fringe terrorist group using the incident as an opportunity to create havoc was a very real fear in his mind.

Colin Hammond, too, was a very worried man. He paced the long corridors leading up to the arrival area of the international flights building, praying that he had overlooked nothing.

For over three hours he had checked and rechecked the security inside the building even to the extent of body-searching a couple of stray newspaper reporters himself, before brusquely demanding their return to the prepared barrier set up for the press. He was very near the point of nervous exhaustion.

My God! he thought in a moment of panic, what if some idiot managed to get past the telephone restrictions to the Embassy and spoke to Fraser. Everything hung on one single thread. Fraser must receive information only from the TV broadcast and the specially prepared seven o'clock news bulletin on the radio.

'Please God, no foul-ups,' he murmured as he dialled the internal number for the control tower.

'No change, sir,' a voice informed him. 'ETA 1830 hours.' He replaced the receiver and fought his way through the crowds to an exit, picking up his team of armed Special Branch officers on the way.

Outside the building, standing together in a specially cleared area, were two huge outside broadcast mobile units belonging to the BBC and the Independent Television network.

A fine drizzle had started and Hammond turned up the collar of his raincoat as the group left the shelter of the arrivals building.

'Never held up a TV station before,' one of the men joked.

Hammond took out his letter of authority.

'There's more ammunition here than you all have between you. Just stand in the background and look as if you mean business. You're the last resort if some fool decides everything should be shown as it really is. Come on, we're getting bloody wet.'

They broke into a trot over the shining tarmac reaching the BBC unit first. One of the men rapped hard on the door.

'Police,' he said. 'Open up.'

Colin Hammond checked his watch. It read six o'clock. Half an hour, he thought. Half an hour and advanced technology, that's all I need to create an illusion of reality.

The door of the enormous transporter opened revealing the mass of equipment in the brightly lit interior, and the technicians staring in puzzlement out at the wet policemen.

Hammond stepped up into the unit, his letter ready.

'Right,' he said. 'Who's the boss?'

6

Alexei Grechko ignited the big jet engine; the roar was a thunderous explosion in the confined space of the copse. Around him the cage of trees shook wildly, showering wet leaves over the fighter as it lifted perceptibly with the down thrust. The air-frame rocked as the fighter's exhaust was blasted back off the low hummocks around him. For a moment Grechko had to fight for control, correcting a violent sway to the right before moving quickly forward through the gap in the trees. There was no time for caution, he had to get out fast, or the sanctuary which had served him so well would be his last resting place with the YAK tipping over and exploding, a victim of its own power.

Night had fallen and he stared down the beams of the landing lights for a few seconds at the terrain of the miniature valley before extinguishing them. In the darkness, hovering a few feet above the wet soil, he felt utterly detached from reality. He twisted the YAK on its axis and was surrounded by a whirlpool of noise. As the thrust was increased on the down-jets, he was pushed upwards as if by a giant hand. The brow of the hummocks fell away and he was back in the land of reality and open space. Looking upward, he noted the heavy clouds shrouding the moon and stars from view. 'Excellent!' he thought as fine rain scattered in crazy patterns on the wings; then, raising his hand in an imaginary toast, said: 'To the stupidity of man,' and gave the YAK full power.

At Fighter Command Headquarters in Stanmore the controller relaxed in his chair, sipping tea from a large mug, his pipe smouldering in the ashtray.

The phone rang and he yawned, putting the mug down on the small table before answering the insistent buzz.

For a while he listened without saying a word, then simply said, 'Thank you,' and replaced the instrument.

'Anyone picked up a tearaway?' he asked calmly through the throat mike. From around the illuminated table pale faces turned upwards, heads shaking.

'Well, I have,' he announced. 'Broken a few windows on his way according to the police. Right! He's below radar so we'll go for a sound print.' He pressed keys on a board before him. 'I'll give you the read-out on the co-ordinates passed on to us but he's way ahead of the game by now.' The computer chattered privately to him for a few seconds and he punched buttons on a visual display panel. 'There you are, plot it from those figures. No time for consultation. I'm afraid this time we're on our own. Put a squadron up ahead of him when we've established the toe of the print.'

'We're assuming it's the Russian come alive, sir?' a disembodied voice asked in his headphones.

'Oh yes,' the controller replied without hesitation. The phone started again by his left hand and he listened. 'Thank you very much. We're most grateful,' he said, and his fingers delicately touched the keyboard.

As he waited, he watched the tape machines rolling first one way then stopping and reversing in the search for information. The read-out spilled in front of him and he studied it.

'Here's another visual,' he said. 'He's up and running – or should I say down and running. Wouldn't mind getting a look at that navigation computer he's got on board.'

'Problem, sir,' a girl's voice began. 'Our prediction gives a constant path over urban areas. We don't have a hope of knocking him down if he stays that way.'

'He will,' the reply was emphatic. 'He knows that we're not

prepared to sacrifice civilians. Looks like we'll need an umbrella in the air to cover him all the way. Put all fighter aircraft now on alert status into the air – and also warn the coastal stations to wait for a scramble order. Can't tell which way he's going to bolt.'

In the momentary lull he lifted the red telephone, relayed in a few precise sentences exactly what was happening, then returned to watching the board.

'Sound gone, sir, a sharp break in the pattern. A crash?' The girl's voice was cool, almost impersonal.

The controller relit his pipe, his mind working swiftly as he studied the constantly moving tapes.

'Do a run on emergency services and come back to me. No talking for a moment, please, I need a minute to think.'

He sat for some seconds absently chewing a rough patch of skin on a finger, then began punching a question into the computer.

Grechko swept over the rooftops, suicidally low, yet he had complete faith in the advanced computer which regulated his mad flight.

His eyes remained firmly fixed to the radar screen, searching for the telltale blips which would let him know that he had been traced. It wouldn't take long before that happened but he knew the pursuing aircraft would not dare attack while he stayed on the present flight path.

They'd track him on sound, he knew that, but felt he could outfox them. He began to cut power.

'No report from the emergency services, sir,' the girl said.

The controller didn't answer but half of his mind registered the question and the hiss of the headphones immediately afterwards.

'No matter,' he said finally. 'He hasn't crashed. We've been misled by two factors. One: the assumption the Russians would use their fastest strike aircraft, and two: that the fighter was damaged or destroyed by a near collision with a B-52. What was the name we were given?'

'Grechko. Alexei Nikolai. Naval commander (air).'

'Yes. Well, Alexei Nikolai is flying a YAK/STOL. They've

played a jet-age version of the tortoise and the hare.' He bit hard in frustration on his pipe stem. 'The bugger is that if we announce that information the game changes from "search and destroy" to "finders keepers"! Now what do we do?'

The faces peered up at him.

'They downed the Nimrod, sir,' one said.

'Reasonable deduction,' the controller muttered. 'Probably flew the B-52 into the ground as well.' He looked down at them his jaws working. 'Sorry, it's tough but we have to go upstairs or it's pensions out of the window.'

He lifted the red telephone and passed over the information and sat, slow fury filling his body as he listened to the reply. With a curt 'Sir', he put the receiver down.

'Hands off. Don't touch. Meaning they're going to fight over what's more important, the plane or the consequences,' he said and watched the faces.

The red telephone gave a high buzz.

'Yes, sir.' The controller listened intently, then repeated the message.

His hands free again, he worked once more on the keyboard.

'Right,' he said into the throat mike, 'they're ready to carry the can. Put it out to the sectors. Fingers off firing buttons or there'll be the sound of heads rolling. Close all the exits, we're to run him around until his fuel's gone and he has to put down.'

'Self-destruct mechanism, sir?' the girl queried.

'Good point. He'll use it too. Tag him with Harriers; if they stay really close he won't risk it – perhaps! It's a chance we've got to take. They say so!' His finger pointed straight up. 'Where is he now?' No one spoke so he answered himself. 'Gone to ground. Well, at least we're learning how effective a V/STOL really is. He'll pop up soon. Let's be ready for him.'

Grechko sat in the cockpit, the engine humming, as around him locomotives pushed flat-cars laden with huge containers around the marshalling yard. The low hum of the jet was almost lost amidst the clang and clatter of the rolling stock.

He'd come in with his engine cut back to such an extent he'd nearly lost control twice, but his superlative ability saved him again.

The approach he's chosen brought him across a polluted

canal and a huge area of disused land, buried under partially burned piles of scattered refuse. Some of it still smouldered in the steady rain.

The YAK was tucked between a large rusted rail shed on the outer perimeter of the marshalling yard and one of the rubbish tips which threatened to engulf him if he moved.

'What a way to end your days, Alexei,' he said. 'Under a pile of garbage!'

At Stanmore the controller sat hunched forward, his face resting in his hands, pondering his future.

How much would the top brass tell the government? Would it even go as far as the Secretary of State for Defence? Or were they too committed already?

Intelligence had been unable to get any real information on the YAK 36 and it was imperative that comparisons were made with the British Harrier jump-jet. Part, if not the whole, of the Harrier sale to the Chinese rested on obtaining accurate information about the Soviet equivalent.

Yes, he decided finally. The Defence Minister would know everything, but he'd keep his mouth firmly closed. The Chinese order was worth millions, and it was only the beginning.

And there was the Foreign Office. And the Americans, who were currently sleeping with the Chinese. And us! Poor sods who sat in the middle of a mass of diplomatic arithmetic we couldn't begin to understand, but which we were held responsible for when the sums didn't add up.

'What have we got?' he said into the mike, a little brutally, causing the pale faces to start up at him.

'Nothing, sir,' someone said, and they looked at each other helplessly.

Jonathan Fraser stood at the window of the KGB Resident's office, unaware of the gathering storm.

He bared his teeth in a snarl of controlled rage, for he had never intended it to end this way. The trial of strength had become a flaccid surrender on the part of the authorities and he felt cheated.

What should have been a last stand – perhaps a little dramatic in such a cynical world, but certainly glorious and memorable – was now no more than an unusual television broadcast. Even the prospect of it being viewed by millions did not extinguish the blazing fire inside him. It was wrong. All wrong.

In an instant of searing pain, he dropped to his knees, his hands reaching instinctively to the cause at the back of his head. His eyes rolled upwards, the whites reddening, as blood suffused his face.

Slowly, the pain receded and he pulled himself up. Weakly he found his painkillers and swallowed a double dose, sitting at the desk to await the mild euphoria he knew would follow.

'Damn them all!' he exclaimed viciously; then the drug swept through his veins and he relaxed.

He checked his watch. Not long now, he thought, rising from the chair to switch on the television set.

A talk-show was featured on the BBC1 channel, discussing the events at the Soviet Embassy and a statement made by an eminent politician stuck at him like a barb.

'Colonel Fraser has won,' the man said, 'because he chose to do battle where it is impossible for the forces of civilized society to fight – in those sensitive areas we call "diplomatically protected". Had we sent in troops we should, in essence, have been invading foreign soil and, although the Russians would have been more than happy to have had Fraser out of that building much earlier than this, I am certain that they would have been most disturbed if our forces had taken the building by storm. In short, the answer to your question,' he said to the interviewer, 'is yes – he has defeated us hands down.'

Fraser watched the screen.

'There is no victory if the battle does not take place!' he observed softly, then sat at his desk again, waiting in the flickering light from the TV set and the dull green glow of the desk lamp. The Torch threw a shadow of moving flame up from the street on to the wall beside him as the first of the men came through the open door. Upon each he bestowed his inheritance.

The Ilyushin touched down a few seconds before six-thirty and taxied to a specially prepared area.

Along the rooftops of the airport buildings and on the observation balcony, police marksmen with high-powered rifles and night-scopes looked down briefly on the massive silver aircraft before returning to their job of surveying the skyline.

It had been decided that the presence of the army was to be shown as minimal, so the roped-off area where the airliner finally stopped was surrounded by uniformed police. But the heavy predominence of armed officers wearing flak jackets added an aura of violence to a scene already made harsh by the glare of blazing arc-lights.

In the BBC outside broadcasting unit Colin Hammond gave a curt nod to the producer.

'I'm going outside to take a look,' he said, his tone holding a note of warning, even though the television crews had co-operated willingly with his demands.

Clipping an airport security badge to his lapel, he ran through the rain, skirting around the arrivals building and out on to the windswept tarmac.

As he arrived on the fringe of the crowd by the aircraft, the rear door of the Ilyushin swung open, revealing the startled figure of a man dressed in a blue denim shirt and trousers which seemed one size too large. Cautiously, he edged out on to the steps, then began a jerky descent. His emaciated face was shining with silver threads and Hammond realized he was weeping.

They came down singly, being released at intervals, and Hammond cursed inwardly at this, afraid of the prolonged camera time on each man. Then, as he saw the group close together at the bottom of the stairway, he breathed out with relief; they were like the photographs of inmates of concentration camps – all different, yet uncannily indistinguishable from each other.

He shuddered, for in a way these were his creations and the knowledge unsettled him. He felt like an imperfect God whose creatures bore the mark of his own limited imagination.

Around him, a noise like the sudden fluttering of birds shook him back to reality and he heard the sympathetic applause for the first time.

The mercenaries were weeping unashamedly, but stood upright staring out with wet eyes into the lights and the cameras.

Hammond, with a policeman's eye, noted the second stairway being rolled into place by the forward door and the hurried exit of the remainder of the passengers, who made for the rim of the roped area where four Embassy limousines, with Soviet flags fluttering on their bonnets, collected them and drove off at speed. Hammond did not see the long cases being unloaded from the cargo doors nor their transfer to a station-wagon bearing diplomatic plates for, by this time, pandemonium had broken loose as the press rushed forward to the mercenaries.

Great! he thought. Get those faces mixed up in the crowd.

In the BBC control unit the producer monitored the row of screens, speaking constantly into a slender microphone in front of his face. Every time a camera moved into close-up he carefully counted off the seconds then switched the shot, concentrating on the group rather than the individuals. To his right and behind him the VTR operators worked like men possessed.

Hammond flung himself into the flying wedge formed by the biggest of the uniformed police and let himself be swept into a heavily guarded secondary entrance to the arrivals building.

The press were cordoned off and redirected to the area set up for them. Only the TV camera crews were allowed access and then merely as a trailing part of the main group, giving them continuous shots of the backs of heads.

The mercenaries were led into the immigration medical unit where they were made to strip with unceremonious haste. The scene, under the hot TV lighting, was one of complete bedlam with only the cool presence of the medical team giving any semblance of order.

Colin Hammond, keeping well behind the cameras, sweated furiously as he worked with a team of two Special Branch officers, gathering up the mercenaries' clothing and putting it inside large black plastic bags.

'Where are the overcoats?' he demanded.

'Right there, sir,' a man pointed to a corner.

'Now I hope you've got it,' he said to the two men. 'Wait for the signal from the cameraman, then get the mercs into our clothing – it's not the same, but the next shot anyone will see will have them covered up by overcoats. At least we know those are identical. Got it?'

The men nodded quickly.

'And don't balls it up – I know it seems a lot of trouble but

Fraser doesn't miss a trick and he'll have noted their clothing, I guarantee it.'

'We won't let you down,' one replied with a barely concealed look of disgust on his face. 'What happens to these poor bastards – sir?'

Hammond did not answer. 'You,' he said to another waiting policeman. 'Help me with these bags.'

Out on the tarmac, the crowd of press reporters had completely dispersed, taking with them most of the police, leaving only a handful of armed men standing at strategic points around the aircraft.

The senior officer made a signal to the pilot as he listened to an instruction on his communicator, and the squat towing-drone started its engine, taking up the weight of the aircraft.

Around the Ilyushin, the armed police, looking deformed by the bulky flak jackets, began walking at a steady pace with the plane until it was pulled safely into a cavernous hangar.

The police slid the huge doors closed, then stood guard on them.

Below the spinning clatter of four rotor blades two men in a helicopter yelled at each other as they traversed the metropolis.

'Hyde Park,' the TV cameraman bawled, pointing down through the perspex canopy to the great swathe of darkness below, black like the beginning of the sea at the edge of a brightly illuminated coastline. 'Next stop Kensington Gardens – then the Embassy.'

'Watch for the lights on the antennae tower!' the pilot called through the intercom. The cameraman stuck up a thumb.

The trees on the perimeter of the Park were partially lit by the street-lamps, giving them the appearance of hollow green balls.

'Bloody hell!' the cameraman cried out in amazement. 'Take a look at that crowd.'

The pilot tipped the craft over with only the transparent canopy between him and the earth.

'God! There must be thousands of them! Go on down,' the cameraman shouted excitedly. 'Go on.'

The pilot shook his head.

'Bollocks!' he swore at his passenger. 'You get a couple of minutes over the building and no more.'

He banked the helicopter, trimming the controls for more height, his eyes searching the darkness for light ahead.

The ominous shapes which were the tall trees backing on to the rear of the Embassy buildings, loomed towards them but still there was no sign of the aircraft warning lights he expected to see.

'The buggers have switched the tower off,' he said and pulled the aircraft up to a hovering position short of the trees.

'Take it easy,' the cameraman warned. 'Those bastards are ready to shoot at anything.'

The pilot nodded, sweeping low over Kensington Palace, making his turn to fly directly up the avenue towards the Bayswater Road gates.

A broken line of white fire burned startlingly through the air towards them but the flat thud-thud-thud of the powerful automatic weapons was lost above the noise of the rotor.

'Shit!' the pilot screamed and tossed the chopper almost over on its back, the blades slicing madly at the air. He regained control white faced, and glared at the cameraman. 'Sod you, son! You want action pictures, get yourself another flyer – I don't get paid enough for this.'

The cameraman looked wide-eyed at the road now far below, seeing the Range Rover and the van blocking the avenue and, further along, the larger shape of the shattered coach which had carried the KGB men to their deaths.

In the darkness he could not make out the figures of Fraser's men who had fired at them, nor could he possibly see, on the roof of a large building opposite, a team of men dressed entirely in black, with their blackened faces pressed to the wet brick.

The Kremlin's executioners were in position.

Fraser picked up the telephone.

'Prime Minister,' a voice said, strung with tension.

Fraser said:

'The next one I'll scatter across the sky.'

'I don't understand, Colonel?'

'The helicopter! Are you people crazy?'

'I have no idea what you mean.'

'Then find out, or I'll turn my men loose.'

Stratton eased him back into the chair, aware that there was nothing he could do to stop the obvious deterioration in Fraser's condition.

He poured brandy into a glass and placed it on the desk.

'Drink it.'

Fraser reached in his pocket for more pills and swallowed a handful, gulping down the neat alcohol.

'You can't take many more of those,' Stratton said.

Fraser looked up at him, his face rigid with pain.

'I've no choice.'

'You really thought you'd be dead by now, didn't you?'

'Sooner.' The familiar smile broke across the stricken face.

The telephone pinged once and Stratton grabbed it.

'Yes?'

'Fraser?'

'No.'

'Is he all right?' The Prime Minister's voice was high with alarm.

'Yes.'

'Put him on.'

Stratton hesitated, the receiver held away from his ear.

'Give it to me,' Fraser demanded.

'Colonel, it seems the Independent Television people thought they would get some dramatic shots,' the Premier said angrily.

'Well, they almost got dramatically shot!' Fraser retorted. 'Next time they won't get a warning.'

'There won't be a next time, I promise you that. For God's sake, man, this is almost over. You're getting what you wanted. Don't let the situation get out of control.'

'Don't worry about *my* control, Prime Minister.'

An audible sigh came over the line.

'Fraser — everything has been done to ensure that the exchange is handled smoothly. Don't let a mistake by over-zealous fools turn this sour.'

'All right, sir,' Fraser replied. 'I shall be waiting. Keep a tight rein on your end.'

'I shall, Colonel. No hasty actions – please.'

Paul Stratton, with his finely tuned sense of survival, felt his pulses quicken as his mind searched for the unknown danger. His instincts were never wrong, he trusted them implicitly, prepared at any time to stake his life on their unfailing accuracy.

'The girl,' Fraser said, interrupting his thoughts, 'she's getting to you. Don't let that happen. It's possible you'll have to sacrifice her if you want to get out of here alive.'

'Just rest,' Stratton said dismissing Fraser's warning, 'I know what I may have to do.' But, as he left the room, he thought, Katrina! I must find her!

Behind him, Fraser stood up, supporting himself on the desk, and turned the sound up on the television set.

Flash bulbs blazed as the mercenaries were released from the airport immigration medical unit.

They were bundled up in long dark grey overcoats, giving them a hideous shrunken appearance, but the pace at which they were rushed through the front of the arrivals building gave no one time to study them.

The press screamed questions over the heads of the heavy police guard but the men had been warned that they must not answer, and left behind them a wake of angry and frustrated newsmen.

Outside a coach with blacked-out windows was waiting with its motor running. The police entered first, taking the window seats and placing the mercenaries along the centre of the aisle. The BBC mobile camera crew entered next, with Colin Hammond the very last to step up into the coach.

All around, police motorcyclists took up position, with two cars to the front and rear, carrying armed members of the crack Special Weapons squad. Their route to central London had been specially cleared and throughout its length the Metropolitan Division had beefed up manpower with men from provincial forces to control traffic and crowds at vantage points.

Travelling at the highest speed possible for the coach, the motorcade pulled away from the air terminal and entered the tunnel underpass for the motorway to central London.

Throughout the journey the television crew kept the cameras rolling.

At seven o'clock precisely, the nation sat on the edge of their seats and watched the arrival on British soil of a Soviet Ilyushin airliner and, some minutes after, had their first glimpse of the freed British mercenary soldiers. They had no way of knowing that the mercenaries had arrived in England some thirty minutes before and were already well on their way to the centre of the capital for a special rendezvous timed to the split second.

The nation, like Jonathan Fraser, had been duped. They were watching a video-tape-recording of the event, presented as if it were live.

On one stretch of the Bayswater Road, blocked at both ends by barriers and armed police, an identical coach bearing the same number plates waited with its engine running.

In the unlit interior sat twelve men who, to all outward appearances, were the mirror image of the mercenaries.

That image was a mere veneer, for the shaven-headed men wearing denims and dark-grey overcoats were volunteers from the ranks of the élite Special Air Service, supremely fit under their clothing, whereas the men they represented were broken by poor health. Colonel Grenville stood on the step of the coach and checked his watch, before making one final inspection of his men. His statement to Hammond came clearly to his mind. 'If the job has to be done, we would prefer to do it.'

In the far distance he heard the unmistakable double-tone of the klaxon horns and knew that the police at the barriers were being warned by radio to prepare. The switch had to be fast and perfect, with every man in exactly the same seat. Hammond had planned it down to the smallest detail, even forbidding anyone to smoke in case the continuity was thrown in the switch.

Grenville recalled him saying, 'They'll have enough on tape when they actually transmit to give us time to check virtually everything, but we could be blown by the smallest thing – a man smoking one second and the next – gone! You think your beloved Colonel would miss a trick like that?'

And of course, Grenville thought, Hammond was absolutely right.

'Right,' he called. 'Everybody out. Here they come.'

In the BBC television control unit the producer studied the

constantly changing numbers on the digital clock before him. 'Prepare for live transmission,' he said.

The motorcade tore past the first barriers, dousing the police in a fine spray as they pulled them aside.

A group of eight men in plain clothes broke away making for the coach at a trot.

Hammond launched himself down on the wet paving.

'Out!' he yelled. The police pulled the freed mercenaries to their feet and followed him out of the coach holding their charges firmly.

As the TV camera crew made their way quickly to the new vehicle, the police raced after them, leaving the mercenaries standing, completely bewildered, in the rain. For a moment they were unguarded, then the eight plain-clothes officers herded them back into the bus, ignoring any protests, and Hammond took one look at them before they were taken back to the airport, and the African prison block they had so recently left. A feeling of anger, disgust and shame welled up in him.

'Ready!' Grenville called and he ran for the new coach. 'All in – everything checked,' the SAS colonel confirmed, then looked pointedly at his watch. He thrust out his hand. 'I'm sorry now I'm not coming along. Good luck.'

'No chance, Colonel. Fraser would recognize you instantly. Thanks. See you when it's over.'

Hammond climbed into the bus and told the driver to reverse to a marked point on the road and then wait.

'Ready?' he asked the cameramen. The two men nodded. 'Ten minutes,' he said holding up fingers, 'and we're on the air – this is it.'

One of the SAS volunteers rubbed his shorn scalp and nudged the policeman at his side. 'First time on the box and I look like a fuckin' coconut,' he grinned.

The producer watched the monitors and studied the VTR machine. Slowly he completed his countdown.

'Live transmission,' he said calmly, and without even a smallest jump the cross-over from tape to live transmission was made. With a certain satisfaction he studied the monitor, but in the dull interior of the moving bus, nothing seemed to have changed from the previous taped picture. 'Clever bastard,' he said aloud, and his crew thought he was talking about himself.

'I'm not going out there,' Stratton said.

Fraser spun round from the television set.

'What?'

'I'm not going out there – don't ask me why, I have no logical reason.'

Fraser was bewildered.

'Paul! We've done it – can't you see?' he pointed at the set. 'Even I never believed we'd pull it off. But it's there in front of your eyes. They're free.'

Stratton shook his head.

'I'm not going out there and that's final.'

'You're needed. You have to come.'

'No. It's over. Whether I'm there or not makes no difference. I'm staying.'

'Bring the girl,' Fraser pleaded, 'it won't cause a problem.'

'The girl has nothing to do with it.'

'Fear,' Fraser said emphatically. 'That's your gut feeling.'

Stratton shook his head sadly.

'You can't make me rise to that. Of course I'm scared – we could all be under the barrels of snipers' rifles the moment we step into the road, but that's not it. *Something is wrong.* And I don't know where to look. So I'm staying.'

Fraser said, 'You'll spend the rest of your life in prison – surely that's worse than death?'

'I'll get out. It's my problem. At this stage it's every man for himself. Wasn't that the way it was supposed to be – in the end?'

'Yes, of course. But they've given us all we wanted and the chance to get out. We'd be fools not to take it. Ask the men! Even with the money split so many ways, they're satisfied with how it worked out. Now, more than ever, is the time to remain together.'

'I'm not walking out into that road,' Stratton said stubbornly.

Fraser turned to the screen, watching the progress of the bus.

'Well, let's arrange a compromise. You think something's been set up for us – an ambush on the journey?'

Stratton shrugged. 'I don't know.'

'No,' Fraser said with certainty. 'If they're going to hit us, they'll do it out there on the road where they've got us contained. They might even risk killing hostages – Davydov warned me that the Kremlin would agree to that – ' Suddenly his face cleared as if all the pain had left him and the old mesmeric fire burned in his eyes. ' – We'll fight them, Paul! To the last man. If that's what they want then, my God, they can have it.'

Stratton turned away from those burning eyes.

'I didn't go through the conditioning,' he said quietly, keeping his eyes fixed on the TV screen. 'I'm a man apart from the rest. I warned you of this.'

Fraser waved the words aside.

'On the roof!' he said urgently. 'You go on the roof – use the NVD – cover the area – be our eyes. If they don't hit us, I'll hold the bus for you and the girl – do it, Paul – do it.'

'All right,' Stratton agreed. 'I'll cover you. You want to kill them all – to take them with you. It's your way.'

'It's the only way. Better than rotting day by day.'

'I'll get the men together,' Stratton turned for the door.

'Paul?'

'Yes?'

Fraser held an envelope out to him.

'The legacy.'

Stratton took it. 'The devil's inheritance!' he said with a brief, tight smile. 'I wonder if God will damn me now.'

7

Commander Alexei Nikolai Grechko was nearing the Thames at Greenwich.

He checked the map strapped to his right thigh and noted the pencilled blue cross he had put there earlier in the day. Ahead, he could see the buildings of the Royal Naval College and banked to starboard, following the oily black glint of the river directly below him.

The radar swept unceasingly on the panel before him and he noted various blips which looked like airliners. Instantly, on the next sweep, four smaller impressions came on to the screen so close to the edge that he might have missed them.

'Now it begins,' he said to himself and opened the throttles wide, catapulting the YAK forward.

The controller let the computer read-out spill on his table as he listened to the serious voice at the end of the telephone he held cradled between his shoulder and chin.

'With respect, sir,' he said, 'I must bring to your attention the fact that, no matter the intelligence value of the aircraft, it is nevertheless a Soviet fighter plane in British air-space. Yes, sir.' He paused, listening for a moment. 'I realize that you are aware of the situation. . . .' Again he stopped. '. . . No. No, sir, I assure you there is no question of our aircraft shooting it down, even without this order. While the Russian pilot holds his present course, we would have to stay our hand. Yes, sir . . . I'm sure the Prime Minister would make the same decision, but if he were informed of the fighting position . . .' He sighed, holding the receiver away from his ear now. '. . . Naturally I realize that these decisions are made by your . . .' Slowly he shrugged and murmured, 'Yes, sir,' then replaced the instrument on its rest.

For a few seconds he stared at it, daring himself to pick it up again and make the call right to the very top. But his courage failed him and the moment slipped by.

'He's turned on the power, sir,' the girl's voice whispered huskily in his ear. 'Heading straight up the line of the river. We could knock him down with minimal risk.'

'Let him go,' the controller said, surprised at the dryness in his throat.

Despite a huge turn-out by the police and the army the crowds gathered in the area near Notting Hill Gate, Bayswater and Kensington had grown to almost unmanageable proportions.

As the blacked-out coach pulled to a stop outside the Bayswater Road entrance to Kensington Palace Gardens there was a surge like a great moving swell in the kaleidoscopic sea of faces. A roar broke from their throats as the door opened.

From the top of a brace of television outside broadcast trucks the cameramen zoomed in on the uniformed officers who vacated the bus. Slowly, almost with reluctance, they walked away from the vehicle and joined the hundreds of their colleagues who fought frantically behind barriers to hold back the tide of people, almost hysterical with excitement.

One voice high-pitched and clear-cut through a sudden silence : 'Fraser! You lovely bastard. You've done it!' and then in complete violent ecstasy shouted, 'The Wolf! The Wolf!'

The crowd picked it up and began chanting the words, swaying back and forth till police helmets tumbled to the ground and the men buckled under the strain. A uniformed inspector waved in the horses and the mounted officers bolstered the heaving lines.

'Jesus fucking Christ!' Hammond hissed between his teeth in a rare moment of profanity. Quite unexpectedly, as he climbed into the driver's seat he saw the face of Johnson, the photo-lab technician, near the TV trucks. The boy's face was flushed with excitement.

'Wolf! Wolf! Wolf!' the rolling sound continued as he turned to the SAS volunteers, his face set and hard.

'OK, out you go,' he said sharply to the two BBC cameramen standing in the aisle. 'You've done your bit.' Gently, he let in the clutch and the bus juddered as his leg shook uncontrollably. 'Shit,' he swore again. 'He's only a man.'

The Wolf stepped out on to the avenue flanked by his pack. Cornwell moved up beside him, a small deadly human weapon fully cocked and held back by the finest hair-trigger of control. At that moment, more than any other in his life, he was primed to kill indiscriminately at the least indication from Fraser.

James Dewey stood, resting his weight on one hip, the big Sterling cradled insolently in one hand, the barrel pointing up into the night.

The drizzle had stopped and the surface of the road sparkled like a black mirror.

'Ever thought of running for President, sir?' he joked quietly.

'Eyes front,' Cornwell said menacingly, but Fraser's lips broke, amused by Dewey's indifference to danger.

Walters, Carter and Peterson, the Guns of August, broke from the line, joined by Jock Mclennan, and moved slowly towards the oncoming bus, two to each side of the avenue.

Lippmann, the Anglo-German ex-legionnaire, and young Andy Fowler faced the rear, their hard eyes fixed on the far gates past Kensington Palace. Fowler quickly crossed himself, his thoughts with his beautiful murdered wife. Ferdy Lippmann smiled and nodded his head encouragingly.

Next to Lippmann, Johnny Hubbard, the explosives expert, watched the buildings to his left. The giant Murray towered above them all, his great body tensed for a flying leap to protect Fraser if they were sniped at.

Sammy Cohen walked out to join them as the bus neared.

'Tape-recorder rolling, sir,' he said. 'The security doors are down and locked in position.'

'How long before the blank section finishes?' Fraser asked.

'Thirty minutes, sir. Then the recording goes out over the transmitter.'

'Excellent. If this is a trick, we can certainly hold for that length of time.' Fraser turned to Cornwell, 'Right, Sarn'-Major, let the hostages out of the vehicles.'

From his vantage point on the rooftop, Stratton stood looking through the Night Vision Device, seeing everything in bright, almost luminous images.

By his side, shivering slightly in the cutting wind, Katrina Lashkova gazed at him.

'If you're cold stand by the fire,' he said, indicating the burning flame of Fraser's Torch.

'No,' she said simply, and moved nearer.

'Keep away. Lord knows what's going to happen next.'

'No,' Katrina repeated, 'if you choose to stand alone now, you will return to the same empty strength as before.'

Stratton pulled her to him. 'I am not sure I am able to do that. I have grown towards you – with you. I don't know if I will ever be able to stand alone again.'

She shook her head. 'There is no need for that. I am with you. What may happen now will not change that.'

'Don't strip me bare, Katrina! By being up here and not down on the street with Fraser I have cut myself off from him. I *have* to stand by the trust he has placed in me.'

'That too should not change. But now you have a *reason* to survive. Which is more than simply the instinct to survive.

Those men down there have no reasons. Life or death? What difference does it make to them, Paul?'

'Survival is more than instinct!' he said in anger. 'It is experience and training. Having reasons for survival causes mistakes.'

'Then make no mistakes. Throw me away as far as you think you can, but if they die and you are left alive it will be me you will find inside yourself.'

He closed his eyes and shook his head sharply. 'Stay then!' he said. 'But expect nothing.' He pointed at the Torch. 'While that burns I am not free.'

'And if it dies too?'

Stratton looked down on the avenue ignoring her question.

The hostages clung together in a terrified group, their eyes flying wildly from rooftop to rooftop. The Military Attaché shouted at them in Russian and Fraser turned to him.

'What's the matter?'

'They're afraid they'll be shot if they have to walk all the way to the gates. I've tried to control them.'

'Tell them to wait,' Fraser said curtly. Davydov spoke rapidly again, in Russian.

Putting the bull-horn to his lips, Fraser called out to the oncoming vehicle.

'Stop there. We are going to check the outside of the bus.' He turned. 'Johnny, check it over.'

Hubbard ran forward, ducking his head low to scan the underside then got down on his hands and knees digging in the caked dirt around the wheel arches.

Mclennan, Walters, Carter and Peterson began methodically to rip open the luggage holds on the sides and rear of the vehicle. After a thorough search they stood back and Walters stuck a thumb in the air.

'Clean,' he called.

Hubbard, covered in dirt, came over to Fraser.

'Nothing, Colonel. If they've wired it, everything's inside.'

Fraser lifted the bull-horn.

'I want everyone out of the bus. Arms above heads. Then stand in a line beside it.'

Hammond turned around and indicated with his hand. The SAS troopers filed out on to the road.

'Good,' Fraser said. 'Now very carefully remove the over-coats – one at a time, please.'

The men began slipping the coats off. 'Throw them on top of the bus, please,' Fraser instructed still using the bull-horn. 'Very good. Now everyone against the bus, arms outstretched ... rest your weight on your fingers only.'

Hammond began to walk forward.

'Stop!' Fraser shouted.

'I'm Hammond,' he bawled over the distance separating them.

'Stay where you are, Chief Superintendent – I want you searched just like the others.'

'These are the men all this is about, Fraser,' the policeman answered. 'Don't prolong the agony – you're their best friend, for God's sake – let's get this over.'

'Back into line, Hammond,' Fraser warned. 'I'm still not convinced.'

'Bloody hell!' Hammond retorted and leant forward on the bodywork.

The Guns of August and Mclennan moved along the line kicking feet out wide until they were satisfied that no resistance could be offered to a full body-search.

'Clean as a whistle,' Mclennan yelled in his Scots brogue.

Inside the bus, Johnny Hubbard completed his examination, rapped on the driver's window and spread his hands negatively.

'Looks like we've made it, Colonel,' Dewey said quietly.

Grechko laughed as he saw the white blur of upturned faces along Park Lane. Ahead, he saw the great illuminated arch. The YAK skimmed the treetops of the park to his left as he approached, then, leaving it to the very last second, he banked to port and skidded through the air sending a blast of sound rocketing off the buildings around Marble Arch.

Holding his path over the Bayswater Road for a little way he gasped in amazement at the enormous crowds as they scattered below the aircraft.

'By God, Wolf!' he bawled in his deep resonant voice. 'You've got them all by the balls!' From the corner of his eye he took in the four blips now holding in a pattern high above him and out of sight. 'What's wrong, children?' he shouted, shaking a gloved fist as he looked up through the transparent canopy.

Fiercely, he threw the YAK hard over, not hearing the screams of the crowds as the exhaust showered leaves over the wide area.

He headed for the gated avenue, his eyes searching for the burning flare and the armed men lining the rooftop of the Embassy, his finger poised on the firing button of the air-to-ground missiles. Destroy completely. Those were his orders.

James Dewey began forward with a magnanimous open-armed gesture to the first of the shaven-headed men. The man prodded his finger inside shoes that seemed too large. As Dewey stretched out to enfold the man like a conquering hero he saw, very briefly, the slim blued needle of high-tensile steel.

'No,' he gasped as it pierced his heart, his eyes instantly rolling back in his head.

Dewey's body slumped in the SAS trooper's arms and for a fine immeasurable moment in time the entire group were frozen.

Stratton heard the sound of the approaching jet first, before the pilot switched on its lights.

Unaware of the silent death below, he reacted instantly to personal danger and with a flying kick smashed the burning flare off the rooftop, then pulled the girl down behind the balustrade. On the rooftop opposite, the Kremlin's execution squad glimpsed the flash of the falling Torch but were too well trained to shift their eyes from the optical sights of the SAM 7 missile launchers.

Fraser saw two things in the same second. Dewey slumping silently in the arms of one of the SAS volunteers and the plunging flight of his symbol flaring through the air.

Before the Torch hit the ground, Hammond's coach exploded as the SAM 7 missile launched by the Kremlin's killers found its mark.

Mclennan, Walters, Peterson, Carter and Johnny Hubbard were blown to nothing instantly.

Fraser was thrown backwards across the bonnet of the Range

Rover, the giant Murray saving his life by taking two explosive tipped bullets in the back.

The second SAM 7 struck the tarmac to the side of the coach as it veered in to the heat source, but, by some quirk, glanced off the road and ploughed into the Russian hostages, decapitating two of them before exploding against the inner wall of the green van.

Jonathan Fraser, pinned under Murray's huge body, tucked his head in behind the ex-soldier's thick neck and felt the thud as a white hot lump of metal blew the body off him. He rolled to the ground and broke round the back of the Range Rover for the trees opposite the KGB building before the vehicle exploded.

Diving down hard over a low wall he shook his head and searched for life in the inferno that faced him. The screams were appalling for a few brief seconds before the third missile struck dead centre between the three blazing vehicles.

On the other side of the avenue, Colin Hammond lay on his back staring at the sky to his left. His body was numb from the neck down and no matter how he tried he could not turn his head to the source of the streaking death which had rained down on all of them. He blinked his eyes rapidly as he saw in the distance two lights in the sky above the trees and heard the high, soulful wail of a woman's voice. He remembered the girl and her blaring music, closed his eyes and died.

Grechko had aborted his attack-run on seeing the first explosion and, making his decision, ruthlessly cut power.

He came over the top of Kensington Palace at no more than sixty feet, turning on the landing lights as he crossed the green. The wail of the jets, when he trimmed the nozzles for a hovering position, seemed louder than ever before.

The aircraft bucked in his hands as he reacted to the flaring streak of the second missile. The third SAM 7 fired by the Russian President's execution squad blasted out of the nozzle of the launcher as Grechko hung in the air barely moving. In reflex action his finger pressed the firing button and his own missiles, already armed, cleft the air, their exhausts like red holes in the night as they screamed towards the source of the SAM missiles.

The building disintegrated across the whole of the top floor and Grechko launched his full battery, watching with detachment the crumbling brickwork explode in a thousand different directions.

Trimming his controls, he lifted the YAK and turned for the sea, his weapons racks completely emptied.

He was defenceless and his reserves of fuel would get him to the coast, but not much further.

'Well, Alexei,' he shrugged. 'It's a cold night to die.'

Epilogue

They stood on the parapet looking down on the carnage below. In the distance, by the gates, blue lights flashed like beacons across a sea of death.

Men waited by the gates, behind the railings, poised like arrows waiting to be released from a bow of tension. The crowds were silent.

'I love you,' she said simply.

Stratton turned to her, startled by her words at such a time.

'You can't love me. You don't know any more of me than what you see now. I am not a man who loves.'

'You have never loved because you only wanted to die,' she stated quietly. 'You did not believe there was any alternative. You sought peace and looked for death as the solution. Love brings peace to the spirit. You don't have to reach it.'

He turned his back on the splayed bodies. Alone he faced the questions. Would he choose to die now? Perhaps by his own hand or, best, by a bullet aimed at random at the walls.

What of her? She had cried silently for his help, his protection and he had walked away. His loyalties, then, were divided – what were they now? They were dead. All of them. He lived now only for himself. They were gone. Fraser. Dewey. Stewart-Smith. Cornwell. All of them. Dead, with British and Russian bodies laying beside them like brothers.

'You can walk out of here with me, Paul. Safe. No one can touch you.'

He turned his head. 'How?' he asked.

'We have identities. A hundred of them. We created people in this place. Their names – their families – their whole lives. Who is to question anything at this time? Please let us get out of this butcher's house!'

He looked down at himself.

'Clothes?' he said, 'I'm wearing a uniform.'

'Come with me,' she replied. 'Check the living quarters for clothes that will fit you. I will get identification papers in case we are stopped.'

Leaving Stratton, Katrina hurried to the office of the KGB Resident officer and opened the vaults with the emergency controls. Down in the archives she pulled from the files a set of papers to cover a married couple with low-grade diplomatic status. Frantically she transferred her own photograph to one set, then stuck to the other a photograph of one of the Embassy chauffeurs who had dark good looks. She stamped both sets heavily, smearing the ink. Not perfect, she thought, but they would have to do.

As she was leaving, she saw the revolving wheels of the tape-recorder – Fraser's insurance against a trick – the blank section still running. With sudden anger, she ripped the brown tape from the reels, the tangled mess spilling to the floor as the motor continued to run. As she sealed the vault once more, the recorder jammed, reels juddering, then clunked to a stop. She no longer cared who won; the battle, as far as she was concerned, was done.

Upstairs, Stratton, dressed in a grey suit that had been thrown in the dust and speckled with blood, stood waiting behind the front door. She paused before him for a moment, then placed the papers in his jacket pocket, her fingers touching the cold steel of the Browning automatic.

She shook her head and tugged out the Browning, throwing it to the floor.

'It's over,' she said, and kissed his lips. Then she opened the door. Gently, as if leading a child, she took him on the longest walk of his life. The journey between death and being born again.

Fraser's Torch lay on its side still alight, flickering in the wind. She held his elbow and they walked the length of the avenue to the arched gates, floodlights trapping them in their beams the whole time.

Men moved towards them, but she held her arm out and walked through. As bulbs flashed she threw a bag across their faces. 'They're dead!' she said to the crowd. 'All of them. All dead. Let us through – please!'

A voice asked if they were hurt.

'He doesn't speak English,' she shook her head. 'He is my

husband – I'm taking him away from this madness – let us alone, please.'

And as though it was meant to be, the crowd moved apart.

The four Harrier jump-jets swooped down on Grechko, forming up tightly around him. He twisted his head, catching a movement in their leader's cockpit. One hand was raised, its finger pointed down.

They forced him on to the tarmac at RAF Fighter Command Headquarters, Stanmore and, as he cut the YAK's engine, a line of vehicles moving fast across the runway closed in around the aircraft. The circle of headlights caught puffs of steam as a few drops of rain touched the white-hot exhaust. Uniformed figures dropped from the trucks, automatic weapons readied.

Grechko's fingers set the self-destruct mechanism but his eyes remained fixed forward, even as the small remote-controlled signal-unit was slipped into the thigh pocket of his flying suit. With a sigh, he slid back the canopy and climbed down from the plane.

One man, the only one in civilian clothes, walked towards him. Grechko recognized immediately what he was. A man who traded in secrets and bartered with lives. The cold eyes in the friendly face that believed in nothing because, to him, there was no difference between truth or lie – simply advantage.

There was a metallic clatter from the automatic weapons as Grechko pulled the small black unit from his thigh.

'Clear the area!' a voice cut hard through the lights.

Gears crashed as the trucks were flung backwards, their heavy tyres screeching on the tarmac. Only the man remained, facing Grechko.

'You can never go back, Commander,' he said. 'You hit the wrong building. Those were KGB executioners you killed. Your people.'

Grechko stood silent and still for a long while, then raised his big shoulders expressively.

'The Wolf is dead?' he asked.

'With the state of those bodies,' the man spread his gloved hands, 'who knows?' His eyes moved to the warplane. 'You must make a decision, Commander.'

Grechko laughed. 'On what basis, my friend? A simple

answer, please – I am weary of political manoeuvring. Come – something simple!'

'Toss a coin,' the man said, smiling for the first time.

The Russian's grey eyes crinkled at the corners and he ran his fingers through his curling iron-grey hair.

'Or this!' he said and tossed the signal-unit high into the air, its black shape swallowed by the night. At the top of its tumbling arc, the momentum gone, it began falling. It cracked on to the wet tarmac on one edge then tipped over flat.

Grechko watched the face before him, the cold eyes fixed on his own, studiously ignoring the deadly mechanism. Breeze ruffled the man's hair revealing tiny points of perspiration at the hairline.

'You win!' said Grechko.

Paul Stratton led Katrina to the mews garage.

'Can you start it?' she asked, and he nodded. The key turned smoothly in the lock and they stepped inside. In the darkness he fumbled for the ignition keys on a ledge, then found the door-handle. The lock clicked and the Jaguar's interior light came on.

Jonathan Fraser sat in the driver's seat, his amber eyes staring at them. Held firmly against his blood-stained uniform by his left arm was the Cambridge File containing the names of the British traitors recruited by the KGB and now safely established in influential positions. Among them, the names of those who had betrayed him.

Katrina bent down into the car and, as she did so, Fraser's right hand came into view holding the big silenced Browning. For a second her eyes filled with protest. Then the weapon flamed, followed instantly by two harsh thumps. The force flung her out of the car and down at Stratton's feet. In a futile gesture Stratton's hands flew to the empty pockets of his civilian clothes.

'Leave it, Paul!' Fraser ordered. 'Leave it!'

Stratton shook his head dumbly. 'I'm unarmed,' he said, his voice a whisper. He leaned back against the wall, his face white and shocked as he stared down at Katrina's body. As he moved, she flopped over sideways between the Jaguar and the wall, hitting the stone floor hard. He let his head fall slowly back against the wall.

Fraser stretched over, keeping the Browning up as he watched Stratton's face.

'The plane,' he explained. 'She must have made contact with the Kremlin. God knows how. You were supposed to watch her!'

'No,' Stratton whispered.

'Yes, Paul! Face the facts. She made a deal. She fooled you.'

'No,' Stratton repeated, and once again his eyes moved down to the girl's body. He saw two bullet holes under her left breast, barely separated, the scorched material of her coat making them appear as one. There was little blood.

Fraser leaned further over on to the passenger seat, the gun steady. 'It's done now,' he said urgently. 'She's dead – nothing you do or feel will bring her back. She weakened you, Paul. Face it! She softened you up.' Warily he lowered the long barrel of the Browning. 'Come on, Paul, get into the car.'

Stratton brought his hands up to his face for a moment, then let them drop, palms flat against the wall. 'She said she loved me,' he said without emotion.

'She loved you or she used you – or both. Perhaps neither – it makes no difference now. Come on, man! We've still got this.' Fraser slapped the Cambridge File on to the leather seat. 'And by God we can make them pay! Paul?'

Stratton shook his head. 'I can't leave her in here.'

'Right!' Fraser said decisively. 'Get her into the rear seat. Put your arm around her. Hold her against you.'

Silently, Stratton obeyed, lifting the girl's body and placing her by his side on the rear seat. Fraser stepped out of the car and opened the boot. Swiftly he removed his blood-stained combat jacket and, after taking out a dark quilted anorak, tucked the jacket behind the spare wheel. He zipped the anorak right up to his throat. Back inside the car he took a battery shaver from the dashboard glove-locker and, using the driving mirror, began to work on his moustache. Finished, his eyes locked for a second with Stratton's in the mirror. Holding Katrina's body tightly against himself, Stratton pulled Fraser's legacy from his breast pocket and tossed it over the front seats.

'The devil's inheritance?' Fraser asked, his eyes still in the mirror.

'It isn't worth the price,' Stratton answered.

Fraser picked up the legacy and placed it in the Cambridge File. Then he held up the document for Stratton to see.

'This isn't an end, Paul. It's a beginning.' He stepped from the car once more and opened the garage doors. He started the Jaguar's engine. 'Ready?' he asked.

Stratton raised his dark eyebrows then, as though tired, let the lids fall, resting his cheek against Katrina's hair.

They drove out into the London night, a driver with his two passengers close together in the rear of the shining car. From the nestling position of the girl's golden head and the strong encircling arm of the man, they were two people obviously in love.

Discreetly, the driver kept his amber eyes fixed on the road ahead.

*On the following pages are details of Arrow
books that will be of interest.*

BASIKASINGO

John Matthews

It was a name of mystery, of secrecy and of vengeance – the one clue linking a circle of death and duplicity that stretched across the globe . . . terror in London, a diamond heist in Africa, a kidnapping in Bangkok . . . All that connected them were whispers, rumours and chance remarks – but they were part of a gory trail with no beginning and the very deadliest of ends . . .

Caught in its spell, the innocent and the diabolical, the hunted and the hunters act out their desperate dance of death . . . Not since *The Bourne Identity* has there been a thriller so intricate, so vivid and so terrifyingly real.

£1.75

THE D'ARTAGNAN SIGNATURE

Robert Rostand

A dying man whispers a name to his torturers and the hunt begins for the D'Artagnan signature – the power of attorney that will authorize the release of a fortune from a Swiss bank.

It is money tainted by violence, money extorted by the OAS to fund its reign of terror in Algeria; and now the scent of death is strong once more as old hatreds flare and blood-feuds are revived.

Again, the innocent are to be entangled along with the guilty, as the hunters – and those who hunt the hunters – draw close to their goal.

£1.50

THE SECOND LADY

Irving Wallace

From the author of such world bestsellers as *The Word*, *The Prize* and *The Fan Club* comes a searing novel of the most intimate duplicity – and of the deadliest deception.

Billie Bradford is beautiful, intelligent, enchanting and the First Lady of the United States. In Russia there exists a woman who is her exact double, down to the most secret detail. They call her the Second Lady.

It is the Second Lady who will share the Presidential spotlight, who will be privy to state secrets and who will sleep in the President's bed . . . just long enough to tip the balance of power away from the West. While the real Billie Bradford must fight her ruthless jailers in a foreign land – with the only weapon she has . . .

£1.75

DEATH OF A POLITICIAN

Richard Condon

Walter Bodmor Slurrie was ex-Vice President, ex-Senator, ex-Congressman – and he was going to be the next President. Until he became the ex-Walter Bodmor Slurrie.

His death could have been ordered by a number of organizations – from the KGB to the CIA, from the Mafia to the Secret Police. He could have been killed by one of his many enemies, or one of his rather fewer friends.

A suspense thriller in the highest Condon tradition, *Death of a Politician* is a novel about America – about those who own it, run it and occasionally rent it out to their fellow citizen.

'There are few funnier Americans than Condon' *Observer*

'Condon writes wildly funny, exuberant yet elegantly controlled and devastatingly accurate satires' *Tribune*

£1.50

THE BETTER ANGELS

Charles McCarry

Women have always wanted and adored Julian. Men have always feared and envied him. He is the second most powerful man in the United States and nations turn on his decisions. No one knows better than Julian Hubbard the realities of America towards the end of the twentieth century: ruthless politics, corrupted causes and deadly ideals.

But on the eve of a Presidential election, America faces a threat that could destroy democracy. As terrorism, violence and viciousness erupt on the campaign trail, Julian Hubbard becomes the focus of a desperate moral dilemma.

Thought-provoking and superbly written, *The Better Angels* is an unforgettable novel of ideas, character and shattering suspense.

'Taut and exciting' *Daily Mail*

'Ruthless and sophisticated . . . sharply readable' *Guardian*

£1·50

BESTSELLERS FROM ARROW

All these books are available from your bookshop or newsagent or you can order them direct. Just tick the titles you want and complete the form below.

PROMISES	Charlotte Vale Allen	£1.95
THE AFTER DINNER GAME	Malcolm Bradbury	£1.75
THE KGB DIRECTIVE	Richard Cox	£1.75
MCENROE	Tania Cross	£1.50
GOD BLESS THE BORDERS!	Lavinia Derwent	£1.25
WELLIES FROM THE QUEEN	Colin Douglas	£1.50
A DISTANT SUNSET	Virginia Ironside	£1.50
ONE STEP AT A TIME	Marie Joseph	£1.50
PAINTED BIRD	Jerzy Kosinski	£1.60
SCANDALS	Barney Leason	£1.95
THE CHAMDO RAID	John Miller	£1.60
PIN	Andrew Neiderman	£1.50
WHITENIGHTS, RED DAWN	Frederick Nolan	£1.95
TORPEDO RUN	Douglas Reeman	£1.50
WOLF TO THE SLAUGHTER	Ruth Rendell	£1.50
THE EXPERIMENT	Richard Setlowe	£1.75
SONGS FROM THE STARS	Norman Spinrad	£1.75
MORE TALES FROM A LONG ROOM	Peter Tinniswood	£1.50
THE FACTS OF RAPE	Barbara Toner	£1.75
THE CLAW OF THE CONCILIATOR	Gene Wolfe	£1.60

Postage ——————

Total ——————

ARROW BOOKS, BOOKSERVICE BY POST, PO BOX 29, DOUGLAS, ISLE OF MAN, BRITISH ISLES

Please enclose a cheque or postal order made out to Arrow Books Limited for the amount due including 10p per book for postage and packing for orders within the UK and 12p for overseas orders.

Please print clearly

NAME ....

ADDRESS ....

....

Whilst every effort is made to keep prices down and to keep popular books in print, Arrow Books cannot guarantee that prices will be the same as those advertised here or that the books will be available.